Going the Distance

Going the Distance

A NOVEL

Michael Joyce

excelsior editions

State University of New York Press
Albany, New York

Photo image © Sascha Burkard / iStockphoto.com

Published by
State University of New York Press, Albany

© 2013 Michael Joyce

For information, address State University of New York Press, Albany, NY
www.sunypress.edu

Excelsior Editions is an imprint of State University of New York Press

Production by Diane Ganeles
Marketing by Fran Keneston

Library of Congress Cataloging-in-Publication Data

Joyce, Michael, 1945-
  Going the distance : a novel / Michael Joyce.
    pages cm
  ISBN 978-1-4384-4798-8 (pbk. : alk. paper) 1. Baseball stories. I. Title.
  PS3560.O885G65 2013
  813'.54—dc23
                                        2012043679

10 9 8 7 6 5 4 3 2 1

For Eamon,
smooth second baseman
and maestro of the stats

Preface

It's been twenty-six years since I wrote this novel, and I've come to love it more and more over the years. Though I have come to be known for other works, in many ways I am fondest of it among all the fictions I've ever written. It has twice been published electronically, first online in 1995 as a very early electronic book, by the now defunct Pilgrim Press founded by Martha Conway and Christian Crumlish; and then republished in 2002 by the legendary electronic publisher Bob Stein, under his Night Kitchen TK3 "experimental electronic publishing" imprint that followed upon Voyager. By 2009, after Stein left off TK3 development and moved on to create the Institute for the Future of the Book, this book seemingly no longer had one.

Despite this novel's electronic lives before this, it was not conceived as a hypertext, and yet like my other print fictions I think it shares the narrative qualities of my hyperfictions. It is in fact a print instance of what I've called multiple fictions, a polylogue of woven voices as if along a river or in memory or a baseball stadium.

For a while before Pilgrim Press first published it, this novel kept threatening to be published in print but something always seemed to happen. In one case a press went out of business just as it was about to be acquired; in another an editor who told me she could recite the first page by heart moved on and away from literary things; and so on.

This novel is dedicated to the memory of a great baseball writer and poet, my friend Joel Oppenheimer. It is also dedicated to my brother Tom, who is quite alive and who always believed that Emma was the girl from Ipanema.

"It is designed to break your heart. The game begins in the spring, when everything else begins again, and it blossoms in the summer, filling the afternoons and evenings, and then as soon as the chill rains come, it stops and leaves you to face the fall alone."

—A. Bartlett Giamatti, "The Green Fields of the Mind"

ONE

All, all is beautiful, careening as we are.

Past the yawn of the dell, past the meadow where the road turns from Oxbow to Rossie, past where the two boys stood off a ways from the blinking man, all watching the silver foreign car as it took the turn past them, tight along the single black lane. They had stopped their work to watch, the curved narrow tines of their hayforks delicately set in the mown grass. They were midway in the field, a hard morning's work behind them in wide tongues of newly mown and pale green hay which they had been forking into narrow strips for the old mechanical baler to gather up. The midday light hung low and thick to their knees, shimmering off in a drifting haze, thin light at their faces. They seemed to float in light and yet their complexions were the scrubbed pale rawness of upper New York, faces he had seen all his growing years. They were primitives, they or their kind had stood in folding hills from the days when British raiders moved through these same counties and skinny boys played club ball in the greens along the Hudson. Two square red wagons sat on rubber wheels at the far end of the wedge-shaped meadow, one wagon already stacked with the squat, regular bales of yellowing hay. The three faces watched him drive past, looking up from the work.

The ball rose from deep in the green meadow, the white leather cover slowly spinning in the high air, light and lofting above their gaze. All sounds receded, it would not be caught. He turned back to face the road, smiling.

They paused long enough to watch the car move through their sight and disappear, gone along the road toward the islands.

It was long gone, already turning heavy, falling, an uncharged particle, a home run.

He fixed them once more in the rearview mirror—they were already turning back to the work—before the road turned away, and then in the same plane he saw his own grey eyes, watching the road and the hillsides receding. Already he would be putting his mind to the next pitch. He knew she was watching him, but he concentrated instead on the waxy cardboard image on the dashboard. His own face, the face in the mirror, a mint-condition Fleer's from the World Series year. He was capless in the picture, short-haired. It was unusual to be photographed without the cap, but he had insisted on that. "It's a shame not to see your eyes, your beautiful eyes," a woman had told him, and so when they came to take the pictures, he did not wear the cap.

It was early in the season when they came to take the pictures, early in the time when it seemed that everyone had something to give you. Two hundred dollars for your picture, a glove for your hands. Later they would begin to take away, each season a slow process of taking away. For a while you went into the spring thinking the hits and runs were yours, the outside corners, the slow curves; always they took them away, just as surely as they took the tone from the muscles, the air from your lungs. You smiled and pitched again. It was all give and take, and now it was all taken. This season there had been no check, no picture, no glove, no season. Only the slow curves, the road running home.

She was watching him look at the card.

"Is that reality therapy or something?" he asked.

She laughed like an echo.

"Do you think you need that?"

He honestly did not know her, he had tried to explain. The thin, blond shoulder-length hair, frosted silver where it framed her tanned, smooth face, jogged no particular memory, sent no juices. It was bewildering, he could not say he didn't know her, he knew a hundred of her, right down to the aviator sunglasses, the smoked lilac lenses. She was evidently bright and pampered, smooth brown skin across the collarbone, cool and fragrant flesh under the cotton shirt. She pressed her knees together, smiled, yet he could recall no common history between them, not even a chance meeting and a slow night. There was nothing beyond the morning and the drive up from Syracuse.

"That is your baseball card, isn't it?" he asked.

"If it's the gum you're after, I chewed that a long time ago," she said, this time laughing like a chime in the wind.

"Really."

"Don't worry," she said, her voice growing darker. She was worried about him, and knowing how much he could not remember about her, he did not blame her.

From Rossie to Hammond the air was plain and the houses mainly unshaded. It was a bleak stretch always, the desert between hills and the river. One newly tinned farmhouse roof flared momentarily with searing white light reflected from the sun. It was flat and painful and too dazzling to look at for long. He had the feeling she was still laughing. How beautiful everything is. Yet I suppose you will think I am lying, he thought she said.

We drove on. I remember.

Suddenly, along the high plateau to Chippewa Bay, limestone ledges marked the beginning of the long, subtle declines by which the road dipped patiently toward the St. Lawrence.

"How far will you be going?" he asked, and she laughed again and he knew she was humoring him.

It's not me, lady, he thought. I remember everything from February to this moment, everything but you. But he said nothing.

The islands, when they saw them, were thatches of emerald scruff; verdant, dark divots detached from one another by thick, grey channels of water in flat light. In the chop of the surface, the light rocked and glimmered secretly, as if tiny mirrors floated there, countless shards, each throat full of the voice of light.

"Have you ever seen anything so beautiful?"

He looked at her without answering.

Sometimes you could swear that you heard each individual voice throughout the stadium, that you marked each pair of eyes, the listless fluttering of cheap banners, the single, errant, floating tissue of white wrapping lofting high in the upper deck, drifting slowly down. Two fingers wiggling between the thighs, eyes behind the grid of the mask imploring you not to go crazy on him just now, the bat slowly undulating like a cobra's head. It was the most peaceful moment on earth.

"I really can't remember," he tried to tell her, making it something like a joke.

"Does it matter?"

They walked down toward the water to where the cove was crisscrossed by a grid of floating docks and a bland and ugly assortment of lusterless hulls. It was like a floating trailer park. Aluminum, fiberglass, and plastic curves slid up and down in the water of the slips; there was a stain of scum and weed slime on some hulls. All over people squatted and crawled upon the boats like grubs on stones, dusty silver stones like the ones you found along the river as a boy, those too stained with slime.

"I am a pitcher of baseballs . . ."

She laughed at this odd way to say it. It was a conspiratorial laugh, she knew he joked like this.

He had picked up one of the stones.

"At a time, I would have been known here. I would not stand by the shore because of the fame."

"Like Odysseus by the ships," she said.

"What?"

"People still know you. I knew you."

"Yes."

He chucked a stone into the water. It was not the pitcher, he threw it like a boy would.

The secret, he remembered telling a young pitcher, is you never really release the ball. Sure it leaves your hand, but you power it, you move it all the way in; you strain your legs and thighs to keep it in your grip.

"That's why, when a manager takes it from you . . ." He shrugged and did not finish. It was a bitter thought. He would not have bitter thoughts.

She pretended not to hear him, or so he thought.

Someone had turned at the sound of the stone's plunk, looking in toward shore from the deck of his boat, perhaps thinking the sound had been a fish. He turned back to the yellow rope he was coiling at his feet. It was a wooden deck, a wooden cabin. Here and there elsewhere in the slips one or another of the boats also displayed wood—an inlaid panel, a cabin, or only a single dark rail—dark and oily wood. It brought back memories, of wooden boats, nineteen-foot rowboats with high prows, long oars of ebony, mahogany, and cherry. He wasn't that old, it wasn't that long ago, thirty years at the most when he first remembered seeing them. Now this aluminum scum.

Even now baseball remained a game of wood and leather, of pine tar, rosin, cotton, wool. Even in the midst of the plastic turfs, with their midsummer smell of new car interiors, the blast of humid heat as the moisture steamed up from them, the damned seams that shot ground balls like mortar shells into the outfield, the ghastly green of Easter basket grass; even now a club would supply wool caps instead of synthetics to those who asked. The sweat would cool along the leather band inside the cap, the merest breeze evaporate the moisture in the wool, cooling your skull. Wolfman Hunt, the coolly silent, very dark-skinned outfielder would stick his bats in the sauna before games in early spring, the ash smell mixing with the redwood fragrance, the cedar benches; and when he rubbed the tar in, it would fill the grain where the sauna swelled it, his hands and the bat the same color where he gripped it. On some summer afternoons the bat rack smelled like a lumber mill and it was nice to sit near it, even on days when they could not get you a run to pitch with, even when your only reason to sit there was to stay out of sight and keep them thinking what a silent-suffering gamer you were not to be bitching for some support out there. Sometimes you wanted to laugh. Sometimes you dreamed of grabbing your own bat and doing it for yourself, a contact fly that carried down the line in the opposite field. That had been the worst thing about being traded, not getting to dream about batting. That was the worst thing, not getting to dream any longer.

Children were laughing. He looked up to the tongue of uncluttered water in the near part of the bay where two kids pumped a pedal raft along the channel from the boat launches to the open river. The sunburned man, too, looked up from where he knelt at the cabin of his boat, the yellow nylon line now coiled before him in a lump. He seemed to think that the children had shouted to him, and he waved vaguely, trying to be nice. The flat hull of the raft slapped mildly in the wake of a departing motorboat. The raft rocked on its pontoons when the twin slashes of the wake crossed them. The kids laughed again and pedaled harder. As the wake stretched toward the slips, some of the slumbering boats began rocking gently at their moorings, the caves of their hulls shrouded with tight canvas. The boats screeched when the wake reached them, a series of screeches as the white foam-plastic bumpers rubbed against the metal docks, the sausage-shaped bumpers screeching one by one between dock and gunnels. It was different from the noise tires made when the boats pressed against them. The tires sighed, the plastic screeched. He turned away from the water.

"Well?" she asked, "Is this it? Do you want to try to stay here? Should we see about a cottage?"

He shook his head.

"I haven't been sick, have I?" he asked, "Is that what?"

"Don't you feel well?"

He chose another stone and chucked it sidearm.

"The best I have in years, kiddo!" he said. "The best I have in years . . ."

"Then why worry?"

Beyond the bay the river made its own sound. A constant distant hiss. Voices somewhere and motors buzzing way out on the river floated on the hiss. It was not unlike the sound in a stadium, once you are used to it. There was a shore breeze. Beyond the inlet to the harbor on one of the smallest islands a couple was embracing in front of their cottage. The island had a sheer bank around its perimeter, a lip of muddy turf with bleached roots—the roots of trees—thrusting down into the water. The island reminded one of an onion just pulled from the soil. You could see the couple in the hazy light, alone on the small onion island.

I am alone, she thought he was thinking.

"No," he said quietly, "let's drive some more. Let's drive to Clayton."

Later, in the honky-tonk river town of Clayton, they ate beef greedily at the bar of McCormick's seafood restaurant. For a while she was the only woman there in the bar. The bartender studied his face as if he knew, but then seemed to decide to say nothing. He might have thought they were arguing, the way they sat there, not speaking, drinking ale. It had been hours since they ate in Syracuse and they filled themselves with Canadian ale while they waited for the beef to be served.

It was no different, he thought, than it would have been if he did know her. He didn't like to talk when he went out with someone, he never had—although he could not deny that he was even less apt to talk in public once he had become famous. For a moment he had considered explaining all this to her there at the bar, but he had not wanted to make talk, not even under the circumstances.

While they ate, a slowly gathering crowd of young men and college girls in tee shirts filled the small barroom. It was evident from their talk that they were waiting for the All-Star game to begin. He had the idea that these people were waiters and waitresses elsewhere, that they were not a summer crowd. That idea made no sense, really, when you considered the time of day and the season. It was just what he thought.

"National League ain't shit this year, all washed-up Cincinnati Reds and a coupla spades from Pittsburgh . . ."

He would not turn to see the face of the kid who had said this. It would be embarrassing to be known. The asshole calls Dave Parker a spade, he doesn't know baseball. Sometimes he forgot how racist it was here.

"There's Garvey too."

"That prick's so square he oughta be a Yankee . . ."

The bartender laughed. You had to admit it was easy to hate Garvey, crouching like a Little League twerp every time there was a throw to first, covering the ball in the glove like he was carrying home Twinkies to his mother.

Someone shouted across the bar, getting into the conversation.

"Garvey can play for Reggie when he doesn't show . . ."

Yankee country here. He knew that, he had grown into it himself, counted Maris's homeruns while never really liking him. Once saw Casey Stengel in Alex Bay, going fishing. It hadn't been surprising to be drafted into the National League; it hadn't been bad at all. He had found himself realizing that he always secretly believed it was where they played real baseball. Then it was bewildering to go in the trade to the other league after fourteen years, to play in Yankee Stadium after the renovation.

It was getting louder now, the talk, and he watched her swipe up a dab of brown mustard from her plate using the last part of her sandwich to wipe at it. She ate like a drinker. She saw him watching her in the bar mirror and smiled—such a friendly smile—and touched his hand.

I should know her, he thought. It was a very sad feeling, sad and frustrating, like trying to clear your head when you just wake up.

"Stop it!" a girl giggled. She laughed like someone was tickling her. Everything was getting louder. He sneaked a look at the girl. Nips pushed against the tee shirt, there was a time when counting nips was a big deal among the country boys, like the beaver hunts Bouton wrote about. Something to do on the road when you're horny and dumb.

"If you don't stop it," the girl told the dude who was tickling her, I'll shove your face under the table and really give you something to lick."

The dude had been licking her arm, really rude and obvious. Everyone laughed when the girl shut him down. He looked back at the bar mirror. The piece of bread she had used to wipe the mustard with was now discarded on the plate, a dry wedge of bread with the shape of her mouth still there where she had bit away the mustard. She looked very skeptical and uncomfortable about the talk in the bar. Yet it was the kind of talk you heard around baseball games, he could tell her that. The game affected some people that way, they talked rude. But she'd know that, if she knew baseball.

It was very loud there, filled with laughter, all the pregame horse-shit starting on the television. A close-up of the Seattle dome, the camera panning to the big suspended speaker that Willie Horton hit earlier in the season. A four-hundred-foot homerun dropping for a single, the speaker being in play. Through the large picture window at the rear of the bar you could see into the dining room. It was like looking into an aquarium. Families, men with rooster knit ties and seersucker coats, women in organdy gauze. He turned back to the bar before anybody could get a good look at him, studied the framed pictures of the great, gone wooden boats of the river. He wondered if he had remembered right at Chippewa Bay, if there really had been all those boats when he was younger or if it was all these framed photos over McCormick's bar that he was remembering.

He felt like a stranger, it wasn't surprising. Always there was the feeling when you came into tourist towns, into places like these, that you alone were strangers. Even the summer people, the fudgies, seemed linked by some secret lore.

They left before the game began and walked down to the dock and watched the river tour depart. The tour boat was full, not every-one was watching the game. It was Yankee country but Canada gleamed across the river, silent and lost in the past. O Ellis Valen-tine, he thought, what a nice name for a baseball player . . .

Andre Dawson.

"Flynn," he said.

"What?"

"Flynn."

"I know," she said. "Do you want to watch the game?"

"Not really."

"I thought you were announcing yourself . . ."

"Do I kiss you?" he asked. "I mean, in whatever life I know you in, do I kiss you?"

She shrugged. It was a funny gesture, a coyly smart face.

"And you?" he asked. "Your name?"

"Emma," she said, looking glum. "You do know that. I told you, you do know that."

"Whatever you say, lady."

They walked from the tour boat dock up along the strip in the cooling night air. The boat was down the river before them, a moving carnival out on the black river. The game was on the radio at the ice cream stand, it filled the night. A fishing guide was checking gear in the air outside his shop, he too had a radio on. They walked, Flynn and Emma, like a young married couple, not holding hands, but close to one another, their hips brushing sometimes, up and down the strip once again, smelling the river in the air, beer from the tavern doorways, a smell like burnt sugar or cotton candy pervading everything.

Then they went to their room and slept, first she and then he, each in a separate bed. It was a lovely, soft evening and the noise from the street seemed far from them, below in another, gaudier world, submerged there like the clam shells gulls dropped in the shallows; iridescent moons each with a jagged hole pecked in the middle.

He woke and wondered what she was dreaming. What hour it was. His arm was already numb, although he could not have been asleep for long. A panel truck, army brown and camouflaged in light tan and green patches, roared down the strip, the faulty muffler sounding like the glass-packs Flynn remembered from his teens. Soldiers on their way back to Drum, the bars closed for the night. He hammered a fist into his arm until it began to tingle with the circulation, then lay back again.

Below there was no noise. Silent lights passed on the visible segment of the river, high somewhere the engine of a small plane labored steadily against the night. She seemed to catch her breath as if frightened, but then laughed softly in her sleep, once and then once again, kicking her leg free from the sheets. The second laugh had been different, filled with genuine delight. If she were awake, he thought, she might have clasped her hands then, delighted. He wondered why he was certain of this, whether he had known that gesture from her before. He remembered other times, lying awake beyond a woman he barely knew, attempting to piece together some personality for the body beside him. These were not happy memories. For some reason he knew that Emma was someone he knew much more about; she had not questioned him when he lay down to sleep without her, she had shown no hesitation throughout this long day.

My unborn sister, he thought, she could as well be that, a cousin, the wife of a friend. He had a dim sense that it was as much the fascination of not knowing her as it was anything else that was prolonging the reeling in of any recollection.

Her breathing resumed a slow, regular course. It made him think of the sound of a trolling motor, it was that kind of rhythm. I cannot be crazy, he thought, if I notice so much; it is just that some things are momentarily in deeper pools. For the first time since they ate he wondered about the score of the game. He slept like someone slipping into black water. As he fell into it he knew his arm was numbing already. Someone moved quietly along the hallway outside their door.

He was absent when she woke. She reached toward the empty bed, watching the sunlight wash across her palm. The bed made her think of shed skin, the wispy silk of snakes; it was as if he had peeled himself from both bed and sleep in a single movement. There was something uncommonly childlike and affectionate about the sight of the white furls of the sheet in the glancing sunlight. She was aware of the scent of his body, and another odor, medicinal and sweet.

She rolled back toward the wall and was surprised to see flowers on the side table. Black-eyed Susans and Loosestrife in a white foam cup.

The key turned in the lock. He had bundles in his arms and steadied them with his chin.

"'Lo," he said. "It is impossible to compose a proper breakfast on the road in America."

She smiled and yawned.

"In what other countries have you composed breakfast?"

"None really," he said smiling, "It's what they tell you."

"Do people really talk that way?"

He ignored her question. "I did spend two winters in Venezuela," he said. "They eat fish there in the morning, I think."

"They eat pickles and rice in Japan," she said.

"Never played there."

On the desk he set out two cups of yogurt, two Grannie apples, a smoked sausage in plastic skin, fat round hard rolls dusted with white, a new plastic thermos. Coffee smell came when he unscrewed the thermos cap.

From his pocket he dug out foil squares of butter, plastic tubs of jam, clear plastic flatware. In the last paper sack there were blueberries, dark and fat, each with a puckered navel.

"The berries aren't in season," she said.

"Why they sell them then?"

"I wish I ate breakfast."

He laughed. "You will," he said, "now . . ."

She too laughed and then slid from the bed, nude, very pale in the light despite her tan, her flesh gold where the sunlight washed her. She shivered slightly although the air was warm, padded to the shower. He poured coffee and screwed the top back on the new thermos.

"National League scored two unearned runs in the sixth and went on to win it by one run," he said.

She could not hear him above the shushing water, he knew. He had stood with the hot water on his arm for at least a half hour that morning, heard nothing.

"I hope I left you some hot water," he said.

"You didn't mention the apples," he said, "Grannies are from Australia or somewhere, I think . . ."

"I thought maybe we would take a run up to Massena and show you where I was born," he said.

"But then you know that already . . . do you . . . ? I don't think I can last long like this . . ."

Careening. A spider had woven a web of concentric circles over one pane of the window, the circles minutely oblongated where the crosswise ties adhered. The web shone like a prism.

TWO

Flynn.

John "Jack" Flynn, b. Massena, NY 11/8/43, p. rh.

The *Selena Marie,* Panamanian registry, rose slowly up toward him, her cargo chemicals. She came up from the concrete canyon of the locks, weightless and huge in the rising water. Gulls squabbled over bits of popcorn and hot dog buns dropped to them on the walk below. Flynn squinted behind mirrored sunglasses, watching a sailor with huge brown arms leaning back against a bulkhead and gazing wryly up at the legs and tits and lonely faces, the cameras and children above him. The children tottered in their parents' arms, held upon the rails of the observation deck despite the warnings of the public address announcer. According to the chalkboard in the snack bar below, the *Selena Marie* was bound for Duluth.

The sailor waved to someone on the observation deck. Flynn looked to see if he could tell who it was. Along the rail the tourists watched the ship rise toward them. They were impatient for something to happen, but nothing would happen.

Flynn was not unlike them in appearance. Khaki pants, blue oxford cloth, summer-weave shirt, topsiders, no socks; a well-conditioned thirty-six-year-old man, alone now.

He could remember many things, even the first time he had seen these locks in operation. The Eisenhower Locks, St. Lawrence Seaway. His father brought him up to them in the boat. It was in July, the day after the dedication, and they passed the Britannia, Queen Elizabeth's yacht, big as a freighter.

"The bloody fucking queen!" his father said, and spat in the water, the gob turning to a silver swirl. "Would have come down myself for the dedication," he said, "but for that bitch. All her damned lah-de-dah battleships tied up the river. Ike wouldn't of had it, Jackie! No sir, there's a democracy for you . . ."

Flynn was sixteen then and the locks were not called the Eisenhower Locks. He didn't understand his father's vehemence, except that it had something to do with the war and a USO in England. He had not much cared, there was a ballgame that afternoon, Flynn remembered. You grew up around events like this.

He remembered. The length of the *Selena Marie,* seven hundred and eighty-five feet, according to the lady who read the spiel on the public address system. Remembered leaving Chicago, meeting with Lenny to go over the schedule for the coming months' engagements. A golf tournament in Moline, Illinois; a series of meetings in Pittsburgh; a quick trip to Wheeling, to Cincinnati, to St. Louis. He had asked Lenny to call for tickets at Riverfront.

"Are you sure?"

"Of course, I'm sure. Whatta ya think I'll stay away from the game forever? Anyway, it's business. People expect that."

Flynn had taken care of himself. He would "never have to work," said Lenny. Lenny did not consider it work to be a manufacturer's representative, which was what he had arranged for Flynn to be. Yet Lenny argued over the amount of money Flynn had drawn for the vacation trip east. Flynn smiled. He paid Lenny to do that, to manage his affairs.

"I want to buy a new car for the trip, Leonard. Consider it a sentimental purpose. Something sporty but stylish."

Lenny had laughed. He did not look like someone called Lenny—or Leonard for that matter. Lenny was plumpish and handsome, the sort of man who never sweat, whose shirts never wilted. Lenny was a white Anglo-Saxon accountant, a careful man with an uncareful name, grey suits, gold at the wrist, a Samsonite briefcase, a wife and children. A good partner to have, a manager.

Flynn could remember everything except her. And yet he sensed the knowledge there. It was like looking at a page of print where a single line is smudged. It was like trying to find your slider on a night when you didn't have your stuff. Someone had run a finger over the memory of her, yet left the gap in place. It was maddening, it made you want to blink.

The boy stood respectfully behind him. How long he had been there Flynn did not know. He had a plastic Detroit Tigers batting helmet on his head, a shirt that said, "My Parents Went To Florida And All They Brought Me Was This Lousy Teeshirt."

The boy's father stood behind him, looking down at his son in that wistful, almost apologetic way you saw fathers do. He was proud of the boy and he didn't want to show how proud. It was beautiful.

"Mr. Flynn—Jack—could I have your autograph?"

Flynn wanted to do something different for the boy with a father so proud of him, but there was nothing to do but take the paper and the pen—a skipping ballpoint, he had to shake it between letters—and write the boy's name on it, "To Brian, all best always, Jack Flynn."

The great swooping loop of the "y" in Flynn dwindled off into a series of smaller loops, the two "n's" and a modest arabesque decoration. Flynn had taught himself to draw his name like this after too many boys were disappointed with his accustomed schoolboyish scrawl.

They'd eat you up sometimes, the autograph kids. Tell you you shit and slug your bicep, spit on you and toss the paper away. There were fathers who'd demand that you sign every page in a scorecard. Even so Flynn always signed. There were too many fathers with sons like this smiling boy.

She stood behind the boy's father, looking as proud as he did, the two of them smiling upon the pitcher and the boy. She could have been the man's wife.

"Sorry you aren't still out there," the father said softly and touched the boy's shoulder.

"Thanks, I miss it," Flynn said. It was as unsurprising as the autograph, he had said this before.

"Should we go, Jack?" she asked. "Your aunt is probably waiting."

Yes. He nodded, used to being managed so. The deck of the *Selena Marie* was at their level now. The sailor absentmindedly rubbed at his crotch, walked toward where the men coiled the cable on the deck. It was sunny and clean on the deck. Jack Flynn signed more autographs as he and Emma made their way down the stairs and to the parking lot.

"Good to see you home again, kid," an older man said.

"Yeah," Flynn said.

"I seen you pitch back in the Legion ball championship," the man said.

Flynn nodded and waited. Often a man like this would say that he had once fished with Flynn's father.

"You could still get 'em out in the bigs," the man said. "You seen the kind of ball they played last night."

"Afraid not," Flynn said. It was an ambiguous answer.

Instead of driving into Massena, to his aunt's house, he drove back toward Ogdensburg. Emma sat beside him in silence, the same smile on her face that she had had when he signed the autograph on the deck. It was annoying, he wished she would say something, he wished she would ask why they weren't going on into Massena. At Ogdensburg, past the exit for the Psychiatric Center and the bridge approach, there was a cluster of relatively new buildings. A Mac-Donald's with a kiddy park, a motel or two. He exited.

Here is nowhere, he thought. She nodded.

She had waited while he went in to register, sat still silent while he drove around the back of the cinderblock building to the spot the clerk had shown him on the mimeographed chart. Flynn took their bags and went up the outside stairs to the room, holding her overnight bag under his arm while he juggled with the key to open the door. The room stank of mildew and plastic. He sat on the bed in the dim room and watched the television, forgetting about her. It was a good hard bed, the air conditioner pumped in coils of damp air. The last major leaguer to prefer motels, he thought.

The television was tuned to the cable station, the screen cut into blue, red, and green bands with advertising on the upper band, Reuter's newswire and the temperature and wind speed and time on the middle band, stock market figures running across the bottom.

Eighty-seven degrees, 2:38 EDT, thunderstorms by evening, small craft warnings will be posted on the river. Two p.m. and 5 p.m. and eleven at night were the long times. He heard her footsteps along the concrete balcony, the scruff of her sandals. She stood in the doorway and looked at him. Her legs were bare and brown and she wore no slip under the sundress. He looked dully at the outline of her thighs. She entered the room quietly.

"Forget about me?" she asked.

"That's a funny question under the circumstances."

She stayed at the door. The cool air from the machine in the window surrounded him.

"Do you sing?" he said.

"What?"

"Songs. Do you sing songs?"

"Are you all right, Jack?"

She sat on the bed next to him, gripped his shoulder and kneaded the flesh there, pressing the muscle with the expert grip of a masseuse. She worked along the bicep, not imposing on him, not saying anything.

"Take your clothes off," he said.

She inhaled deeply, continued to probe and push against his bicep.

"I don't think that would be good," she said quietly.

The slap glanced off the loose flesh just below her cheekbone. Yet his fingers had caught just under her eye, he could see that when she stopped crying, when she came back to the bed with the washcloth. Her face was already swelling, a puffing bright contusion with pale white sparks at the center where his fingers had caught. She looked grotesque after this assault. He was terribly ashamed and very sick to his stomach. He wished she would leave him alone so he could try to sleep and forget what he had done.

That's it, he thought. I've lost it.

Already the flesh under her eye had begun to grow smooth and purple. She would have a shiner. She could call the cops. He would just sit there and wait for them to come, try to explain, drive back with them a half-mile to the psychiatric center.

The bruise was already so tender that she winced as she pressed the cold washcloth to it. She dipped the cloth into the ice bucket. He tried to remember her going to get the ice. It could not have been there in this room, yet he could not for the life of him recall her going. He could not even say exactly where the ice machine was. Sometimes all you could do was to pack your arm in ice until the weariness fled.

Despite himself he could not help looking at the flower of bruised flesh. It was oddly beautiful, pale lavender, moist looking, plump and soft. It was terrible to think this. In the awful light from the television screen it appeared to be some grand and delicate tattoo, a tropical moth, a lilac web.

"You do that again, Flynn, and I'll cut your balls off, I swear."

He nodded and fell weeping into his own lap.

"I swear," she said.

Both times she had spoken softly, very sure of what she was saying, yet very soft. He remembered this in his dreams.

He woke at night, no one was there, no overnight bag, no scent of perfume. Even the ice bucket was drained and dry, overturned on the Formica ledge next to the sink. The nerves in his arm screamed with a deep and subtle pain, throbbing there like a serpent under the knotted muscles. It made him grate his teeth and flee into the night, the river air, the promise of whiskey. He left the key behind on the dresser, the television on and still shining dreamy information across the triple stream.

"You're Flynn, right? Jack Flynn? Fished with your dad once."

The bartender wore a red vest over a stiff white shirt and black bow tie, a red garter on his arm. It was a Gay Nineties idea, although nothing else here suggested that. It was cool and black dark within the bar, river bottom cool. The bartender was toothy and narrow-jawed with dark little eyes behind rimless spectacles. A muskellunge sort of fellow, very fishlike in all. It made Flynn laugh.

The bartender grinned with Flynn's laugh, preferring to act as if they shared a private joke. His grin showed needly teeth, and he leaned confidentially toward the pitcher.

"What really happened, Jack? Were you washed up or did they force you out?"

Why either? Why not a taste for perfection? A preference for the game perfectly played with at least enough strength left to accompany the guile necessary to compensate for lost power. Why settle for three seasons of fifteen and eight or thirteen and ten?

"To tell the truth, friend . . ." Flynn sipped the last pool of Wild Turkey from the glass, felt it enter his blood as the bartender leaned still closer to hear this confidence. ". . . got so's I was making too much money, I swear to god. You're the first soul I've told the truth to, since I retired."

Flynn sipped at the ice to see if it would yield, but then cupped his hand over the glass when the bartender moved to refresh it.

"Manufacturer's rep," he said, "Sumnabitchs'll pay more to play golf with you than you can make pitching baseballs."

"But you were losing it too, weren't you?"

Flynn looked him dead in the eye. Nice man. People always want to know the inside of everything. Can't blame him, an honest guy, you could see it in the eye, behind the watery shallows of the rimless lenses.

"That too, pal," Flynn said and hopped off the stool. "I'm not the kind to settle for a nine-and-seven season."

The bartender called after him. "Hell no, Jack, you're just right. You could walk to Cooperstown on what you got already."

Flynn tipped an imaginary hat and went out into the cool, thick air. Across the river the distant light of Brockville appeared as a smear, giving way to the discrete Canadian lights of Prescott and Johnstown beyond the bridge. He thought of going north, off down the MacDonald-Cartier to Cornwall and Coteau-du-Lac and Montreal where the world turned French and crazy.

Had the bastard leaning in on the two and two, he thought, and he fouled them off until I fed him one. Muskellunge were that way too, tease you and tease you and jaw right through the cable and the steel leader both. Flynn had to laugh, it was something to do, laughing along Route 37 downriver toward Aunt Bertie and her scrapbooks and talk of Joey, Flynn's father, and her talk of children and how they were disappearing from the world, and why didn't Flynn do something about that, make a family like Joey and Nell had, make a family and live forever, do something with your life.

"I married at an early age and we did not want children."

That was a sad thing to say and Flynn wondered about Emma. It hurt to think about her. I have never hit a woman, he said, meaning before this she thought. It was an awful thing to be, ugly, to have done this thing with the world so beautiful and all the lights along the river and all.

A whole lot of being going on tonight, boys, Flynn thought. It was turning out to be the theme for the night. What to be? Leonard favored manufacturer's rep, Bertie husband and father.

Emma?

Why do I have to be anything? I was not prepared for a life in which you had to be.

Hah. Be on the black, be on the best, be on the river.

Flynn chose the black, the very edge of the pancake universe, the pitchers' name for the corner of the plate, the shadowy stripe where the rubber gripped the brick dust, the clay, the sand.

On the whole it's been a good life so far I have to say. No complaints about playing a game for a living, let alone doing damn well at it. Nossir. No sir.

Cooperstown could be reached in a long night. Down along 56 into the forests. And then what? Three and 30 and 20 and down some highway he didn't know the number of. Pretty good memory for so long away from home.

He pulled into a rest area and checked against the map under the dome light. He was right. US 20 and then 80 into Cooperstown. Miles of forests first: 30 twisting among the lakes through the Adirondacks. Babe Ruth's bat and all that crap. John Samuel (Johnny) "The Dutch Master" Vander Meer, not enshrined, also known as "Double No-Hit," because he did that back-to-back and on the black, one more than Flynn, and then, like Flynn, never again, ending up unlike Flynn, on the short side of .500 lifetime—maybe 119 and 121, Flynn would have to check it.

I've lived my life in numbers. Joe Flynn knew the charts in his head, the shoals and reefs, the depths. But he was no fool, no old-fashioned guide all greasy and plopping French toast into the boiling fatback. Nossir, Joe Flynn was among the first to use fishfinders and sonar and all those number machines. His eldest son, Jim, died at 30—Flynn's age when, later, their mother died—drowned in his car in the river in four feet of water. Jack, of course, became a well-known major league pitcher.

Flynn sat in the car and looked at the row of sleepers, the semi drivers in their cabs, their running lights like boats on the river. It was time to sleep and he would drive to a motel in Massena, unwilling to wake Aunt Bertie.

Frightened, he wondered was Emma someone of Jim's? Someone who had known his brother? No, it was silly. Unlikely. She was thirty tops, which would have made her ten years younger than Jim.

I've lived my life in numbers.

Was Jim in the boat with you then? When the silver gop boiled on the hot surface of the river and your father damned the Queen of England?

No. Jim was twenty, twenty-one then, already going bad, or so they said. Jim was never much of a one to go out on the river after he grew. Thus Flynn was now about to buy a charter business.

That was it. He would call Leonard in the morning and begin to have him work up figures on a boat and business. An investment merely, Flynn would never—could never—run it. Although maybe the thing to do would be to buy some cottages too, a whole damned resort. See then if a film of sweat forms along Leonard's ivory accountant's forehead. We're into extra innings, Lenny.

Hah. Flynn drove on, leaving the stream of cab lights behind him. Like boats on the river, he remembered, boats on the wooden river.

Emma, she went into Canada early, vaguely sailing, mildly hurt. At the bridge they asked her if she had a revolver in the car. Bien Venue au Canada, and yet the green-clad custom's officer was not smiling. No joke, no gun, no citrus fruit. I plan to stay a day or two. Au Canada, O Canada, my home and native land.

I am the very model of a model English gentlewoman.

The custom's officer stared a little long and grim, at the bruise no doubt, which he must have thought a butterfly, something dark and deep and faintly mysterious. Likely, really, he thought she was running away from home, from a husband who beat her, which Flynn was not, she did not suppose. Something in how clean the custom's man was made her think of Grannie Smith, the globe apples which Flynn had brought for breakfast, like the apple of de Chirico which fills a house and John Cheever made the cover of a book of lovely, sad stories, fathers and sons.

Emma remembered the faint, faint perfume of the apples. The smell of liniment which had taken her the longest time to figure out. And now the custom's man seemed to pause at the astringent smell, the perfume odor of 10-06, Emma's heal-all and cleanser, antiseptic and balm, but then he waved her off, diffident and wholesome, into Canada where she soon found a cottage, a bed and breakfast, unlike Flynn the motel man, with a little woman who served tea and said to come out after and look on the river, her nose wrinkling briefly, mouselike, as she surveyed Emma's fragrant injury.

She slept, thinking the episode ended. In his dreams she rose toward Flynn, the *Selena Marie,* mother moon, young and lovely the girl from Ipanema. She just doesn't see.

THREE

It was possible that Aunt Bertie could have been the kind of aunt who is maternal. Plump, tight in cotton dresses, smelling of powder. Or she might, like her brother, Flynn's father, have grown to become a river rat, dressing in denim Oshkosh, fingers that smelled of worms and the bait bucket.

At times she had been both of these, but now she was settled into someone tailored and a little cold, a little skittish. It happens to furniture too, Flynn thought. The little stuffed chair in the parlor at a certain age is covered over in brocade, never sat upon. A smell of naptha.

"Hello, Jackie, running up and down the river again, I see."

Bertie kissed him by pressing her cheek against his. She has learned these ways, this style, from television soap operas. She has decided to become the still-attractive but matronly woman played in these dramas by the women who model mature clothes for mail order catalogues.

Bertie has no special insights. She knew what Flynn had done because he stank and had not changed clothes when he awoke in the motel in Massena.

"I got your lovely note." Bertie gestured toward the drumtop table where Flynn's postcard sat propped against two baseballs.

"You will sign those for the neighbors, won't you Jackie?"

Years before Flynn had told her how they brought in the cartons of baseballs to be signed in the clubhouse. Bertie was impressed by the fact that the players receive a check for this use of their property, and she began to find baseballs a worthy project. Each time Flynn saw her, she had more baseballs for the neighbors. Often they were the slippery, vinyl balls sold in discount stores, sometimes they were Haitian leather, gaping at the stitches, the kind of flaw you hoped to find once or twice a game before the umpire discovered. A pitch would dip or flare when you could spin a cut stitch off your finger.

"What happened to the ones I sent you?"

The balls on the table said "Little Leaguer" and felt like they had rocks inside. Flynn had sent her a mint-condition box of the real thing two years before.

"Pardon me, Jackie?"

Bertie came back from the kitchen where she was no doubt making tea, something she always tried to foist on him.

"I'm going to make some eggs and a pitcher of Bloody Marys, Bert. No tea, thank you."

"I hope you're not drinking, Jack."

Was he, he wondered. Blackouts? No, too Ray Millandish.

"What happened to the new balls?"

"You are very popular with the people in your hometown, Jackie."

"Even when I never signed them?"

Bertie gazed innocently upon him. She probably had a closet upstairs full of baseballs, like the old men of Flynn's youth who saved tires and string for the next war. In the event of nuclear war, Bertie would be the new commissioner of the World Baseball Association.

"After the revolution," Flynn said, "Castro gave each child in Cuba a ball and bat."

Bertie smiled and followed him into the kitchen and sat at the table, her tea steaming under the needlepoint cozy before her. She wrinkled her nose when Flynn poured dry mustard into the eggs, but helped him find green onions. He made the Bloody Marys with V-8 and Worcestershire and Mohawk vodka he found in the usual place under the sink. She had no Tabasco, so he stirred cayenne pepper into the juice.

"Your arm hurting you, darling?"

Bert had noticed. Flynn had disdained the hot shower that morning, drove left-handed into town. It hurt like hell.

"Likely will until my grave, Bert." He spoke with his mouth full, she did not like this much. "Price of admission, darling. Remember when I used to say I'd give an arm and a leg to play in the bigs? Well, they collected."

"Your leg hurt too?"

Flynn laughed too hard and splittered yellow specks of egg on the tablecloth. Wiping it off made it worse.

Well, yes it does, but that don't count, sweetheart. The leg at least feels like it's still part of the same body.

Bertie began to cry. The tears did not suit her new personage, and Flynn wanted to comfort her. Yet there was a sinking feeling within him, a sour mix of the tinny vegetable juice and the eggs and mustard. He knew she wouldn't cry like this because he laughed at her.

"Poor, poor Jackie," she said, "I'm sorry you have so much sadness to bear. How long will it take, do you think?"

Flynn stared at her in perfect terror, yet feeling his face compose, showing none of what he felt. There are certain small rewards for a life given to a game.

So it wasn't just a single smudge, not just Emma who was out of place in this flight of his. What else was there? He couldn't ask Bert, so he merely continued to stare, benign and blank and—he thought—the perfect picture of the woe or grief or whatever it was he supposed Bertie thought he felt now.

She let him off.

"You'll want a shower, of course, won't you, Jackie? There's no need to run off into unpleasantness first thing."

"No," he allowed, thinking perhaps he could call Leonard and ask what it was he should know.

On the way upstairs, he signed the baseballs and looked at his own postcard for a clue to what should be done.

Bertie,
I know you share my feeling. I will be there in three days after a drive up along the river. Thank you, darling

He had signed the card, Jack Flynn, in the little-boy scrawl.

The shower covered his shoulders and drummed against the mass of muscle in the triangular hollow below. Flynn loved water because it was never anything but itself; he loved it in all its forms. It was an unusual thing for a river dweller, for water was what you went upon, looked on, or plumbed through with lines, sticks, or the blunt paddles of a motor prop. It was never to be known, only used, seen there in the distance, the white glare of the ice sheet in February light. Yet each of the showers, in Clayton and now at Bertie's had the tang of river under the chemical sniff. The water itself held memory and dim knowledge. Mud and eelgrass, a fragrance like the flesh of bullheads. During eighteen years, his half-life, he had come to use water as a tool, the swirling salt of the trainer's whirlpool, little blocks of cloudy ice in a plastic tub, your arm dead and white under the blue mound of cubes. At some early age Flynn had learned why water was said to be an element, long before he had known how to think in those terms. Water sliced itself into segments, it held like gem and then dissipated with its own will, it divided and subdivided and merged, caressed, attacked, surrounded and drowned. It came from nowhere, it obeyed only itself and the murmuring commands of falling, welling, pooling, boiling. He loved showers and baths and swimming and rain. The drip from the dugout roof in a rain delay, the sheets of rain curling in from the power alleys and across the infield tarp, the cat's paws of rain on the river, the steaming needles of the shower turning his arm red and alive as he soaked it. The end of it, the last few drips like breath, evaporation, the river disappearing as the road cut inward.

He was looking for Emma now. She knew.

Ogdensburg was flat and dusty and old in the sunlight. The cinderblock motel was surrounded by a sea of tarmac. The maid would have turned the television off, the screen dimming in a slow glare in the empty, darkened room. Flynn tried to remember if Emma had screamed when he hit her.

He had not been able to stay long at home with Bertie, although he left his things there, intending to go back. Massena was cool under the tunneling shade of its trees, its clean white bungalows and broad houses adrift on emerald lawns—everything Ogdensburg was not this afternoon. Yet he had to go out.

Bertie had been watching the soaps when he came down from the shower, perched on her La-Z-Boy, her feet hardly skimming the carpet. She sailed through the afternoons this way, he knew. Before she was aware of him back there in the room, he watched her watch the television. She moved her lips minutely, silently whispering the words of the characters as they spoke, the whispering sometimes interrupted by a surprised smile, an expression of woe or fear, the near-smile of scandals.

Under the soft sloth of her face her brother's face lay in outline like a statue under a sheet. Flynn's father's long bones and nose and his tough, fibrous lips were shadowed in his sister, silked over with puffy flesh, a hint of ladylike jowls. Bertie's eyes were more deeply set, wider than he remembered his father's, but she had his broad eyebrows, dark still though her hair was grey, unplucked though she had blued the eyelids with silvery shadow.

Flynn looked at the creases and chiseled folds of the face of the cowboy before him. Remington's bronze was tobacco brown, like leather really, which was how they talked of cowboys. It was a mistake to look for Emma here in the museum of the cowboy artist. She would have no interest in lariats and the pained grins of rearing horses. Emma would be found near flowered teas, chamomile and lavender, purslane.

"Oh Jack, you scared me," Bertie had said.

He had studied her face then, witness now instead of spy. She was frightened of something, you could see that, perhaps frightened at the events unfolding on the screen before her, perhaps frightened by the effort of being what she must be this and each afternoon, perhaps by what Flynn could not remember having come here to do. Yet she was also beautiful and kind and all those things a boy remembered about an aunt; it was not really fair to think her cold, she had merely made choices.

"I think I'm going out for a while."

"There?" She caught her breath with the question, making an expression like she made when the soap opera surprised her.

"Maybe."

"Would you like a roast, or something light?"

"I'm not sure about dinner."

"I can turn the air conditioning on, if you like. I don't use it much for myself."

Flynn nodded. Bertie was already paying more attention to the program before her than to this commonplace talk.

He would let her go on sailing. Whatever it was he had to do could not be so urgent. He had allowed it three days in his postcard, and Bertie seemed unhurried about it now.

She was whispering along with the actors again.

"I'll call if I'm not coming back tonight."

"Emma was here, you know. Early this morning before you came."

"No, I didn't know that," Flynn said.

"She has a nasty bruise," Bertie said. It was news solely, she gave no sign of purpose in it.

Flynn nodded and left.

On Water Street he found her, walking in a yellow sundress, the street empty otherwise. It had not been long since he left the Remington Museum, three or four turns around concentric blocks of river town tenements, two long glides down one-way thoroughfares, and then here to the blind end of Water Street.

She entered a new Buick and drove off. A rental car, Flynn knew by the "Z" plates. He tried to keep her in his eye, she had not seen him. As she drove away, Flynn could see that she kept her windows up, using the air conditioner no doubt kept her fresh in the yellow dress. Flynn, on the other hand, kept his windows down. You had to hear to drive, his father could hear the river above the burring noise of a trolling motor, above the roar and growl of the main outboard. He could hear fish down through the surface and depth of water.

He was a hero.

Flynn lost her in a change of signals out near the highway. He saw her weave the auburn Buick up into traffic and along north. Women were weavers, the good ones at least. He would not chase her. If she had come to Bertie's once, she would be back again.

Flynn headed for Canada but stopped short of the bridge at the little-league field. Walking across the cinder parking lot, he stopped and for a long time studied the towers of the old mental hospital in the middle distance. There was something familiar there, more than the still-adhering childhood fears of the substantial dark brown towers, the bony parapets and the severe, square walls of the Victorian nut house. That castle of rumor had become offices now; the kids who played on these fields—on land ceded by the state from what had been the hospital's dairy operation—would not recognize the castle for anything more than it was, an official place with stones, only darker than the old limestone armory in town. Even the iron gates were gone, and the claw-topped iron spike fences were replaced by the same chainlink that also surrounded the outfield of each diamond. Cream brick bland buildings clustered in a little campus on the grounds behind the old hospital. These were the new hospital, now called a care facility, and only the helplessly mad and the frail were no longer released into halfway houses in surrounding towns.

The remaining patients roamed within sight of the diamonds, up and back on simple paths through the green, the nurses or orderlies standing among them like creatures of salt, crisply white. The moaning rose up.

"Hey batter hey batter hey batter hey . . ."

Everywhere they moaned so now, kids did. Infield chatter had become foreign, the endless singsong of mullahs, something sad and distant and hypnotic, ceasing at the release of each pitch.

Flynn resisted turning to the games for a moment, still staring at the dark brown building, its mullionless renovated windows like so many eyes blankly staring. He was reminded of his father, in the time when they had first operated on the cancer. He too was a shell then, seemingly benign. Flynn believed neither.

His feet turned in the soft stones of the parking lot, a familiar sound. He squinted ahead to the ball fields. You do not recall this bleakness, how it was all sunlight even then, glaring burdock along the roots of the chainlink, ragweed outside the outfield margins, small boys holding gloves before their own squinting eyes like great soft shields, kicking dirt and helpless in the sun, steamy and choking dust in the center of the scrubby infield.

These days they returned to red plastic drums of cold water, Eskimo coolers like the big leagues, instead of the long-handled dipper and pail.

It has not been that long for so much to change.

The moan rose up again and stopped with the pitch, the magnesium ping of the metal bat, whipping the ball back and out as the colors shifted in the field. The umpire, tanned horribly brown as the Remington cowboy, walked toward the water cooler. He drank and spat and leaned against the backstop watching the pitcher warm up. He was a skeletal and ominous man, dark patches of sweat under each arm of his faded black tee shirt, beancap pushed back on his skull, an equally faded pillow protector slung from an arm at his hip, instep guards flapping.

"Play ball!" he shouted in a drawl, nodded toward Flynn.

He was so thin when he died we draped the white tee shirts around him, tucking the excess under his bony hips.

Until even the touch of the cotton tortured him. Then we propped the sheet with Styrofoam cups so it wouldn't touch him.

"SteeeReyekk!"

A bovine moan and click at the hip. He thumps the pillow protector up under the chin, squats to line the strike zone up, the iron mask leaning over the catcher. One and one, Flynn figures, fastball on the fists. The metal bat thunks when he saws him off, a bloopy sound after the ball falls foul, exactly like a rock makes sinking into deep, still water.

One and two. Waste one away.

But Flynn shakes it off. Inside curve and take a little off, in this kind of sun you can catch him anticipating you'll go by the book.

A perfect pitch sails in and trims a little space of white at the knee. The iron mask turns away and the hand drops to click the count even.

Flynn comes four steps off the mound to take the ball and stare at the cowboy eyes behind the iron.

Fitch slips the iron off to meet Flynn's gaze. Cerulean blue and placid eyes dare him. Flynn shakes his head and walks back up. Fitch is mopping sweat and unready to crouch yet. He too was fooled, Flynn knows. Sometimes the smart pitch catches everyone unready even when it trims the white. Two and two, Flynn rubs the ball, steps down and off for the hand to mouth, rubs both palms against the leather until they buck and skid. Fitch is ready to crouch.

Flynn asks for another ball, lofts this one in with a girlish fling. Fitch looks at its innocent face and drops it back in the pouch, throws out the same skiddy bastard Flynn's twice rejected.

Flynn promptly throws it back and Fitch smiles, pressing the smile in his lips so it doesn't show. Hamburg gets up from his crouch and strolls out with the new ball, rubbing it gently with splayed fingers, knuckles like purple knots. The home fans boo the visiting Flynn as Hotshot walks off to find the pine tar rag.

"Tired, Jack?"

"Never felt better, Hamburg. Asshole missed it, didn't he?"

"Sure he did, Jack, but you gotta pitch to Hotshot not to Fitch."

Hamburg takes the opportunity to grab his cup and rearrange and air the contents. Flynn laughs toward Fitch and turns back while Hamburg jogs back down.

"S'a count, Fitch?"

Fitch shows it like he really didn't know. Even Hotshot laughs.

Flynn fires a pisspea off and low, really smokes it. Fitch pulls the rope and bellows and Hotshot stands there long enough to hear the boobirds while Flynn walks in.

"It's a unfair world, Hotshot," Fitch says, and he too walks back to get water.

"Bad weather for a fireballer, boys," Flynn announces.

The skipper thinks it's funny. Wolfman rubs his constant bat, glaring at the skipper. Wolfman is a jujuman and he thinks Flynn speaks voodoo magic, and he don't like anyone to joke when Jack throws.

He proves it by hitting one out, high and long and disappearing slowly into stretching hands in the deep right-field upper deck.

"Just gotta go with the pitch, boys, don't you see?" The skipper cackles at this wonderful joke of his own, but this time it's okay since Flynn is up a run, and up the steps of the dugout waiting to give the jujuman five.

It ends that way, proving the validity of magic and the virtues of the book. Flynn goes to eleven and five, three point two ERA.

Smokey Joe's Band prepares a red carpet of white towels to lead the way to Flynn's locker. It is the first time in five starts that they have not had to work, and Flynn's complete game has enabled them two games of spit-in-the-cup in the bullpen. Flynn is a hero.

The press has decided so also for today, so Flynn fixes a new wad of Beechnut and Levi Garrett to enable him to think of quotable quotes. Wolfman, in his opposite cubbie, also sacrifices a post-game brew long enough to meet the press. The jujuman doesn't look the reporters in the eyes. Instead he glares at Flynn. It is love, Flynn knows. Wolfman believes that Flynn produces home runs for him. Flynn tips an imaginary hat to the Wolf during one of the glaring moments; Wolfman nods and lights another of the smelly French cigarettes the skipper believes to be impregnated with hashish. The man from the Morning Herald slips on one of the ceremonial towels, twisting his ankle. Serves him goddamn right, Flynn thinks, and he heads off to get a ham sandwich before his shower.

Flynn sees bony, purple ankles in high-back slippers next to him. The faint spray of burst vessels under the white skin reminds him of the catcher's knuckles, reminds him of Emma's delicate bruise. The leather slippers are covered with a skim of fine white dust from the cinders. Above the slippers the cuff of the grey trousers is frayed where it barely laps the ankle; a blue seersucker bathrobe ends at the thighs, it is tied at the waist in knots. Under too short sleeves skinny, hard arms end in huge hams, the fingers long and faintly blue. On the inside forearm facing him is a tattoo: LIVE FREE OR DIE. This is an old warrior.

"Afternoon," Flynn says.

"I was your bird dog, Jack, remember me?"

It is Ichabod Crane who speaks to Flynn, white strands combed akimbo over the craggy Dutch forehead, reddened eyes blazing in the deep, dark sockets of the skull. Flynn smells Old Spice and chaw, Mail Pouch: treat yourself to the best. The old man squits through the teeth, making brown dots in the cinders. Flynn begins to walk and the fellow shuffles after him, slippers scuffing fast and light as a firewalker.

"Oh yeah?" Flynn tests. "What'd I do the Legion champion year?"

"Seven Oh, three shutouts, no hitter where they allowed a flukey unearned run on ya!"

Old Ichabod squeals a high laugh and, squit-squit, dots the cinders.

"Hey batter hey . . ."

"Called Fred Billings in Albany after your first game that year but they didn't mind me. When you wrapped it up, he called back and said I could offer five thousand smackers to sign right away and I only laughed at him. Knew there was scouts already offered your dad twice that and the cham-peen-ship was coming up . . ."

He-he-he, Ichabod's wheezing laugh acknowledged an old wisdom: baseball organizations were sometimes slow and stupid. Flynn nodded.

Flynn stared at his father, unused to such guile in him.

Joe Flynn had made the vice president of the Cardinals come down to the boathouse with them. He rummaged through the tackle boxes, shaking the trays more than Jack had ever seen him do before. It was the only sign of anxiety in the old river guide.

"Rappala," Flynn's father said and held the jointed, silver minnow up for the vice president to see.

"Fine bass lure," the VP said. They were not stupid men.

His father held a bright thing up.

"Double ought spoon," the VP said. It was a game.

Flynn wondered why he was there. He decided then that

whatever they decided he would reject it, he did not like to be played with.

His father held up a banana curve of wood with great hooks.

"Afraid you got me there, Mr. Flynn."

"Muskie plug, my own design." Flynn's father placed it in the VP's hand. "You can have it. Don't work worth a damn, maybe you can figure what it needs."

"Jack's a fine young man," the VP said.

"So say he does sign up now. I heard there's boys never see these big bonuses. Play ten games in some mountain league and then they find out the damn bonus' got as many twists as this river."

"There are performance features in some bonuses, yes. This one too. Not, however, in the matter of the twenty-thousand signing bonus. That I assure you I am prepared to present today."

Flynn watched his father catch his breath as he pretended to hunt through the rods on the rack. Suddenly he felt sad. He wanted his father to say yes right now, take the check and pay off the business debt. He wanted to ask the VP if he and Dad could talk in private, tell his father he loved him, loved how he bargained with this clean-smelling, tailored man.

"Although . . . ," the VP tantalized. Flynn's father turned too quickly from the rack, the VP could see he had them hooked. Flynn knew that.

"I would like," the VP spoke softly, paused to drag it out, "I would like to set up some photographs of the signing, and we'd need the check for that." He smiled like a man with a fish.

"Jack's going to college," his father said.

Flynn blurted no aloud, his father stared him down.

"It's been a pleasure talking to you, sir," his father said, "and I know you have Jack's interests in mind, but his mother and me have always wanted him to go to college."

Later Flynn's father spat it out. "Trim bastard's afraid I'd run and cash the damn check before he gets his picture! Screw 'em! We ain't about to sell you cheap, Jackie. That money'd get you a house and . . ." He was going to say business, Flynn knew. ". . . a house and all and set you up in case it didn't work out, but I'll be damned if we let 'em cow us, son. Your mother and me, we want the best for you, and there's some fine colleges want to see you play for them."

That afternoon they went out to visit his sister. Flynn watched her crazy eyes as their father tried to explain it all to her. She understood money well enough, it bought candy bars and oranges, but Jack knew she couldn't follow the part about the vice president and colleges. He saw it build up in her until she cried, then he stood uncomfortably watching his mother wipe the tears away from the overgrown girlish eyes, watched her stroke the huge and tender skull.

"I'm sorry, Jackie," his sister wept, "I'm so sorry, Jackie . . ."

Flynn knew she had convinced herself she did something wrong that lost him this chance. He stood and rocked on the burning soles of his sweating feet, unable to say anything. They had led her away from the dayroom still crying. Flynn walked out to the car alone to give his father a chance to cry also.

Now he walked with the old bird dog to the side of the backstop.

"You make any money on me, Mr. . . . ?"

"Willard," the old man said, "Willard Walker, called me Restless Willard when I pitched in Triple A."

Hell yes, Flynn knew him, looked him in the face again to see. They were all there under the changing skin, the dead and the old, there under the aging flesh.

"Pleased to see you again, Will," Flynn said and extended a hand.

"Sorry, I can't," Willard said, then he whispered, "I catch diseases easy, can't stand to touch no more. Caught things from nigger boys and fish. Used to fish with your father, especially when they tried to sign you."

He whispered again, "Don't use no coins anymore, nor no spoon nor fork neither. Studied up more immunology than most doctors. I'm eighty-three and I'll live to be two hundred."

Willard blinked a few times and then leaned in toward the fence using the gaps in the chainlink like goggles. He kept his hands pinned behind his back and his feet planted three feet from the fence, leaning gangly and fragile as a bony boomerang, careful to touch nothing.

The boy pitching threw from the extreme left side of the rubber and still came inside with his heat. He was plump and sweaty and mad at himself, and between pitches he stole glances to the bench where a tan, hard-muscled man, his thigh swathed in ace bandages, stood and nodded.

"Don't open up your shoulder, remember what we talked about

when I warmed you up. Is he inside, Kenny? Is he inside? He says you're inside, get over on the rubber."

Flynn knew the man had to be the pitcher's father. The other coach, a stocky man with blinky eyes, could not disguise his scowls each time the pitcher's father spoke.

The little mullahs moaned and stopped, moaned and stopped as he loaded the bases.

"He ain't extending his arm," Willard said, still leaning at the absurd angle. The umpire nodded vigorously behind the catcher, he and the bird dog seemingly used to this running color commentary.

"Shouldn't ah listened to his danged father. Boy needs a coach."

Umpire nodded. Willard tensed with the pitch. The batter, a Mexican-looking lefty, ponged a neat little single into right field. The right fielder, charging, scooped the ball on one hop into his floppy mitt, pulled it out and reared back in one motion, pegging a true one-hop to the plate. The relay man waved to the throw as it passed him, and the catcher, a scrappy little kid wearing glasses under his mask, placed the tag and threw right back to second, his Yeager-style throat protector flapping.

He had caught the Mexican kid stretching the hit and bunching two runners between him and third. The second baseman waved a tag down in the proximity of the sliding man. The umpire waved him out from halfway up to the mound in noisy appreciation of two good throws. The Mex kid had beat the tag clean but it didn't matter.

Flynn hunted for the plump young pitcher and found him walking off toward the shade, his father's arm slung heavily around his shoulder, his head bent to his ear. You could see the tension in the rigid way the kid walked; with an arm like his, he'd end up a catcher if he played.

The umpire leered through the fence at them, resetting his bean cap over a sweaty thatch of yellowy silver hair.

"Right fielder's a prospect, Red," Willard said to the ump.

"Got a rifle, Willard." The ump spat a gob of brown, bit a fresh wad from the rope chaw in his bag, then extended it through the fence to Willard. "Looks like your escort's nearing, Restless."

The ump gestured beyond. Flynn turned to see the orderly ginger-footing across the cinders in floppy thong shower clogs.

"You know Jack Flynn," Willard said, as pleased as could be.

The ump nodded and stuck two crabbed fingers through the

chainlink for Flynn to shake. The fingers were brown and dirt caked. The ump was a nice man and liked to work kids.

"Come on, Mr. Walker," the orderly said, reaching for Willard's shoulder.

"No need to touch him," Flynn said as Willard angled away from the grasping fingers.

"Guess not," the orderly said. He and Willard started slowly back across the hot stones.

"Here!" Flynn shouted out, and went after the orderly. "This is to buy him chaw, and I want it in his account, hear? I'll give a call to check on it."

"Sure thing, Mr. Flynn," the orderly said, unblinkingly honest. Flynn felt awful about checking up on him and peeled another twenty off.

"Here for you too, for looking after him."

"Can't take tips," the orderly said. "Thank you anyway."

Willard waved from the gate near the hospital grounds.

"Damn decent of you, Flynn," the ump said and turned to shout, "Play ball."

Flynn wondered how the orderly knew his name. Had he been near enough to hear Willard say it, or had he known it from somewhere?

A woman in a yellow dress walked through the distant hospital grounds. Flynn felt the dust coating his throat.

Yessir, there's some places in the big show where'd it come in right handy to have the nut house gate next to the park, boys . . .

He didn't stay to watch the game.

FOUR

A woman floated on a rubber raft, not far, not close to the dock. Her dark, dark flesh was crossed by two thin bands of electric pink bikini. The surface of her back shone with sun or oil, and her hair was a phosphorous blond, beautiful at this distance, though it would have seemed hard-looking on shore.

There was no one else out on the lake and it was already eleven in the morning, but this lake was private and surrounded with year-round homes, a great oval green water where businessmen sailed sunfish after work and cast phosphorescent pink plugs and neon plastic worms at the bass they had paid to stock here. The woman floated, unmindful of all, her arms folded before her in a perfect diamond, her head slightly turned across the infield. The raft seemed to undulate slightly in an unseen series of waves. Flynn imagined that her toes trailed in the water where she turned them under at the end of the raft, the flesh barely licked by the cool water.

He imagined that the ride on the water was something like an endless orgasm for her. Still, warm, away, and slightly tremoring.

It was because he was young that he had thought something so foolish. And, too, because he had just come out from one of those houses, where he had spent the night making love, with more enthusiasm than skill, with a woman he had met whose husband was away.

He was an hour late for the bus, a bonus baby miles away from the park of his rookie league club.

In many ways he thought it the first memory of the big leagues.

The lady had called him Meat, likely because she knew players and the language they used.

"Oh more of that, Meat, please. I like how you touch me, darlin' . . ."

She hadn't really, Flynn knew. He was not very good, nor apparently possessed of the stamina she was used to in her ballplayer friends. She let him know with sighs, and by teasing him to keep him from dozing off.

He had wanted to sleep because he was tired. That seemed simple enough. He had pitched well and won a game—not his first but his first won right—and by three in the morning he wanted to sleep.

"Meatsy wants a sleepy bye, does he? He's gotta give Momma a kiss."

She pushed her groin toward him. He knew he was supposed to laugh and act, one way or the other. Either play the ballplayer and slap her ass and laugh, call a cab and go; or bitch her out and laugh and drink another glass of her bourbon and snore, farting on her bed. But he was tired and wanted to sleep.

And he resented her calling herself Momma.

He had called home after the game. They spoke to him, his father, Jim and then his mother, bothered by a summer cold like she was every year. A bronchial wheeze on the phone, long pauses as she choked on her cigarettes.

Flynn imagined something like the Lou Gehrig story, or some such film, a mother cured—or dying happy—at her son's success.

"Struck out ten, allowed three hits, and pitched mostly ground balls."

"Oh, that's good, Jack."

She tried to understand. She was ill and there was a lot of noise on both ends. Jim and his wife and kids were there on the river, the assholes in the clubhouse were shouting "Hi Mom" and stealing quarters from the payphone ledge in front of him.

"I wanted you to know," he whispered, "I'm on my way."

"You're coming home."

"No. You know."

"We believed in you then, Jack, we believe in you now. You're the only one you have to prove it to now."

He nodded and began the goodbyes. The guys in the clubhouse were throwing his game ball around. He had had to pay for it, the club had no provision for memorializing someone's first rookie league artistic success. The game had drawn two thousand and four-teen on a Friday night.

"We love you, Jack," she said.

He nodded and said, "Goodnight, Momma."

The guys on the club called him Sweet Momma for weeks. For a while he thought it would stick, but he was one of those white pitch-ers who would never be nicknamed, never a Dutch Master, Flash, or even Righty. He was always too good for that, like Seaver, Carlton, or Palmer, though even Seaver got stuck with Tom Terrific for a time.

Some pitchers just had a kind of intense presence, a lordliness that kept them from having any nickname stick other than their own. Gibson did. Early on, Flynn too knew he was one of them, he had to admit it. He grew tan and silent.

The game made him become something, it wasn't what he wanted. He had begun playing baseball for noise and for the secret reason most boys and men have for the game: it authorized intimacy and companionship. Not the pat on the butt that writers liked to notice in witty or thinky columns, not even the high fives and dou-ble clasps shown in slo-mo. Rueful smiles were what Flynn remem-bered, VFW-style practical jokes, looking into someone else's face to see how the pressure showed on him. Roommates watching eleven o'clock news on television, reaching to pick up the phone and answer a bed check call, all the while still watching the news and making an asshole face. Rows of colored bottles—of aftershave and cologne and herbal balms—on a locker shelf; the wood click of rows of men in spikes along a runway from the clubhouse to the dugout.

Women's reasons, Flynn supposed, but then his mother gave him the game. She thought it would be good for him to get involved in organized play; not, he thought, to keep him from following his father into something as solitary as the river, but to make that inevi-table choice have a reason to it.

The reader shouldn't get the idea that the elder Flynn opposed the lad's choice of such cooperative athletic endeavor.

Nossir. His father loved baseball, though he understood it little.

Times on the river at night. Mel Allen on the Yankee network from the Syracuse station echoing on the water. Humid air, mosqui-toes druggy and fat. Clear nights, planets in a row on the horizon, a stripe of shimmering moonlight making a river within the river.

On all kinds of nights, they listened together, the sound of the radio slapping off the resistant water, echoing and pooling in the night air, exactly like haze. Dodger games out of Watertown, the reception fading to whispers and then Red Barber's voice booming out so loud you heard men in other boats hooting it down. Whether they had a client in the boat or they fished alone, baseball was there.

His father loved the outfield, the range and darkness of it. It was like water, something Flynn came in his own time to recognize as well. The swirling eddies of the left field corner, the lake of right, the fanning channels of the power alleys, the oceanic—yet breachable—expanse of center field. To Flynn's father all baseball reduced to a single play. Flynn recalled being taken to see it in the newsreels at age eleven.

The catch. Everyone called it that, everyone had a way to describe it. Mays, in deep, deep water, in shadows, turning his back to the ball and swimming out to the mark where the stone already began to sink through the slow water. A loping, certain stride, like the old men with goggles and rubber caps you sometimes saw in the river, distance swimmers, their bodies dark with grease and tan, as dark as Willie's. On each great stroke of their paddlewheel arms, they would look up over their shoulders, as Willie did, almost stopping in the water, the next stroke pulling them through a long glide before the arm came up again, Willie turning coolly and making the throw in a while, falling back down in the water. Wertz and the Series gone.

It was one of two times Flynn's father broke his allegiance—an allegiance, Flynn sometimes thought, based on the patriotic directness of the name—to the American League. The other time was in '47 when Robinson came up. Flynn was only four years old then, he couldn't have remembered, yet he liked to think he did.

His father said something beautiful once about all that.

"When you see something like Jackie Robinson," he said, "you know how beautiful America could be if we would let it. People have a beauty all their own, son. You have to see it."

It was unusual for him to be so eloquent, but not so democratic. He had fought at Normandy during the war. He was silent about it, he had seen too many people die. Once Flynn pressed him and he was shocked at the bitterness of the story his father told.

"We had been there some time, mostly mopping up. It was a long time after we hit the shore, a long time. This one morning we were in the woods near the beach, you see, doing all the shitty little odds and ends you never hear about in war. This fresh-faced lieutenant comes up to us and he has us measure the frigging tree stumps. It wasn't that strange, Jackie, there were always these bullshit jobs to do. Finally someone asks and this pisspot says we were responsible for the damages to the trees. We had to measure so we could pay the owners . . ."

Flynn asked who the owners were.

"No one owns a tree," his father said blankly.

"Who?"

"When we marched out, we seen it. Up over the road was this horseshoe arch, a sign like they have up at Alex Bay. Chase Bank of New York, it says. I learned right then that we fought the goddamned war for the banks and not for people floating in salt water with their guts hanging out . . ."

It was during the time that there were troubles with the bank over the loan for the business. "Let 'em come, Honeybabe," his father told his mother once. "I'll blow their asses off with my twelve gauge."

"It'll be the sheriff, not the bank," his mother said.

"I'll fill his ass with lead too, he knows better, he's a veteran."

Even so, Flynn did not doubt the story. It marked something for him. He marked it and fed it back to the old man in 1967 when the war came, and later when Ali lost his championship because he would not go. His father couldn't argue, nor could Flynn. Team doctors assured him he could not be drafted. It made little sense—it would be grandstanding—to make a public statement.

Still he signed a letter against the war in the New York Times, his name listed with actors and singers. And he went to Washington while Nixon watched a football game behind a wall of buses. Flynn had something of a box seat and saw a sea of people waving together, singing, "All we are saying . . ."

And whenever he saw a clip of the catch, or saw or heard Jackie Robinson's name, he had the kind of family feeling you have when someone dies who you knew as a kid, when someone comes up to bat who you played with in the minors.

Still he wondered if that was not how his father came to call him Jackie. And he remembered how no one owns a tree, and how people have a beauty of their own, when, in college, a bearded little man made him read Walt Whitman.

"The sun falls on his crispy hair and moustache, falls on the black of his polish'd and perfect limbs. I behold the picturesque giant and love him."

Flynn still has the book somewhere, a critical edition it's called. There's a picture of Walt Whitman inside; he looks like God.

Flynn looked into other poems since, but none were the same. There was a poet with the Pirates in '72 or '73, he was writing a book with Doc Ellis. The guy was a big teddy bear, awkward, and yet real pleased with himself. Flynn wasn't very impressed, but the guy had a poet's beard like Walt Whitman and a pretty fair belly. He huffed playing fungo.

Flynn headed back upriver toward Clayton, sure somehow Emma had gone back there. In the sun along the highway near Chippewa Bay, a car was pulled over in the shimmering heat of the shoulder, its hazard lights flashing like a spaceship. The man behind the wheel sat staring ahead, patient and weary, his hands gripping ten and two on the wheel, while next to him a woman shook the child on her lap, violently angry, the woman and child both screaming, the child's baseball cap shaken off as Flynn went by. They had paused for this. Life—even on vacation in the islands—had too much anger to it.

Kids often made Flynn sad. Especially hearing them in some game gone beyond salvation, down six runs in the bottom of the ninth and two away, a whole section of Little Leaguers chanting, "We need a hit, we need a hit, we need a hit . . . ," high in the grandstand behind them. The afternoon seemed closed around them, and only they did not know. You could already hear the traffic outside the stadium, see everyone in the dugout getting on their postgame faces and beginning to dream of beer and roast beef. The kids kept chanting. We need a hit, we need a hit.

Flynn was that once. It was why he played. The best was the kind of baseball disappearing now; everyone showing up at the park after school, choosing up with an absolute sense of relative forces, with neither kindness nor lies. Later in the summer, the kids would come out early before the haze quite burned off.

"Flynn has to pitch from behind the mound or we don't go."

"Make him pitch both sides . . ."

"No."

Even then he should have known he could never be one of them, that he would end up the tall, handsome man without a nickname.

"We'll only pitch him three innings and then he goes to right field."

"He has to throw something we can hit."

"I try, I really do."

"Bullshit, Flynn. You can't do shit but throw the ball fast. I'd like to see you really have to play."

"Leave him alone."

He didn't play baseball to be alone and yet that was how it worked out. Something in you chose you for it. The muscles of the thighs and back, an appreciation for the rhythm and concentration a game requires, the goopy look about your face that when you grow up makes you handsome, but when you're a kid gets you laughed at and called names.

His mother's hero was a goop too. Something of the Catholic in her made her latch onto Don Larsen and the concept of a perfect game. Flynn imagined she saw it like the unblemished soul the nuns talked about. He always imagined the soul as a milk jug, white and cool and full; but what form sins took in this image he couldn't say. Perhaps specks of dirt, or a housefly afloat on the creamy surface. Larsen had allowed none of these specks. There was a picture Flynn remembered, number eight with his mask still on in Larsen's arms, Yogi like a fat frog in the arms of a prince. It was about this time that Flynn turned against the Yankees.

The stupid Yankees! Mantle, the big hick, hit a homer. Meanwhile Maglie pitched a sweet little five-hitter and no one remembered that until trivia games started to get popular.

They had The Barber up that year for the annual father-son communion breakfast and Flynn made his father go, but then everyone asked questions about how it felt to see Larsen do what he did. The Barber was a guinea from Niagara Falls and he answered all the questions like a priest, real quiet and dark, nasty eyes.

Lifetime The Barber had it all over Larsen. Like they say, you could look it up. But the goop's who they remember.

Flynn saw Maglie again when he was pitching coach for the Seattle Goddamn Pilots that Bouton wrote about. By that time he was a real goombah-looking guy, king of flatfoot and lost-looking but still mean in the eyes. They didn't talk.

It had to be because of Larsen that his mother made him play ball in the leagues. He was thirteen years old then, late to start, baseball, if it hits you it should hit you at twelve.

Flynn remembered running out on the porch and down into the shady street, shouting because the Dodgers won the Series. He was twelve then and Johnny Podres threw a shutout. There was no one else out on the street and he jumped and shouted awhile and then went in, feeling foolish and lost.

Hodges batted both runs in. Sandy Amaros robbed the fat turtle Berra of at least a double down the line, then doubled up McDougald, the throw going Reese to Hodges.

For a while that first high school season, after they made Flynn a pitcher, his mother would ask, "Did you pitch a perfect game, Jack?" when he came home. He finally explained when she pissed him off once too often with it after a game where he got knocked off the mound.

She was still alive for the no-hitter. Only Hooton and Pappas and Stoneman did it with him that year, and only Hooton's was on the books when Flynn pulled his in July. It wasn't on television, which was good because it was fairly boring when all was said and done.

"It wasn't a perfect game, Momma, but it was a long time coming," he had said on the phone.

"At least there weren't any questionable plays, if you know what I mean, Jack."

He knew. It was a clean, workmanlike no-hitter by a lord of the game. There were no errors to question, but he had walked three, so it was also far enough from perfect to take that out of his mind. Once he had it in his hand, there was nothing special, it was like climbing a hill. But you couldn't say that. It was an exclusive club and it had been a long time coming.

How does it feel, Jack, to be part of an exclusive club so long denied you?

He wanted to say, ask Seaver or Carlton. Not being a smart ass, but really. Ten to one they'd tell you the same. It's a hill you climb, and when you get there, you go back down.

Tom Seaver, the hardest hitter I ever faced.

He wanted to say that once before he quit, but never got the right chance. Seaver was so damn smart-looking up there, so certain of his body. Flynn was jealous, Seaver a year younger.

Johnny Bench and Foster.

They were hills you got up and then came back down. Sometimes Bench seemed worst because he seemed to know what every pitch would be and where you'd place it. When he twisted all around missing a fastball, he'd sort of nod at you as he settled back in, as if he was saying nice pitch, I didn't expect it to rise so much but otherwise it was right on the money where I wanted.

Other times Foster seemed worse because you never really knew if he wanted to play that day. When he did, he would murder you, he was like Wolfman that way; and when he didn't, he would scare you with an easy cannon shot falling just short of the fences.

"What's wrong?" she asked.

"Nothing. Why?"

"You have a look on your face. I thought you were in pain."

Flynn turned to Emma.

"Do you like the car? This car?"

She laughed. "Yes, I like it, of course."

"Good. I'll give it to you when I'm done."

It hurts to reminisce he thought she knew.

Why.

They turned inland at Alex Bay. "I don't want your lovely car," she said. He nodded silently, he did not mean to insult her, not even to have her think he thought the gift would even things up.

"Can I ask you something?"

Of course he nodded.

"Why," she said, "why when we came up from Syracuse didn't we stay on 81? Why'd we cut back through the country?"

I wanted to see my mother.

He remembered it was very clear turning now back there.

"I understand you saw Willard Walker today," she said.

"Yes."

"I didn't know you knew him."

"Why's he in there?"

"Shouldn't be. Nowhere else to go, and he does lose it now and then."

It? Yes I know him like the duck knows the bird dog.

"He says black people drove him crazy."

"He's a sick, old man, Jack."

Nodded. Heading toward Redwood and then to Theresa—pronounce the "h" and drop the "e", lisping like: Thressa, like Plessy for Plessis up the road. Down between the two lakes.

The woman floated on the rubber raft.

"Have to be pushing off, Meat?" the married lady asked.

She wore a long jade-colored bathrobe, embroidered in gold.

"Wanna screw her too, big boy?" She pointed out on the water. "In Johnson City there are mucho available women, Meat. It comes with the territory." She laughed ugly. "A territory where no one comes, except the 6:15 train."

The woman floated, Flynn had to hitch into town because the married lady was expecting something.

When he caught up with the team, a taxi fare of thirty-some dollars, everyone whistled as he came into the shabby clubhouse. They knew the married lady. The skipper did also.

"Listen, peckerwood," he said behind the thin folding door that was the visiting manager's office, "you want to dip your stick into every honeypot that sees you pitch one, that's all right with me. The word has come down from the front office: you, Flynn, are certified stuff! You're gonna be the next Bob Gibson . . . ha! You pitch every five days, whether I like it or not. And you may not ask me now whether I like it. But!—" and here he shouted, Flynn heard the room hush outside the folding door, "you miss my goddamn bus or any of my goddamn pregame warmups and I'll have you run your pecker off, which if I'm right will begin to run by itself soon enough, seeing as who you've picked for your hall-of-fame flop in the hay-hey-hey."

Flynn looked at him.

"What are you waiting for, flat ass?"

Flynn didn't know, so he let himself out the folding door.

"Shut it please, Mr. Pitcher Flynn," the skipper growled.

When he entered the squirrely little room, they greeted him differently. He was certified stuff, even though he didn't play baseball to be alone.

Within weeks he was up in the New York Penn, the old PONY league, "a short-season 'A' league," the Irish commissioner insisted to him, "not a damn rookie league!"

He was moving up and near to home, fans already coming down out of North Country to see him at Utica. Local boy makes good. Alone.

The woman floated.

"Which of the young men does she like the best? Ah the homeliest of them is beautiful to her."

"What's that, Jack?"

"It's a poem," he said. "I learned it in college."

FIVE

Why'd you choose Iowa, Jack?

(Laughs) It probably sounds hokey, but in a way Iowa chose me. I mean, I think my old man was half bluffing when we turned down the Cardinals, and I don't remember that we had any applications in, you know (laughs) at colleges, I mean, other than maybe this Regents scholarship they had in New York.

So they recruited you?

Well, we had a lot of colleges in this big packet my father set aside. I mean, you win a Legion championship like that and the word gets around. So my father flips through the packet one night, he and my momma—uh, my mom, I mean—and it's like my father is looking at mail order ads, you know, to see who has the best deal. (Laughs loudly) They didn't really say anything, those letters. There's all these NCAA requirements and you know . . . baseball coaches are a far piece from basketball coaches, in recruiting I mean . . . (A great smile crosses his face.) I think my father wanted to have our cake and eat it too, you know. I mean we had just turned down twenty-plus thousand bucks.

Did the Cardinals suggest Iowa?

Hell, no. They take care of their own. They wanted us to think about somewhere in Missouri, and they mentioned Arizona and a community college down there in the Southwest. They really didn't have a lock on me, you know.

So . . . Iowa?

There was a river there. (He is speaking softly now.) Honest to god. That and my father got the idea that I would definitely be playing in the Midwest. It's hot as hell there in the summer, he said, corn's as high as your eye, and all that . . . Plus there were two minor league teams in the state, and that impressed him, why god knows. Also he liked the Hawkeye . . . Herkie.

Pardon.

Herkie the Hawkeye. He's the little mascot, like the Chicken. On the letterhead they had this Herkie figure smacking a baseball glove. My father was a very simple man, he was easily swayed by advertising. My father . . . (he pauses here, unable to find the words) . . . you don't see that kind of man much anymore. Oh, there's dudes playing in the majors still something like him, simple farm boys, despite the fact that they're hyped that way. Catfish was supposed to be that, you know. I never really knowed him.

(Flynn seems able to lapse into this regionless dialect at will. It is not an affectation so much as what one imagines to be the speech of baseball fields, a bit of Indiana and Georgia combined. The dialect does not unsuit him, it is just unconvincing. Jack Flynn is clearly one of life's true aristocrats, a graduate of the Communications and Media program at the University of Iowa, a man destined for life beyond baseball. The effect is rather like Bill Bradley talking jive. You are disconcerted. You look for some mockery in him when he speaks so. There is none. It is as if he always longed to be one of the boys and knew he would never be.)

My father . . . (Flynn pauses and shakes his head. He is clearly having trouble getting this out. For a moment it looks like his eyes are glazing over, but then the Flynn control reasserts itself.)

Talk about him, Jack.

I'm trying to (laughs), seems like I'm always trying to. You know what a shore dinner is?

In restaurants, you mean? The seafood platter?

Yes and no. Those things're named after what the guides do, you know, when you have a fishing party? My father . . . my father, he prepared the best goddamn shore dinner you ever tasted. I mean he loved making shore dinners! He was as careful as my Aunt Bertie baking a pie . . . First there'd be this big deep skillet full of fat back, cooked right over the fire 'til it crisped.

Cracklings?

Yeah, that's the idea. Me and Wolfman Hunt, sometimes we'd chow down on cracklings in a bag, you know, like chips. Gave the rednecks shit fits . . . Can I say that?

It's a transcription, you can say anything. Hell, I can print almost anything.

Anyway, my father, he'd take those crispy pieces of fatback and put 'em up on bread with some onions, and that'd be your appetizer you know. Heaven really, on the river. The twilight coming down and this big, careful man leaning over the fire, watching to see that the whole party ate, just like some big surly lady waitress. (He quickly makes himself clear, his voice rising.) Now don't get this wrong, goddamn it, my father was a man, one helluva man. Tougher than shit. My brother come back from running the Rangers basic training, back in the 'Nam days, and my father decked him, clean out . . . (Pauses, considering) Can you leave that out? That's real private and will hurt certain people. My brother died—not in the fight, I mean, later—but it was one of those things. Say that when I grew up, I always confused my father with Paul Bunyan. For a while I even got the idea he had a blue ox! (Laughs)

So, where were we?

Onion and fatback. There was this story I read for a class in college. It was mostly bullshit, but with some real beautiful stuff about hiking in the pine forests, and about the river. Anyway, the guy in the story takes an onion sandwich with him when he goes out to fish. I knew when I read that, that that was right. I sorta sat up and paid attention if you know what I mean.

Hemingway.

What?

Hemingway. Ernest Hemingway.

Yeah, whatever. Anyway, while people's eating this sandwich, you set the water boiling on the fire, and you set that rendered fat boiling with it. Two iron pans. Sometimes you get 'em too close and the steam will settle on the fat—or you'll splash them—and the fat roars like a railroad train, or thunder or something. Real boily noise, all crack-crack-crack! So . . . you set your corn boiling and your boiled whole potatoes, little sweet things . . . (Laughs) You can tell I'm Irish, huh? Irish caviar, my father called mashed potatoes! (Laughs) Then you put in your fish. Doesn't matter what it is: pike, bass, anything, it tastes wonderful, you know. Dropped in that hot fat, fried in it. The air smells of it, it mixes with the river smell.

Batter?

Huh?

You put some batter on the fish?

(Laughs loudly) Jeez, I thought you wanted to get back to talking about baseball.

Well (laughing), I do eventually, unless we can sell this to House and Garden.

Field and Stream! (Flynn laughs again. Finally the laugh is becoming comfortable, not the wary punctuation it was earlier. You begin to think Flynn would be fun to know, a good friend, behind the priggishness, the awkward quality he carries around with him like his lifetime ERA and his bad arm.) No, they don't put batter on it! That's for Arthur Treacher's, Brit shit. This is the real thing . . . After the fish comes steak if they order it as an option. I could never tell my father's position on steak, but I think he just went along with it. Oh, I mean, he liked his steak at home or a restaurant, but I think he thought it was treachery, you know, a lack of loyalty to the river, to have steak with the shore dinner. But . . . business types liked it and the markup was good. (Laughs) My father had to have an eye for the markup, we were always right on the edge, you know, until I signed.

What about your signing? There are stories . . .

(Laughs) Let me finish the dinner! (Laughs) My father'd kill you if you didn't tell about the dessert—I mean he would of, if he was alive, you know—just like he'd like to kill you if you didn't eat it when he made it.

Well, I wouldn't want to get anybody killed . . .

(Flynn pauses strangely, not catching the joke. He has a wary quality.) So, where was I?

Dessert.

Oh yeah. French toast, these big slabs of bread, you know, cut them from the loaves in blocks. Soak them in batter—Dad used a little nutmeg in his, said a Frenchy guide taught him that, and it makes all the difference—and then plop 'em in the same fat.

The same fat?

Yessir! I know you'd think it would stink with fish, but you got to imagine how hot this grease is I'm talking about. (Laughs) Once the old man somehow kicked the pot over, this great big iron fryer, you know. A whole gale of flame struck out! Leaping tongues of fire! (Laughs) You can imagine the loss there, the whole dinner depends on your grease.

Somehow he made it through . . . (he seems to lapse into memory here, just dipping in for a moment and swimming right out) . . . somehow. So you slide these French toast slabs into the grease and it seals 'em right up, instant-like, crisp as a carnival waffle. You serve 'em up and put on butter, some maple syrup—the real thing, Dad tapped his own—and then a tablespoon of heavy cream, a spoon of brandy. You'd think you had died and gone to heaven or someplace like it . . .

Sounds like you wouldn't mind doing it yourself. Do you get up there often, to the Thousand Islands?

(Flynn is in thought and he does not answer immediately.) I just might do that someday. I really might. You can't just be a guide though, not the kind my father was . . . (Thinking again) No . . . no, not much anymore . . . there's really no one up there except Bertie and . . . (Again he sinks in thought.)

And?

And so we went to the College World Series (laughs), but of course we didn't make it through. It's unusual for a Big Ten school to do that. (Laughs again, almost devilishly; the sense was that he had gone so far and then retreated, it was a feeling something like what hitters must have felt when Flynn worked against them.)

I take it you want to get back on track.

Want to? (Laughs) No, have to, right?

So . . .

(Flynn interrupts.) It's important to say . . . I mean what got me started on all this horsecrap was how my father was easily swayed. It's strange, isn't it, a big man like that, you know, the rough-tough, wise river guide, that you'd feel you had to protect him? He was a very simple man, with simple needs and simple joys, if I can say that . . . I . . . I remember, when I started playing ball serious, that was my mother's doing, but my father got into it, you know. He'd warm me up or just play catch every day. I can remember the light slipping, the sun going down in a haze like it does by the river, and we'd try to use as much of the light as we could . . . Fish would be rising and maybe a ship would be making its way down the channel, something romantic, you know? A ship from Panama . . . Liberia. We'd throw 'til the mosquitoes chased us in, hardly talking, maybe Red Barber or somebody on the radio, the ball going back and forth, smacking in the gloves. I'd watch the rotation of the stitches when he threw it to me, you know (laughs), maybe I was still thinking I could have been a slugger, and two home runs careerwise aint half bad! (Laughs, then pauses in thought again, very pensive and almost sad) My father (sighs), he was something, yes sir. Hell, you'll end up writing the whole piece about this, won't you? (Makes a gesture as if setting out a headline) Flynn: His Father Was His Secret Source of Strength! (Smiles oddly) Maybe that's all I really wanted to say about him. I mean, I remember when we first started playing catch—when he first offered—I was worried about him, worried that I'd hurt him, or show him up, or, really, that he couldn't do it. He threw like a woman, sort of, he threw like he casted a rod really, but he had a hell of an arm. He could whip it in there, keep you lively, you know? And he had an old, big-fingered glove he drug up from somewhere, a strange thing he greased up with mink oil and polished again and again with oxblood shoe wax. He was always careful with his gear . . . and he surprised me, you know? The way he played catch? I guess I learned something about him in those summers . . . He thought the world was lovely, my father did, bad with the good, for him it was all a holiday until the end . . .

"What about your mother?"

Flynn drove with a blank and resolute quality, a wholesome caution she found quite annoying. They crossed the Indian River into Theresa.

"Aren't you making too much of that white knight quality?" she asked.

"What?"

He did not waver.

"All that crap about a natural aristocracy of pitchers . . . the white young men with destiny upon them?"

"You make it sound like the Ku Klux Klan," he said.

He negotiated the village streets with care, looking for something. He is coming around.

She smiled and asked him to forgive her.

"But really," she said, "isn't it all too goopy?"

She got through. Flynn slowed and parked carefully, stared at her.

She saw it dawn he knew she thought.

"My mother is buried here. Here in Theresa."

She looked at him.

"You knew, didn't you?" he said. "Why did you use that word?"

"Goopy?"

It hurt not to know her. He tried.

"I knew—I saw—great black pitchers. Gibson, Ellis . . . Fergie Jenkins strung five twenty-game seasons in a row. They had a certain quality, I . . . I just mean that I . . ."

He began to cry and she was sorry but it had to be done. She had felt the same way when he struck her.

"Don't you see . . . ," he cried, "I can't remember!"

"I know that," she said sharply. "You've told me that before."

He wiped at the tears with one knuckle. Men were dear.

"It's something," he said, "a natural state . . . I tried to speak it so I could get out from under it. It's not just pitchers. You see it in other sports, in life . . . senators, teevee anchormen . . . goalies . . . there's a scrubbed quality about them, a state of grace . . ."

He studied her with a glazed understanding.

"You're putting some things together, right?" she asked.

"You're from Canada," he said. "You know about goalies."

She nodded happily.

"Guy LeFleur," he said. "He has it too, the goopiness . . ."

She nodded again. Yes, yes, Flynn, it is coming back.

Emma LaChance, she thought.

He started the car again and maneuvered through the village to the hill where she lay.

"You want me to tell you everything, Jack, and it's the worst thing I could do. Amnesia, if that's what it is, isn't any virus. Nor is it a knock on the skull, at least not usually, and then it's almost always retrograde. You know too much . . . What you have is a block, no? You're familiar with that phenomenon, much more familiar than I."

"I suppose so," he said, "but there's more than you, more I can't get straight . . ."

"I know that too," she said. "Shall we go up?"

She let herself out the door and stood, unfazed, crisp, coolly pastel, waiting for him in the shade by the gate. Stones in an arch like the woods outside Normandy, spike iron fence and a mossy, damp smell like the old hospital in Ogdensburg.

The car door had the curve and fit and weight of the hatch door to a jet cockpit. Wolfman Hunt was a pilot and they wrote it into his contract that he could not fly. This was long before Munson went down, before Clemente. Wolfman ignored them and they suspended him; he ignored them again after they reinstated him.

Flynn still held the door open, and he looked at the wood inlay on the dash, the rows of black dials with lime green numerals.

"Considering the other expenses you are likely to undertake in the coming weeks, I have to advise you that a Maserati is not a prudent investment," Lenny had smiled then. "Besides, where will you get it fixed up there, the corner garage?"

"I didn't expect it to be the kind of Maserati which breaks down in the first two weeks," Flynn said.

"Touché," Lenny said, and then he had signed the purchase order.

He walked to her at the gate.

"What am I supposed to do?" he said.

"Keep remembering."

"And?"

"Do what you have to do. You're the white knight, Jack."

It was not easy. Inside the gate, up the slope of green where the markers made uncertain rows like chess pieces against the shaded turf, a man stared down at them, coiling hose into a black doughnut at his feet. He wore pressed, crisp work clothes, the forest green gabardine Flynn's father favored, alone among the guides not wearing flannel shirts or khaki. The gravedigger bent at the waist to coil the hose and he peered at the two of them with interest but no suspicion. It was hot and he was working, and there was an attractive woman entering the grounds. He brought the hose in slow circles, the nozzle slithering through the grass toward him as he coiled it. Flynn climbed the gentle hill toward the Coghlan plot where Nell lay, a Flynn in death, and like the Flynns, dead by water.

Pneumonia was a kind of water death. Cancer too. Six years before she had not survived the annual onset of vapors: the spring bronchitis thickening, a flu following upon it, the pneumonia setting in. She had drowned in herself, just as Jim had drowned in the river, just as her only daughter had begun to drown in the womb, the water setting in upon the skull, making it bloom but pressing the brain into something like an ill-formed chestnut, a shriveled thing, a constant childhood.

Flynn had received the news in spring training. He was in the outfield with the other pitchers, after running, taking turns at taking lofty fly balls in gentle sunlight, neither pushing nor holding back, just feeling his body come back to him, slowly in April, but sure it would be there.

This would be his year. He was coming off a 20-10 year on a last-place team. In any other year it would have been enough to get you in the record books. It was enough, that and a no-hitter; even if Carlton had won 27 with a team that finished a percentage point back, even if it was with the Cards, where Flynn was supposed to have made a lifetime, before Carlton came up.

He felt good. They were kidding out there and stretching their legs, and the boys were talking to him, joking at him. It was what happened when you had a good year under your belt, it gave people a license to razz you. It felt good.

"Look alive, Flynnie!"

The ball pokked off the fungo bat and rose in a looping arc, high in the sun. Flynn turned his back to it and the boys hooted and made like to faint. He jogged out after it, gauging where he thought it would drop, turned and saw it there, like a Polaroid snapshot, the red stitches grinning at him like a clown face. It was like the ball had just stopped in the air, the bottom falling out. He stuck his glove out under it and felt it thud off the hard ridge of the heel.

As he chased after it, he could hear the boys squeal.

"Ooooh-eeeee! No-hit Flynn bobbles the catch!"

"Take the spring out of there, Flynn!"

"Steve Carlton goes to the wall and snatches 'em, Flynn!"

He laughed and threw it in, lobbing it to preserve the arm. Karen sat in the wooden stands in a yellow bikini, her face buried in her hands, laughing with the other wives. Another fly ball pokked out toward the group of laughers. Someone was waving toward him and shouting, "Come in, Flynn! Come in . . ."

The boys were still laughing when he jogged in to the infield.

"Told you, boys, no-hit, no-glove, he's gone!"

There was still some hooting in the outfield when he made his way into the clubhouse.

"Said it was important, Jack," the clubhouse boy said.

Two reporters nodded to him as he took the phone.

"She's bad, Jackie," his father said.

The way he wept sounded like the boys hooting. It was a yipping sound, it made Flynn afraid to hear his father yipping like that.

Pneumonia is a backwash, like when the bottoms flood over after spring rains, the soil so saturated it becomes a swamp, too wet to drain, rich and dark and skimmed with algae and mosquito larvae. Only the sun could dry the shallows again, only the sun could retrieve it from the marsh grass. It was sunny in Arizona, sunny and dry and eighty; snow and thirty degrees in Massena.

"She just can't get her breath, Jackie," he yelped again. "They're trying, but it's bad enough to come, son."

Flynn lying in the outfield grass, the sun so good upon his face and chest. Just can't get my breath yet, Skipper, need to stretch out some and soak the rays.

The Skipper laughing. This would be his year.

Karen didn't take the plane then. Flynn had told her not to, but he hadn't really thought she would listen to him. He had wanted her to come.

"You can stay with the girls here, I'll call you to come up if there's anything serious."

"You sure, Jack?"

"Sure I'm sure."

He wasn't. He thought she would say that Mama Nell needed her. He hated when she called her Mama Nell, but he wanted to hear her say it now.

"I'll come back and pack for you," she said.

The girls were watching him, he hated them now for the same reasons that he loved them usually. How they hung together, all these wives. They were like sorority girls—hell, most of them were sorority girls. They took care of their own. Death was bad, but so was being traded. They were watching to see what he would say.

Karen ran a finger under the elastic at her waist. The tan line. She was looking to see how her goddamn tan was coming while Momma was dying in the snow and shitty slush.

"No need to do that, hon'. I'm used to packing . . ."

The girls smiled. He had shown the right stuff.

"Anyway," he said, "you'll be better here with the girls. I won't worry about you so much . . ."

"Autograph, Jack?"

"Screw it!" Flynn said.

It was an old codger in a Hawaiian shirt, grinning through a leather tan, liver spots all over the hand that pushed the Holiday Inn placemat forward to be signed. The old codger's face turned yellow with the shock of rejection.

"I'm sorry . . . I'm . . . ," Flynn tried to tell him.

"Jack's had some bad news," Karen explained.

"I don't need that," Flynn snapped at her as he signed the placemat. "Sorry," he told the man.

"No, I'm sorry," the man said, "Hope it works out, Jack, this is gonna be your year."

The old man tipped his terrycloth fishing hat to the girls. They were all staring at Flynn. He had snapped at Karen when she was standing by him.

He kissed her and she smelled like coconuts from the lotion all over her body. The lipstick had that strawberry, waxy taste. She wiped at her lip with a finger.

"Call me, hon'?" she whispered, baby-like.

"Yeah."

Yeah. Karen was there for the funeral, tan and in a Saks white linen suit. Wolfman, too, wore white linen, carried a black walnut stick with an ivory and gold handle. It was formal wear. Wolfman didn't have permission to leave training camp; he came anyway, bringing his own jet into Ogdensburg, a voodoo pilot.

At the funeral breakfast, Flynn's father commented on the cane. He appreciated good work. Wolfman gave him the walking stick, wouldn't hear of him turning it down. Flynn's father had seemed touched, he muttered thank you through watery eyes.

Yes! The same man, the gravedigger in gabardine, was working that morning high on the farthest corner of the slope, uphill of the funeral party.

Flynn remembered the loop of water in the sunlight, like a spray of diamonds. The beauty of the air, spring setting in on Theresa.

He had gotten his mother a hand-rubbed cherrywood box with brass fittings, the best they had in Massena. It too shone in the spring sun. Everyone shone. Karen in white, her tanned arms gilt with soft, bleached hair. His father wearing a black wool suit and tie, polished English boots Flynn made him buy because the black utility shoes wouldn't shine up right.

It was like some festival under the tent on the hill, all of them there. The traveling secretary from the club stood within inches of the white and violet arrangement the club had sent, the Padres' SD in dark roses near the center like a bow.

Wolfman had tiny white roses in his arms, a bouquet of hundreds he had brought on the plane with him. Aunt Bertie edged near him when the priest began to talk, and Wolfman took her arm.

There were people everywhere around the green gape of the grave, the mat of thin Astroturf covering the hole and the mound of wet clay.

People everywhere. Theresans took care of their own.

Guides Flynn hadn't seen in years, standing in an awkward row like an honor guard, nodding back and waving fingers in salute when Joe Flynn acknowledged them.

The cherrywood of the coffin burnished with an auburn fire in the wood. The brass handles softly gleaming.

The priest in white, singing the words of the "Our Father."

Joe Flynn crying, bent near the casket as they left.

It was all so beautiful, a spring morning and Wolfman's walking stick, the priest in white and the man in grey gabardine spraying diamonds through the sun sparkle.

And Emma there, on the fringe, with a dark, beautiful child. And Esther's broad forehead and hair ribbons and blue silk dress; a thirty-three-year-old child, with wise eyes and violets crushed in her fingers, violets she had picked on her way in through the horseshoe stone arch of the cemetery.

Emma was there.

SIX

Molly LaChance feared dolls' eyes, the blue foil eyes of chocolate rabbits, bathrooms, the musty-smelling hallway at the entrance to their second-floor apartment, voiceless phone calls, wind, nights with too many spinning stars, and two or three of the men her mother had dated after the divorce when she changed their names from LaChaise to LaChance.

There was a man with a gold crown inset with a star-shaped emerald. His hair fell in oily dark strands, like braids, and he ate only vegetables. Jerusalem artichokes, kale, alfalfa sprouts, and the awful sawdusty bulgur. Once he had a boil on his arm and she knew it was from pickled beets.

He liked to hug her. He was genuinely warm and gentle and never too distracted to play. Yet he made her angry insisting that Ken and Barbie had retired their motor home, making it into a shack for their pigs.

He kept pigs though he did not eat them. Once he slaughtered one for them and the bacon he made made a noise whenever they cooked it, a low squeal. The noise reminded Molly of the sound Emma made when she made love. Groaning then squealing on the chirping bedsprings.

In the morning the emerald star man always awoke before them and sat bare-chested in blue jeans in the kitchen, drinking raw eggs and wheat germ and orange juice made in the blender.

"He's just an old hippie," Emma explained to Molly once.

Forever after, Molly thought of him as a moundy brown animal with great slow jaws and blunt, scaly teeth. There was a temptation to connect the image with sex, but Molly was careful not to burden herself with fears. "You should never burden yourself with fears," her mother had said once. "Not of sex, not of anything . . . It isn't fair to say so, but that's what I've done. I'm only now learning to crawl from under."

Molly understood. She and her mother could talk. Once on her grandfather's farm, a mink had crawled from under the long wood-pile. The sun burnished it auburn, there were diamonds floating on the water of the pond. Hippopotamouse meant river horse.

Molly loved the river, softball, geography, younger children, David Cassidy, her father, the etchings of William Blake, and Jack Flynn.

Her father had remarried a smiley woman with fat legs and macramé hair ties and two other children, one older, one younger than Molly. They were all vegetarians, sometimes it seemed the whole damned world was vegetarian. Even Emma ate only chicken and fish. Lacto-ovo: it sounded like health education class.

The ovaries were two pale apples at the top of a white tree with curved trunks that had the texture of octopus legs, but were pearly and soft.

"The roots are your pubic hair."

Emma laughed when Molly said this, but she meant it, sort of. In the bathtub, pubic hair softly waved with the movement of the water. It was a wise old goat's beard, it was like the flowing weeds under the river. It was smooth and secret when it first came.

Lactation should have sounded nice, but it was an icky idea. A baby sucking on you, just like some men do. She wanted to understand how it could be nice, but instead she thought of Eva, the name she gave the Tiny Tears doll her mother had saved her.

Eva had a little bottle like they feed mice with. The nipple was a nub, almost a tiny tube, and Eva closed her scary, sad eyes when you laid her back and fed her.

Emma had no breasts anymore. There were scars there now, two pale pink hooks like someone had underlined where her breasts were. Emma explained how they took much of the muscle too. She said "they took it" and the way she said it sounded like in a dream. Sometimes when they would talk while Emma took her bath, Molly looked at the scars and her mother's chest, and the way the skin was tight against the flat bone made her seem brave and vulnerable both. Emma was plucky looking.

"She's a plucky lady," another of Emma's boyfriends told Molly. He was the English professor and he wore black suits and cleared his throat a lot. He gave Molly the book of Blake prints and she loved them right away and he seemed to like that, even though she wasn't so interested in the poems that were supposed to go with them, like the one about the tiger which her mother had read to her about eight hundred times before.

Still, plucky was a good word, like skipping rocks on the river, and the drawings were real weird and scary in a happy way, with colors that looked like colored chalk does after a rain.

The English professor cooked icky stuff, like snails and noodles with smelly sauce and water chestnuts that itched your teeth when you bit them. All of Emma's boyfriends seemed to cook, but only the English professor grunted and kept saying, "Ah, that's good, that's good," when they made love.

And he didn't like to play with her like the hippie did. He was always blinking and drinking white wine so cold that it made the sides of the wine glasses sweaty and wet. Sometimes when they drank wine together, he and Emma looked at poems they had typed to each other the night before. Though they never said anything real, there were times when the poems made them hold hands and look at each other. Molly looked at the poems whenever she felt like it, but they didn't make much sense. There were things about people with flowers the size of their faces, and baskets of fallen leaves brought in the night, and a fairly nice one that had a story about a woman and her daughter who couldn't play the piano.

Molly knew that was about them.

"I'm not serious enough for him," Emma said when the professor went away.

"You're always serious . . . too serious," Molly told her.

"No, I mean he wants to marry someone," her mother explained.

She laughed then like she had laughed once when they went through Syracuse and Molly told her that there was where her life would be, in the city, near the tall buildings. It wasn't a laugh that was making fun, it was more sort of surprised, and it was one of those things that Emma remembered to tell her boyfriend—either the hippie or the professor—later at night, when she thought Molly was sleeping.

Molly didn't want her mother to marry anybody but her father or Jack Flynn. David Cassidy was who Molly herself would marry, although she really knew it wasn't true, and she always kind of thought he was queer even when she liked him. He was way too nice, like people sometimes are, especially at school or at family parties, but she kept thinking of him a lot, so she didn't give up on making him her fantasy.

Fantasy was what you called it when it couldn't be true. Like marrying her father again, now that he was with Bethany and the two vegetable eaters. It couldn't be so, even though you wanted it, and even though he was starting to love them more than he did her. More than both of them.

Jack Flynn was a fantasy because her mother only really knew him when she was little and he was bigger already. But he still was a better fantasy because he lived around there and came back to visit his family; and also because she had liked him even before she began to play softball on the team, or before she even knew that her mother ever knew him.

He was such a fox. She saw him on television first and also had his picture in a scorebook, which she tore out and put up on the corkboard with David Cassidy and a bunch of other weirdos she couldn't even remember liking.

Sometimes, when he pitched against the Yankees, they would put the camera so you looked right into his face when he was starting to pitch, and you saw the blue eyes blink as he got the signals, saw him nod when he was ready, and then saw him lift his leg up and kick so you thought he would fall over as he came down on the mound and let it go, making an L in the dirt with his front spike.

He was so cool. Like when there was a home run against him how he would watch it go out, real blank-like, and then turn back and hold his glove way out in front of him with a stiff arm, waiting for the ball to start pitching again. You knew he was angry, but you also knew he was smart enough not to show it.

"It was a million years ago," Emma said, "and I really knew his family better than him. He probably doesn't remember me. They had a lot of troubles, that family did."

"All families have troubles," Molly said. "That's the way they are."

Her mother looked at her the way she did whenever something she said was supposed to be eerie. That was one problem with living with Emma, she was always looking for eerie things you said.

Once there was supposed to be something eerie about what she said about Jack Flynn. It was when she was almost ten and she had just discovered him, the year before she began to play softball and he was still with San Diego. Flynn was pitching against the Phillies, his old team, and they were really bombing him. Molly got madder and madder each time they showed McNamara in the dugout, chewing away at his tobacco and just looking out at Flynn with innocent eyes, never blinking.

Flynn was real sweaty. He kept parading around the bottom of the mound after each pitch, wiping his eyes with his glove, taking his hat off and putting it on again; and when he pitched, he scrinched his eyes up tight and weary, like he was looking for some way to fool the batter. It was Mike Schmidt, Molly remembered, because she liked him too, sort of, since he looked like somebody real.

Anyway, there was Flynn, all tired and getting beat bad, and with McNamara just watching. Flynn pitched to Schmidt and he hit a long, long foul ball that just sort of disappeared into the stands like a pigeon flying away, nice and easy.

Emma was sewing something in her chair, a dinky needlepoint or something. She was supposed to be playing Othello with Molly, but that was okay since she was watching Flynn-boy anyway.

This catcher they called Hamburg threw out a new ball to Flynn, all the while talking and joking with Schmidt. It was like they knew Schmidt was going to hit a homer and they were just sitting around there, the three of them, waiting for it. Even the umpire was talking and laughing.

So Flynn got the ball back and walked off the mound to rub it up and check it like they do. Next thing you know, he's windmilling his arms over his head, like he's trying to loosen them up, and even then McNamara is only watching.

"He looks like a drowning man," Molly said.

Now why was that supposed to be eerie? It was a pretty normal thing to say, if you asked Molly, what with Schmidt and Hamburg and the ump laughing there, and McNamara chewing his cud, and the whole infield and outfield just staring into Flynn's back while he sweated away out there, down seven runs.

Still Emma thought it was eerie, so eerie she had to go and tell Grandma about it on the phone when she called.

"Yes! The Flynns, Mom," Emma said. "From over by Massena,

the one who was a river guide over near Alex Bay . . . Isn't that something? I mean, sometimes I think the child is positively eerie. She has a kind of vision, you know . . ."

Molly did not know.

"Yes, I know about the brother, Mom . . . That's the point!"

Sometimes Emma was meaner to her mother than she was to Molly, it was like she thought Grandma didn't know anything.

Finally, Schmidt tripled, the ball thumping into the cushioned outfield fence so hard and low that it didn't even roll back and Winfield had to go and dig it out of there like it was a lost Easter egg. Meanwhile there's Schmidt again, this time talking and laughing with Rader and the umpire at third, with two more runs in and Flynn drowned for sure, even though all five runs were unearned because of the error earlier.

McNamara came out to get him and even then Flynn jogged back in to the dugout, his glove held high next to his chest.

So nothing was really so eerie, you know.

"He's still gonna win twenty games, and those runs don't count against his ERA because of the error," Molly told her mother, making it sound pissed off because she was in a way. Both because of the eerie crap and because Flynn got knocked out.

"How do you learn all that?" Emma asked.

"It's easy!" she snapped, because she was still pissed about the weirdness of her mother, and about Flynn. "They tell you all that crap on teevee, and there's books you can read . . ."

"I don't like that talk," Emma said. "I don't like that word from you."

"It's just math, Mom, just math . . . They have it on the baseball cards . . ."

"Yes, it's a regular tutoring session," Emma said in her weird way.

"Math and reading and some geography thrown in . . ."

Molly had to laugh. Emma was weird and a creep but she could make you laugh. She went back to sewing at the different herbs on the sampler.

Probably going to frame it and hang it in the kitchen, Molly thought, she's just weird enough."

Still in all she gave Emma a baseball card of Flynn for her birthday in the fall. It was the one from the World Series year—not his rookie card, that was worth bucks and hard to find—but it was the only one without his hat, and he looked real young and goopy like they did back then in the sixties, not boss like he did when he went to Philadelphia in the seventies and started to let his hair grow long and wavy.

Emma kept it in her purse with the other pictures in her wallet, which made it okay.

"You met him once, you know," she told Molly. "You were just a little girl, and we went to his mother's funeral. He said hello."

"No! I didn't know that!" Molly snapped and stomped off. What a dip she was sometimes, Emma was, she wouldn't tell you anything until you about crapped your pants.

Flynn and Emma stood by the stone a long time. The gravedigger carried the black doughnut of the hose down the gravel path, scritch-scritching his way to the little stone shed, where he locked the hose away.

"I always come to see her," Flynn said.

Emma did not know what to think.

"She was a good old girl," he said, and bent to touch the stone.

"That's a load of crap, Flynn," Emma said. "Don't pose like that. Say what you mean and let it take care of itself. You're better than all that . . ."

"Than what?"

"Than who you pretend to be. Jack the Witness . . ."

Flynn had to laugh. It was Emma who was posing. She had pulled the nickname out of the hat like Little Molly Magician, letting him know she knew all about him. Some New York writer had tried to stick him with the nickname in 1970 after he had lost a no-hitter to Singer, the second such loss in two years and a record as far as anybody could tell, although it turned out not to be, only a record for modern time.

Stoneman had got him in '69 and then Singer in '70, and the writer was trying to make it a big thing because of the angle: "Flynn witnesses but never gets one."

It went away long before he got his in '72, although somebody dredged it up again in September when Pappas no-hit the Padres and Flynn was supposed to start but got scratched because of the arm.

Emma could have known it from then, or she could just be some kind of Baseball Annie with a numbers jones. But he didn't think her the kind.

The gravedigger scritched along the cinders again on the way to his car.

"I loved her," Flynn said, "even though I never figured her out. She got kind of lost in my old man, you know. Drowned . . ."

"That's better," Emma said.

"Glad you think so," Flynn said and turned from the stone. "Where to now?"

"Willard," Flynn said. "Got to visit old Willard Walker at the hospital."

Emma looked benignly on him.

He thought Emma thought the cinders reminded him.

Out on the warning track, finding the clown's eye in the high sun.

"How's your daughter?"

"She'd love to see you, you're her hero."

"Let's see her after Willard."

"She's with her father. You remember."

Pale mint, Flynn remembered. Doctor and nurse in mint caps, the nurse hating him for being there, her eyes burning dark above the mint green mask. The doctor coming in, late and distracted, he too in mint down to the booties that covered his shoe tops.

"Howdy, Karen . . . Flynn."

Still the nurse stared at him.

They weren't going to let him in there, Flynn had to throw his weight around to get the doc to agree, and then again to get the hospital administrator to do his job and follow the doctor's orders.

"My Dad had a bird dog," Flynn told the doctor, "and when he put it down, he went in there with it. I can at least do the same with my own. There's doctors in this world who will agree with that if need be . . ."

"It's Karen's decision," the doc said. He wore those half-moon auburn glasses that made him seem sad-eyed, a raccoon. He was putting Flynn off.

"You want me there?"

Karen peeped and began to cry. It was the only time he was mad at her. If she wanted this so damn much, why should she cry now?

She cried because she knew what it was, he knew. He could not fault her. Maybe she was made of spun sugar and department store dreams, but a woman felt this, he knew. It was not right to hurt her.

"Honest to god, honey, I won't if you don't," he said softly.

"I do," she peeped again. "It's just that I think you'll hate me for it."

Flynn looked at the doctor.

"I'll make some phone calls," he said.

They wheeled the little cart to the table, a two-wheel cart like a battery charger, it too mint green and dull chrome. There was a bottle a little larger than the bottle from a blender, set down into the chrome cup halfway. The wire-reinforced translucent hose was coiled within a cloudy plastic bag to keep it sterile.

The nurse helped Karen get her legs up in the chrome stirrups, and she was kinder with Flynn's wife than she had been with him. Karen was trembling, she said it was cold there and she was shivering in a rhythm, although a film of perspiration coated the blond, delicate hairs of her upper lip. She looked pale and afraid without her makeup, with her blond hair covered by the sterile cap. She nipped at her lips with her fine, white teeth and she squeezed Flynn's hand. Where she bit at her lips they flushed pink, the pink washing over the whitened indentations where she had bit.

Flynn felt an incredible longing wash over him. He wanted to get her away from here, get her where they could be alone together and he could hold her as he had when they first knew each other. There were less people than he had imagined there would be—only doc and the angry-eyed nurse—but still it was too glaring there, too public for something so intimate.

The OR lights shone yellow on the green linen. It was exactly the light of a night game: full, metallic and oddly softened.

Oh Karen, he thought, this had better be right for you.

The nurse extended the starched green shroud of the sterile field out from Karen's hips. It was as if she were attached to a kite, a taut green square of sailcloth. The doc stood on the far side of the sail, staring inward to her center, looking with distracted interest on the preparations, his hands held before him, the surgical gloves like skin about to be shed.

Flynn felt discordant images. Karen leaning over the aisle seat of an aircraft, handing him a drink, the fabric of her skirt tight and pressed smooth as the flap of the sterile field. The child he could not imagine, the fetus a kidney bean, a small, tumbling astronaut moving weightless through space.

The doctor grunted to the nurse and she peeled back a green covering from a tray of chrome steel instruments. Karen's hand gripped him hard.

"We'll dilate first, darlin', just like normal . . ."

People, when they worked, tended to talk in a drawl. It was something Flynn noticed.

The nurse smiled once at Karen. At least it seemed like a smile from what you could see from her eyes and the flesh around the mask. Then she gave all her attention to the doctor.

Flynn gave all his attention to Karen's eyes. The cart and the blender bottle were still there in sight, although the doc had hootched it over with his leg, maybe to get it closer to where he would work, maybe to keep Flynn from seeing.

Karen looked up at him like from underwater, trusting now, already a little uncomfortable as the doc opened her with the chrome rods.

"They'll be some discomfort, darlin' . . ."

The doc paused, stopped still. Looked at Flynn.

"If you even think you're losing it," he said sternly, "if there's the least tremor in your gut, I want you the hell out of here. You understand?"

Flynn nodded yes.

"Good," the doc said. "It's this little lady I care about now, Flynn, and I don't care if I never see a damn cent from you."

It was right, Flynn knew. The doctor had done what he had to, and now he was getting back at the implied threats Flynn had laid on him when it all started. It was right. There were times Flynn had done the same thing. Someone hits one off you and then rubs it in with a Mr. Kodak trot around the bases. You wait if you have to, sometimes months, sweet as can be, then throw him a little chin music because that's what you have to do.

Face ball, Flynn knew.

He nodded to the doc again. Karen rubbed his hand, soothing him, for chri'sakes, can you imagine? He touched her cheek.

He didn't know how he felt. No man can ever know before it happens, he'd found that out, talking around. I mean, either you think of the thing like a little homunculus, a pint-sized little you all white and bald, or you think of it like something important that you cannot remember. Serious and sweet, and even happy, but you're damned if you can remember.

That was why he wanted to be there, to remember and—as much as the nurse or the doc might not believe—to be with Karen. He'd seen enough of doctors to know that their show wasn't all it was cracked up to be in the reserved seats. They knew diddlesquat, most of them, and the good ones would be honest enough to tell you.

Tendonitis, rotator cuff, hyperextended whatsis. It was all guesses and being around for a while.

"Don't matter how they do you," Wolfman used to say. "Use steroids or herbal tea, use knives or little Chinamen needles in your neck . . . It's all the same, man, mistakes and magic, magic and mistakes . . ."

The compressor had the sound of an electric trolling motor, a sweet little humming engine. The doc fumbled with the wrappings of the hose like a kid with a Christmas present; he studied the fitting for the vacuum, tinkering with it like someone tinkers with the family Hoover.

"Here we go, Karen," he said. "You will feel it, darlin', but it won't be nothing you can't stand. Just a sensation of voiding, if you know what I mean."

Flynn knew. Drowning. The little lima bean man would let go in a whoosh and come tumbling through the tube in a tide of blood and salty fluid. He would come tumbling down into the center of the universe, the Milky Way, another star gone wrong, a comet briefly appearing, a footnote on the stats.

Poor Karen, he thought, as he heard the liquid enter the jar. She had discussed it with the girls, with Flynn, with the girls again; it wasn't right yet, they were still moving around too much to settle down yet. It was a mistake and this was the right thing to do; when they did it, they wanted to have it right. They needed something more than a place between flights.

The lights went down on the emerald park. He cut the trolling motor and drifted into the shallows. The air died and the kite sailed downward. The tail of the comet streamed off in a flash of diamond ice and sparking dust.

It was all right. He loved her, and he felt sorry whenever she felt sad afterward.

SEVEN

Restless Walker was very like a spider, an old Daddy Longlegs, holed up in his airy private room at the corner of the bland cream building of the care facility. Set back in the farthest corner near the open screen window, the better to enjoy the germ-cleansing qualities of the breeze, within sight of the Little League fields, which he gazed upon from time to time although they were empty now in the afternoon sun, he stretched upon a plastic webbed lawn chair, the seersucker robe pulled loosely around him, his bony butt perched on a tuft of toilet tissue, spread so it covered the whole surface of the seat.

"He sprays it down with Pine-Sol and water three times a day, don't you, Willard?"

The black nurse who had led them to Willard's room seemed comfortable with his fixations. She laughed as she explained the disinfecting procedure, and she seemed to take real care not to touch the tissue-wrapped artifacts of the room.

There was tissue everywhere, carefully spread to cover the top of the enameled metal bureau, wrapped around water glasses, the radio, the top rails of the bed and chairs. Even the mirror, the faucets, and Willard's shaving brush had their white wrapping.

Willard, for his part, did not seem to take any special precautions on the black woman's account. Nor did he seem to mind her laughter at his precautions.

"Had my sister's kid get me this here lawn chair," he explained. "Air flows through it, you see. Germs got nowhere to land but on the metal, and I take care of that."

He and the black nurse laughed conspiratorially.

"I'll let you's alone," she said.

"Good thing too," Willard said.

The nurse paused. Flynn and Emma waited. But Willard was not being rude, he was merely continuing his initial conversation.

"Ain't seen the child in two, three years," he said. "She brung the chair for me, then hightailed it . . ."

"She live in the city, Mr. Walker," the nurse said. "You knows that. She live in New York City."

"Niggers," Willard said, and the nurse went out, a hushing, admonishing look on her face.

"You shouldn't say those things, Mr. Walker."

Willard screwed his eyes at Emma. He whispered to her.

"It's nigger boys, miss," he said. "She knows that as well as I do. Their own kind know the diseases . . ."

"That isn't true and you know it!"

Flynn was not sure there wouldn't be a fight first thing. Emma was rightly riled; Willard seemed to draw his eyes back into his head as he crouched further toward the corner in his chair.

There was a pulse throbbing in the web of purple veins at Willard's ankle. Sashes of toilet tissue hung from the window shades, there were white paper packets tucked into shelves opposite the bed.

Like a spider, Flynn thought. He's packed these spittly white things away to devour later.

Suddenly Willard cackled, he-he-he, like he had that morning. The deep red eyes and the bony, large forehead bobbed with the laughter. Willard stretched a long arm down next to the chair and removed a covering of tissue from an open coffee can. Squit-squit, he spat brown into the brown of the can, then covered it up again.

"She's a fireballer, ain't she?" he said to Flynn.

He-he-he, he scratched at the purple web of the ankle.

"Yessir," he said to Flynn again, "girl throws smoke, doesn't she?"

Flynn nodded stupidly.

"Don't envy you none living with that one," Willard said.

"I don't."

"I'm truly sorry to offend ye, ma'am." Willard bowed his head as if he were about to tumble from the chair. "You're not the first to call me on it, I admit. Prob'ly not the last neither . . . all I can say is I have my reasons, don't you see? I have my reasons."

Emma nodded glumly, settling for this much. There was a

charm Willard had. You felt sure you could not pin him down, that he would just crawl up clockwise to a higher strand of his web.

"Take a chair," he said, "and don't mind the prophylaxis . . ."

"What?" Flynn said.

"The paper! I can string it out again after you left. It'll be time then for the pine wash anyways . . ."

Why are we here.

You have to know some things.

"You two okay?" Willard asked.

Flynn nodded and, careful not to disturb the bunting, walked to the window. The bridge rose in a bow toward the salmon-colored Canadian shore, it too was spider work, a spoked, bolted web. Emma had once lived there, within sight, came over with her Canuck husband before the gates to heaven closed, before everything began to be screwed down, people afraid of nigger boys, of Mexicans, Haitians, Cubans, and the floating leftovers of a war, the Indochinese gypsies, taking all the jobs. There was work then for a Canadian kid, a woodworker. In '67 people wore flowers in their hair, a cabinet maker could sell small boxes of cherrywood and brass, make oak furniture hand-rubbed with tung oil.

Emma was a gypsy then, with long flowered skirts and sad eyes, and her long hair held back with kerchiefs and beaded hairbands. She walked in sandals made of water buffalo hide, a loop at each big toe holding them on. She was pregnant and played the guitar, she threw pots on a foot-powered wheel. There were art fairs in Clayton, Alex Bay, Syracuse, South.

What now he wondered she knew.

The three ballfields spread out in the middle distance like a fan of brown and green, the silver ruffle of the outfield fences at their ends, glinting where the sun caught the chain. The river was silver and blue and sun hazed. A boy rode up to the empty diamonds on his bike, red baseball cap backward on his head. He walked out onto the diamond with his glove and bat, set the bat on the dusty mound, and began to throw the ball into the chainlink backstop, chase it down, walk back and throw it again.

Bertie could give him a bushel basket full, Flynn thought.

The hollow sproing of the ball against the backstop was a familiar sound.

Willard wheezed air up into his nostrils.

"There's a girl comes there, Flynn, ever' now and then. Throws like a mule and can use her glove. Be women in the bigs, someday, now that it's all niggers . . ."

"Goddamn it, Willard!" Flynn stared him down until the red eyes dropped way back in the sockets and his jaw began to shake.

"It's like I was saying," Flynn said. "Baseball's been the testing ground, you know. My father went over this bridge and upriver to see Jackie Robinson in the minors, the Montreal Royals Triple A . . . There was people used to write to Aaron when he was chasing down Ruth's record, told him no nigger could ever beat the Babe, no matter what the numbers say . . ."

Flynn was staring at Willard.

"You didn't say any of that, Jack, not before," Emma said. "You were thinking it maybe, but you didn't say it . . ."

"I want to get you out of here for a time, Willard," Flynn said. "Take you out on a pass . . . I think you need to see some life again. Maybe go down to the Cape and see Gerard, talk about bird-dogging . . ."

Willard's eyes brightened, he leaned a little forward.

"I'd need a mask, Flynn," he said, then squitted into the spit bucket. "They got them in the hardware store, three for a buck or so, works for germs and such . . ."

"Could be arranged," Flynn said.

"You have other things to do, Jack," Emma said.

She was not cutting Willard, she was reminding Flynn. He knew that. It ached still, whatever Bertie and Emma seemed to know he had to do.

"There's still time, isn't there?" Flynn asked.

"I think so," she said. "I can see if you want me to."

She was going to go then. No, Flynn thought, don't leave me yet.

"I'd like to talk to you in private myself, Flynn," Willard whispered.

Emma waited by the door, silent, questioning. Flynn nodded and she let herself out, careful with the tissue-wrapped handle of the door.

Willard watched the door as if he could see her through it, seeming to watch until he was sure she had cleared the cream-tiled corridor, the screened-in day room, the outer waiting room. Then he rose and moved toward the shelves, making his way slowly in a windmill kind of walk, as if he were stepping on slippery stones.

It's his arms make him a spider, the ham hands on bony pendulums, the fingers splayed.

His knees were bony also, he was all bones, skull to longlegs.

"Ya throw heat, Willard?"

"Hooks," he said. "Yellow hammers . . ."

He kept making his way toward the shelves, arms moving in clocklike strokes. A curve ball pitcher, Flynn thought.

"Was three strong boys ahead of me on the chart," Willard said. "Eyetalian kid, a Polack, and a fireballer with less meat on 'im than I had . . . I had something fair for heat, but it wouldn't make it. Hell, I knew it then . . . started thinking about managing . . ."

"Ever try?"

Willard had reached the shelves, was unwrapping a white packet. He raised his white eyebrows high at Flynn's question.

"Over there ta Clarkson College," he said. "Coached a season. All assholes! College never was a way to play baseball, it was different then, Flynn. It was a hard way up the ladder and not everyone went. College kids is spoiling baseball . . ."

"I went to college, Willard."

"I knowed that, Flynn," he answered with a vinegary tone. Flynn was getting on his nerves.

"What you come here for anyway?" he said, setting down the partially unwrapped packet. "What'd you come and spoil my afternoon for? Why don't you look after your sister?"

My sister's dead, Flynn thought. Then no, "Emma . . . ," he said.

"Nice girl," Willard said, real laconic. He took up the packet again, unwound the toilet tissue wrapping. "Kind of a nurse, isn't she?" he asked. "Comes around a lot . . ."

"I don't know," Flynn said. "I don't know why I came. I guess I owed you something . . . I owe something, and you were here."

Willard set down the unwrapped object, a small leatherette ledger book with gilt-edged pages, and JOURNAL stamped in gold on the cover. He quickly unwrapped another packet. Pine-Sol and a sponge. He rubbed down the cover of the ledger book and began to unwrap still another package.

Old Spice. He washed it generously over his face and arms with a huge palm.

"You pitched with that kid used pickle juice," he said.

Randy Jones. Flynn nodded.

"Smart kid," Willard said. "Musta been an old-timer give him that secret . . ."

Must of been, Flynn thought. He had seen a hundred balms: Ben-Gay, bear grease, mink oil, Lydia Pinkham's, mayonnaise, Vitamin E, DMSO—you could make a list a mile long. Everyone still hunting for Ponce de Leon's magic arm lotion.

"This here conditions your skin and wards off micro-organisms," Willard said. "You'd be surprised how many bad arms is really a result of micro-organisms, burrowin' into your muscles like chiggers . . ."

My sister was the moon, her eyes oceans. She could not live beyond twenty, she was that in '61, when I went to Iowa. Micro-organisms had burrowed into her spine, meningitis. Flynn imagined microscopic larvae, maggots or corn borers. They affected the seed and husk in opposite ways, the pressure expanding her skull, a forehead wider than Willard's, soft and white and broad, the dark Dutch bangs falling over them in a straight line, like a fringe.

The brain, Flynn imagined, the brain was like a bad clam, something dark and grainy, almost liquid.

Joe Flynn once boated a perch with three eyes, the gills all encrusted with fungus. It saw too much to defend itself from ill. It was a monster, life made monsters, some were beautiful and round as the melon moon on an August night.

A bad clam. A slug within a cave of mother-of-pearl.

"I'm glad you come," Willard said. He thumped the book against a closed fist. "I'm glad you come, Flynn. I'm closing out my career and I need some company . . ."

"I know about that feeling."

Willard extracted a pouch of Beech-Nut chaw from the seersucker, extended it toward Flynn, who declined. Willard looked up from the chaw with bug eyes, kind eyes.

"Suppose you do, partner," he said. "Suppose you do . . ."

His long legs crawled over to the spit can. Squit. He turned back toward Flynn, then settled into the web chair, rearranging the tissue below his bony butt as he lowered himself.

"I'm makin' a book, Flynn," Willard said, "and you're gonna be in it."

Willard extracted a fountain pen wrapped in a plastic sandwich bag, taking it from the same pocket where he stowed the chaw. He opened the ledger book and wet a finger to turn through the pages, stopping at a point midway through the gilt pages. He unscrewed the cap from the fountain pen, then held it up for Flynn to see.

"Parker Brothers," he said. "You bought it fer me the other morning."

"Glad you could use it."

"It shits," Willard said. "Uses little tubes of ink, not the real stuff from the bottle."

"Sorry."

Willard nodded impatiently, put the pen to the page, and looked up at Flynn expectantly.

Flynn did nothing.

"Begin," Willard said.

"Aw Restless . . . come on . . . ," Flynn said.

"So whatta ya want, a million-dollar advance?"

Flynn laughed and sat down. "You should be telling me," he said.

"I never hit the big show, Flynn, you know that. That's where I want your part to begin . . ."

"How many parts you got?"

"You gonna pitch or bitch, Flynn?"

I suppose it was magic then, coming out between the lines and into the sun beyond the shadow of the grandstand. You know how it is when you first sit there at Alex Bay, down behind the Monticello where my dad used to live . . . Scenic View Park they call it, but it's fairyland, Willard . . . When Mom first went to the Noble hospital there, the pain was so bad she'd turn her head toward the river and just sail on it, you could see her fly, Willard, out there among the islands, like the moon navigates through the tufts of high clouds on a summer's night.

I guess it was magic. I remember creeping out there as a kid, moving across the limestone boulders of the bluffs on hands, knees, and toes, blinky-eyed and scared but dying to see it . . . moving like a water strider in little circles on the rock, and then feeling the world let go below you, flying out on a stone pillow the size of a cloud, holding my breath with wonder . . .

It was like falling into a storybook, one of those things where cardboard elves and gremlins leap out at you from the page and there's too much to see . . . Flying, Willard! Flying through your eyes out into the islands, the river there like an enchanted sea . . .

Boldt Castle out there on Heart Island spinning in your eyes like Disneyland in an upside-down helicopter, all that gingerbread stone, towers and parapets and rough walls pushing up above the green. I was always afraid I would fall, swirling down through the islands, bumping along like a bass plug on the current . . . It was like those dreams you have, especially after pitching, where the world falls away and you go with it. I'd hold my breath to keep from puking and fix my eyes on the stone arch at the beach, then work my sight gradually over the choppy, glinting water until I saw Imperial Island and the house with eyebrow windows, the red roof, mustard walls, and green landings and trim. There you could rest, you could rest your eyes, like when you're on a plane coming into New York say, and the whole cabin's leaning over on a wing and the air is bumping and filled with little pockets of rushing, empty air that'd just as soon drop you as throw you up, and you try real hard to focus in on something to keep your balance, the statue out there in the harbor, the Trade Towers like two bald cliffs, and the stewardess is making her way back along the aisle to check the seatbelts, holding herself with the luggage rack to keep from falling over into your lap . . .

You could rest your eyes . . . and then move on slowly, upriver, where the lights were softer and the house on Cherry Island with the round porches and green gables always seemed to drowse. The Queen Anne orange roof of a boathouse like a witch's cap . . . I got so's I could name most of the islands, you know. The Millionaires Row they call it, the Manhattan group. There's something to names, Willard. Virgil Trucks, Enos Slaughter, Honus Wagner, and Early Wynn . . . The islands, up and down, are like that: Pine and Little Zavicon, Deer, Douglas and Lotus Islands, Fairyland, Comfort, Fiddler's Elbow and Estrellita, the little star, always making me think of my sister Esther . . . It got so I was as afraid to crawl back in from that ledge of rock as I was to go out there. That's how it was, like when you first see it, not now when you climb up the hill from the hotdog joints and souvenir shacks, and it seems a floating circus; speedboats cutting the wake of chipping oil tankers, the Gananoque tour boats like white buses, hurrying in and out of the channel and through the International Rift . . . Now it's all kind of tacky and noisy and fast, but when you first see it, you think you finally grew up to find the land where the giants walk and trolls hide and lizards fly, you know . . . It's like looking into the eyehole of one of those old Easter eggs with sugar shells and painted scenes inside . . .

"Cut the crap, Flynn, I'm an old man and I can hear the sleigh-bells and I want to know."

"I'm telling you!" Flynn said, and then he calmed down. "It's that way when you come up, Willard, I'm telling you. Now give us some chaw . . ."

"I can hear the sleighbells, Flynn . . . I know it, even though I know none of us knows anything, and that's half the problem. My better half is gone now and I got only a runt bitch from my litter and I know, Flynn! I know . . . I'm the end of the line, the last stop. We rose in the west of Vermont, up near where it wasn't sure whether you was a Canuck or not, depending on what side of the bed you plopped out on. Up ta Alberg, Vermont, you know it, Flynn? No one knows it . . . We rose there. Always seemed a joke in that, you know, Flynn? A rose in the west . . . It's like the sun's a flower, you see what I mean, Jack? The dawn light laying upon the horizon like petals lit-tering a windowsill where the first bloom's blasted . . . You know that word, Flynn, blasted flowers? You ever read Lord Milton's poems? "O fairest flower, no sooner blown than blasted . . ."

Rose came up when I did. We were in PONY league the same time and he never hit me. Fellow says that first time Rose shows up to Geneva he walks into the club office, you know, happy as can be, and asks a guy, "Who's the second baseman around here?" Turns out the fellow he asks is the second bagger—it's that kind of story—so Rose says to him, "I'm the new second baseman . . ."

It was like that, Restless, like the world was brash and what the hell. I spent two years in college before I went to Rookie League, a half season there before I rode out the PONY. The whole world was new, Willard, like looking out into Millionaires Row. Musial and Gibson, White, Groat and Boyer. Rose came up and won the Rookie of the Year. Even the strike zone was wider, just for me, you know . . . It was like the stars spread out in the sky, like you suddenly got to pitch up through the wrong end of a funnel . . . I was hurting to go up to the big show, Willard, hurting to go . . .

O Jackie, we've been alone so long.

Alone so long here we don't intend to be no longer. When you resign from human touch, Flynn, you can get powerful alone, so it's welcome to friends and friends of friends and stammers from afar. I haven't had a city or a friend or a decent thing to say about anybody short of my mother for years now; haven't touched no one purposely in a year or more, not since this little girl was here with her long hair and brown eyes and I made her give me a piece of gum, just to see if I could still touch . . .

I remember shaking Gib's hand, those dark intelligent eyes drilling into you like two big pile drivers. I was fresh as new shit, the Skipper at Johnson City told me I was certified stuff and I come up on the train thinking I'd move right into his locker, you know, and then those pile drivers hit me. Most powerful man I ever met, short of Wolfman. You can say what you want, Willard, but I tell you in this country black men know things . . .

Gibson was quiet for sure, you know, but good enough about it, welcoming me to the team and all, me standing at this locker that still said Bauta from before they traded him. Everything was mellow, Willard, everything but me. They'd come off an eight-game losing streak before the break and then set out to winning, eventually it was nineteen out of twenty . . . I was stuff, like money in the bank or a long weekend off. I've seen it since, I've seen fellows like me come up, young arms like red meat in the supermarket bins, ready to throw that meat into rags, you know, make hamburger of it for the cause . . . You need red meat arms for a pennant race . . . They dropped a ball into my flannels while I had 'em down to hitch up my stockings, I pulled 'em up with a Major League tug, a red meat tug, and jammed my balls with the ball and saw The Man laughing by his locker . . . I decided then that that was my job, Restless, to cheer them up through August and win a few games along the way . . .

Was on his way home, Flynn, eighty-some years ago. I heard the bells coming, you could hear the sleighbells through the cracking cold night, him and his brass bells out there in the black ice of night, the sled long past Rouses Point and on the lake ice heading home. Couldn't of been more than four years old, Jack, and I remember my brother all bundled up in furs and out there in the night. Shouting, "Come in, Father, come in . . ." You can't come in farther than he did that night, Flynn, and that's a fact.

The first time I came in I remember hearing a vendor in the stands clear as a bell, shouting "Hotdog here, hotdog here . . ." I mean all that sound up there, a river of it swirling around you, sometimes spilling out over the flat, and you hear this one foghorn voice . . .

I must of looked up at it, Willard, after I warmed up; came in down three runs after Broglio went one and a third, two years younger than Sadecki. We was to be the future of the Birds.

I must of looked up, cause this voice comes out of the Cincinnati dugout. "Yeah, he's calling you, hot dog!" and they all laugh, the laugh spilling over to our own boys, even Bill White, over there at first like he was all year, covering his face with a glove . . . Struck out six straight, Restless, I know you got that in your book. Two in the second, three in the third, one in the fourth, tied a record Richert tied the year before with LA, most consecutive for a rookie pitcher in his first game. Karl Spooner held it before us in '54. His first two games for the Dodgers he never let a run, goose eggs for an ERA . . .

Went eight and four and two-nine-two myself that year, and couldn't understand it when I didn't get to come in against the Dodgers when we needed to win in September. I was that fresh, Restless! I thought I could pitch with Koufax then, in a year he won twenty-five and pulled a one-eight-eight ERA.

I was four or five years old. I heard my brother calling and then come in. We could hear the sleighbells far away in the night, could hear the wolves and the wind singing as one sound . . .

They thought he was dead, they did. We all did, we thought my father had gone out and died. And then that sleigh come in . . . rails on the snow making that soft sound like someone chewing ice, little balls of icy bells on the horse's mane, my old man upright on the seat, whip in hand and beard gold with frost in the lantern light.

He was dead as dust.

I remember Gibson's eyes, Willard, when he came in after Dickie Nen hit the homer in the ninth to tie us up. Nen was red meat, too, Restless, just like me, a transfusion of meat for the pennant race. Gib came into the dugout and he just stood there and looked at me. I couldn't tell if he was trying to show me how it would be, or if he was blaming me 'cause I was red meat too. After we dropped it in the thirteenth, I didn't dare look at anybody, especially not Musial. The Man would never have his World Series and red meat was to blame . . .

Dead as dust. He'd frozen stiff, upright on his seat, outrunning the wolves, and none of them there at the house had half an idea what to do with him. So the five boys, my brothers and my uncles, they hefted him up off the seat and sat him in the barn, stiff as a statue and his eyes crusted over with frost. They waked him there, Flynn, and he disposed of his first night's death with as much wit as you can find in hot mustard, a whiskey stuck in his ghost white hand and his arse on two bales of fine timothy hay, and a white cloth over his face.

Toward morning some of the freeze in his flesh let up, along with the death rigors, and he nodded once before they packed him up, as if to say, "Well, that's it, boys." And they packed him up, buck upright still and still wary of wolves, off to the mortician 'cause this wasn't your normal case of burial and they needed an expert to straighten things out, if you'll excuse my phrase. Took a coal fire burning two weeks on the burial ground before they could open it up and stow him. Story is my dad waited it out under a tarp in the ice shed in town, or so they say . . .

Used to stack up the dead like cordwood in the early days of the Vermont frontier, or so some say. Bury 'em all when the ground turned muck and no sooner . . .

Gold, frankincense, and merde, Flynn . . . , life's all shit sometimes but even then at least it's got its fragrance . . .

He laughs, the high cackle.

Merde's what the Frogs say up Kay-beck way . . . Knew enough Frenchy loggers in my early years, Flynn. Played my first baseball with an ash branch and a buggy bolt wrapped into a ball of deerhide. There wazza fella named She'll Bear, a Frog lumberjack, craziest man I ever knowed. She'll Bear used ta sink his axe into the center of the table ever' time he sat down, slicing his bread over the open edge and otherwise feeling over it with his greasy, leather thumb, always looking for nicks . . . He laughed like a loon but he was the sanest man I ever knowed after his fashion. Ever' week or so the cookhouse boy'd have to replace the table slab where She'll Bear split it with his cutlery . . .

Yessir, Flynn, 'tis the quiet frogs you watch for, in cookhouses and clubhouses, as well as life as it's led on the larger pond . . .

He laughs again, memory a flash in his rheumy eye.

Time in Vermont . . . he-he-he . . . just over the border, four of us'n skinnydippin' in a spring pond and the frogs was stacked up like green flapjacks humping away, and old Roger here's feeling the mood rise in him and his wand cuts the top of the water like a fat pink reed . . .

He-he-he, the girls that was with us ran for their clothes and prob'ly clear back into town. Hellfire, even I stayed away from him, Flynn. Only man I ever knowed was riled by frogs . . .

Koufax spun out fifteen K's the first game of the Series . . . Koufax was what I remember most of the early years. I learned something there, Willard. Turned from bein' only red meat watching that man . . .

Christ, I remember things . . . That's my curse, in fact, Flynn, that's why I'm making a book. I remember things but when I coax 'em to my tongue they go away like fireflies when the dew settles. Left wet's the story of my life, Flynn, or anyone's for that matter. Never knew scheiss about weather. Fellows could look at a blue sky and pretend to spy some haze there. "Rain by five," they'd say, "rain by five . . ." You want to sit out in the drizzle and deny it, they were so damn fine-minded about it. Best I could ever tell was that a slap of warm wind in February meant you'd freeze by morning. The Lord's torture on the heathen is a warm Feb'rary breeze, Flynn. A yawn from hell and three days from the Yukon . . .

He cackles again.

"It's the water will kill you, Willard," Flynn said. "My whole family went by water of one sort or another. Ain't germs you should worry about, it's water. Begin there, end there . . ."

Willard walks sprightly to the closet and cackles, opens the door to show the shelves of bottled water, in plastic jugs and ball jars, each holding a little wave, glinting in the late sun.

EIGHT

Bertie Flynn lined up the cigarette filters like spent cartridges on the table before her. She allowed herself ten Virginia Slims a day and no more, having read once that you reduce your life by ten years for each pack of cigarettes you smoke. She was willing to sacrifice five.

Outside the kitchen window hummingbirds backed in and out of the orange funnels of the trumpet vine against the side of the garage. The vine was slowly ripping the garage apart, one thick and woody section of it had already thrust itself between the shingles of the roof and the sheathing, popping the nails. Another section, thick as a baby's arm, had all but ripped away a two-by-four fascia piece.

She didn't know who she would call, now that Mr. Rosebaum the carpenter was dead. A woman alone had to find people to care for her.

Jack couldn't do it. Sometimes she wondered if he knew anything more than how to throw a baseball, and now even that was gone, with him holding his arm at his side all of the time like it was a dead child.

She smiled. The fresh ham in the oven crisped and spattered, the aroma in the room. The central air conditioning hummed and sighed. The birds held themselves in the air before the orange trumpets like boats easing into a slip. Jack would enjoy a good meal, it would give him strength, for the arm, for the awful task ahead.

On the television news there was word of an accident on the river. A couple were fishing near Edgewood when a large unidentified boat struck them, throwing the wife in the water. A boat captain from nearby Cherry Island assisted in getting the woman out of the river. The larger boat returned and inquired about possible injury before steaming off. The Coast Guard was investigating.

Bertie considered the idea of a wife in the water. Jack would like the story, she felt sure, although she did not know why.

Maybe because always the big boats steamed off.

A week or so ago, a man had sailed one of the old St. Lawrence skiffs off Summerland Island. His name was Herrick and he was out of Cape Vincent and Bertie thought perhaps she knew them.

Oh, you didn't see the skiffs anymore. The captains leaning fore and back, dancing along the grating to keep her on the tack, making up with their weight for the lack of rudder. There were great old boats on the river once, and now they were mostly in the museum in Clayton, or paraded out on special occasions. Once the old Narra Mattah had come all the way up to the Eisenhower lock on a dinner cruise. If she'd known, she would have gone to see it. There were some ladies from church took a day trip down to Calumet Island and they sailed out on her, on the Narra, after dinner. It didn't cost a cent extra, and she should have gone then too.

Weather promised hot but there was an elbow of low pressure closing in, and it was clear the jokey kid on the teevee didn't know what was going to happen.

Joe knew the weather on the river good as most.

Bertie thought she might cry. It was stupid sitting here with the weather on the teevee and a roast cooking in the oven that Jack might not come back to eat. It was ugly to be alone.

There! She'd tell him that when he came back. Ugly and cruel with the flowers eating up your garage.

She lit another of the beige, flower-enscrolled cigarettes. Three to go, two if you saved one for after dinner. She did not cry.

Jack was never her favorite. Jim was. She was as excited about him going into the army as she was about Jack going into the Major Leagues. All Jim needed was a chance to straighten out, and President Kennedy would give it to him.

Protect any foe and fight any friend, he said.

No, that was backwards, fight foes and protect friends, JFK had said. The wind was blustery then and that old Vermont poet kept grabbing at his papers to keep them from flying away while he read his poem, his white hair flipping in the gusts. Ike sitting there like a potato. He was younger when he came down to dedicate the locks;

he and the queen could of made a couple, no matter what kind of foul talk Joey spread about her.

Jackie was the queen of the US, and you just had to ignore all that talk about the policewoman with the Hanes legs who was on the teevee all the time now talking naughty with Johnny Carson.

The sports came on the teevee and she turned to see it.

She laughed.

"Well, there you are," she said aloud. "Old habits die hard . . ."

She was wondering about news of their Jackie, and there was none, of course.

Bertie had chosen a life alone, there was no question about that, and no regrets, really, about the decision, only about the ugliness of a roast turning brown alone.

She had had a sweetheart and lost him, the gentlest man who ever lived. He used to take her out on a wooden skiff with long oars; sometimes he'd use one oar to pole her through the shallows, watching fat old frogs plop from the banks.

Pneumonia took him. The red-haired and fair-skinned ones hardly ever survived in the days before sulfa was in general use.

He wouldn't tan, the freckles only spread and darkened.

Pneumonia took Nell, too, that and some virus they didn't have a name for. It was the damnedest family for viruses. One that touched Esther in the head, and Jim himself had to be crazy to go off like that and end up in the river.

Cancer, they said, was maybe a virus, too, and that's, of course, what took Joey, shrinking him down before letting him go.

Could be that there's a virus infects the tobacco plant, comes in your lungs when you smoke and just grows there like worms.

She counted the cartridges on the table. Four beige filters.

A life alone saved you from complications. Sex drifted away though you never lost it. Only the urgency, you know. Like that blond with the legs flirting with Carson and having evenings at the White House. Or Marilyn Monroe, warm air pushing her skirts up.

There was a big fuss last year when a bunch of nudie dancers starting making the rounds of the North Country clubs. All men, wearing silver jockstraps someone said down to church. The women rushing out to spend ten bucks to drink a beer and see them, shoving dollar bills into the jockstraps.

My Red was a handsome man, poling the skiff along in his white linens, brushing away the gnats from his face, singing, "Sailing, sailing . . ."

She turned the roast down.

You never lost it. A woman was an open receptacle, like the flowers of the trumpet vine.

Emma was trouble. Jack should try to fix things up with Karen, have some children. Life was children.

She wanted to cry again. There was a story on the teevee earlier in the summer, a young boy almost electrocuted swimming off near Sylvan Island. Turns out the electric company forgot to disconnect a power line from an unused cottage. They said on the news that the shock sent his arms flying into the air, and his face contorted with an awful pain. He managed to swim to the dock, but it was his grandma who saved him. She called the power company the moment she saw the boy in trouble.

It was the kind of story gave you dreams.

Jim was the dreamer in the family. They didn't give him that. Oh, he was rough, and sometimes mean-spirited, and he gave Nell lip, but there was goodness in him. He did things. It was Jim who crawled up on the ladder and pulled leaves from the eaves trough each year for her. It was Jim who painted the back side of the garage. He'd look in on someone, come driving up in that loud car with the spangly paint he called candy apple, and the chrome things hanging down the side, and he'd jump out, looking surly and grim and come walking into the vestibule like he was daring you. What's wrong now, Bert, he'd say. It was defiance. You saw a lot of defiance in them then, in the kids. It wasn't like what came later, the beards and sandals and sloth. All the whining.

Bertie liked defiance better, though she cried for days when the two waves met just once, in 1970, when the little girl was laying dead in a puddle of her own blood there in Ohio, her friend looking up with all that defiance and pain on her face. America had gone wrong sometime there, Bertie knew. You couldn't go into your schools and kill your young like that, and you couldn't send them off to be killed either. It was Jim told her that. He had come back somewhere in that time, a real man by then, one of the Rangers, strapping and dashing in his beret and his scarf and his patent leather boots.

"It's crap, Aunt Bertie," he told her when they sat in the front room drinking beers together, just them two.

"Hell, I don't blame Jack for signing that thing in the paper, Bert. I'd do the same if I thought it would get me anywhere. I'm thirty years old and I'm supposed to be a leader of men . . . They're boys, Bert. Poor, dumb farm boys, and river boys, and black kids and they're scared, and I'm scared, and the boys in pajamas we're fighting are scared too . . . Everyone just floats away, you know, Bert. We just float away all night and stumble out in the morning to kill something . . ."

She didn't know. She hadn't known, but she didn't like to see Jim in pain.

She didn't know then that he was taking pokes at his pain with tiny needles, putting them in his eye, and ear lobe, and ankle to keep from being discovered. He drank beers in nearly one swallow then, and he poured himself a water glass of gin and drank it too in gulps, but she didn't know he was a hophead.

They had laughed because he was on a river, despite himself. Everyone knew Jim didn't care much for the river, but Bertie, almost alone in all the world, knew that the river was as much the problem with Jim as the way Nell babied Jack.

A river can be a daunting thing, by day or night. It's like hearing your heart beat sometimes; you just want to get out of whatever this thing is that goes on without you. It hit Jim that way. He was fair-skinned and fey as her Red had been, and the sun on the river always made his eyes squint, and the river nights chilled him, and there was Joey, so strong and handsome, almost always on the dock, about to set out on it, and Jim had to defy him. He was one of a sweet generation, grown into defiance because they had nothing else. Jim had to defy Joey because he was afraid of the river.

It was too easy to say all this, of course. Jim had to take the blame for himself. And there was the virus or chromosome or whatever it was that affected the Flynns and made them so sad. But you had to wonder whether he might not have made something more of himself without the river.

Certainly he would have lived to be something more if the river hadn't been there to take him when he ran off that road that night after fighting with Joey.

But even in Viet Nam, he was stuck to the river. It made him laugh, made her laugh with him.

"They call it a patrol boat, Bert, but it seems about ten feet shorter than Dad's guide boat. Hell, I have half a mind to take some gear back with me and continue in the family business, over there . . ."

He drained a beer and stared at her with reddened eyes.

"'Course the fishin' might not be so good with all that gunfire and them stinking bodies floating in the river . . ."

He just shook it off—she had admired how he could do that, just shake off an awful thought, like a dog drying himself—and he stared at her in silence for a while. "Well . . . ," he said, "what's wrong now, Bert?" and he laughed, but unlike old times. "Better get me on the job before these brown screamers get me . . ."

He held the beer bottle up, brown screamers was an odd name for it.

(Flynn laughs. For some time now in the interview he has been trolling deeper water, as it were, his forehead and eyes showing a darker mood. Now, suddenly, when you would expect the question to throw him still deeper, he bobs up again, laughing.) Oh yeah, I took hell in the clubhouse for that protest. They'd call me Red, you know, Flynnik, or more creative things. You gotta understand that baseball appeals to the All-American type, the hulking farm boy type. (Laughs) 'Course you could look up how many of them spent any time in the service in them years, whole lotta 4-F's or 1-Y's or whatever in the majors . . . But from the columnists and Sporting News types . . . I mean, I was used to it, you know. My father was a war hero, you see, and my brother was as near we got to heroes in that war . . . Hell, even my Aunt Bertie gave me guff about getting involved . . .

(He seems to consider a moment, then continues in a low voice.) You just shake it off, you know, like a hunting dog in the rain . . . like a bad sign. You know that song, "Born under a bad sign . . ."? Sometimes it seemed that way . . . for all of us . . . (Once again he is trolling deep; it isn't a time to ask questions. All one can do is wait out the pause; Flynn is a moody man. He begins slowly again, as if picking his way through underwater weeds.) Lotsa bad signs in those days . . . Lotta bad, bad medicine . . . . You remember what they called '68? (I shake my head no. He laughs grimly, as if tasting the irony.) "The Year of the Pitcher . . ." Hah! McLain won 31, Bullet Bob won 22 and the series. Nellie Briles, the new right-hand hope over there after they traded me, came up a game short, went 19 and 11, and he's a year younger than me. Chri'sakes, Gibby won 15 straight, pitched near that many shutouts and twice that many complete games and ends up flirting with an ERA of one . . . (Flynn mellows momentarily, lost in the deep water of memory. It is clear that Bob Gibson is a personal hero of his.) He never changed, you know . . . I'd see him around in later years, but never around the batting cage, never smiling, though maybe if he wasn't goin' that day he'd nod, you know, for old times, and those eyes of his were still deep wells, you know, miles deep and calm water at the bottom . . . That man could pitch! I mean he was angry inside but calm and cool as some old black bass, you know . . . He ate 'em up in the series, he really did. Seventeen straight K's in the first game and McLain is looking on like it's a pitching clinic . . . (Flynn leans forward, speaking earnestly now; he's anxious, it seems, to establish his credentials, as if that were necessary.) You know I covered that series for the teevee. I can still see that rope that Northrup hit . . . There's Hoot watching that sucker shoot out of there, and Curt's got the damn thing printed, you know, like on a fish finder . . . Then suddenly you know Flood's misjudged it—it happens that fast, when you watch the fielder, not the ball—and he knows he's lost it, and Hoot does too, and it skips through to the wall, and two guys are in . . . After that Gibby's rhythm is broke—you can see the way his back arches, see it in the weight on his shoulders . . . and Curt's out there with his hands on his knees, wishing he could get it back, but knowing, like everybody does, that the Tigers are gonna get the rings . . . (Drops his voice) My whole damn year went like that, you know . . . my whole damn year. I'd been two years away from the Cards and when you're in a broadcast booth, you ain't supposed to take sides . . . but my whole damn year was gone . . .

Maybe they were right, you know? Maybe it started when that damned ad appeared in the Times, but you know when I think it began?

No. When?

In '67, when the world was burning up, you know . . . when the cities went up, and there was Bobby Kennedy and Martin Luther King and all those kids trying to hold it together, and the whole damn world went up in smoke . . . By '68, you knew it was gone. When they shot Kennedy and King it was only finishing it off, you know, the late innings . . . When Wolfman left, I couldn't blame him. I was surprised Richie Allen didn't go with him then; it wasn't any time to be a black man in America . . . Wasn't any time to be in America . . . I tell you my old man and me had it out then, but he was smart enough to know there wasn't any grounds to stand on, you know? I mean he didn't have the heart to fight, and he was worried about my brother . . .

Where'd Wolfman go then, Jack?

You mean you don't know? (Of course I didn't know, no one did, but I tried to stay calm about it. It was a kind of scoop, however many years after the fact. No one really knew the motivation of either of the fabled Philly boys.) He flew away. He took those broken wings and learned to fly . . . (He laughs painfully here.) That was maybe the worst blowout the Wolf and I ever had, before the real parting, I mean . . . I was playing that song, you know it? From the White Album . . . ? "Blackbird singing in the dead of the night . . ." I was real excited about it. I mean, it all seemed to mean something, and I had it on the tape player in the clubhouse down in Florida, you know. I was playing it kinda loud so the Wolfman could hear it, though I didn't say nothing or nothing . . . All of a sudden, he smashes the tape player, you know. Blam! The bat comes down and cracks the tape player into splinters and the tape goes all flooey . . . Crack! (Flynn stares directly at me, there is still some shock in his eyes.) I was twenty-five goddamn years old and I thought the world was some crystal palace, you know . . . I was Mr. Flake, the Flynn-nik, and suddenly it was all crazy and ugly . . . I just looked at him, you know, just stared into those burning black eyes . . . "Honkey motherfuckers gonna tell us how to do it, huh?" He said something like that and laughed, fishing the bat real gentle-like through the mess he made out of my tape player . . . "No thanks, Jack," he said. It wasn't my name he was saying, it was like black dudes talk, they call you Jack, you know . . . "No fuckin' thanks, Jack!" he said. "We be on our own from now on, mother fucker . . ." I could hear the other soul brothers laughing, real mean and low like in the back, but I didn't look back. I just gathered up the pieces of the player and tossed it in the trash barrel. It meant something . . . I felt like a goddamn fool, and I knew why he was pissed . . . He gimme a C-note for it a week or so later, but I wouldn't take it, you know. I felt real damn embarrassed and dumb-assed and . . . white . . .

So where did he go? Wolfman? Where'd he go when he jumped the team?

He ran away to Copenhagen. (Laughs) He and his girlfriend. They took a commercial flight to Europe the morning after King got shot. Wolfman was convinced they would be hunting blacks in the streets, and he felt sure someone would try to get him on the field, you know. He was so damn open out there in the field. He knew it would only take a fair shot with a rifle to get him . . . He wasn't far from right about that, you know?

Why'd he come back?

(Flynn skewers my eyes with his, giving a look as if he feels he has told enough. He considers a moment and you can see the decision cross his face. The sense is that he thinks enough time has passed to tell this story. He tells it blankly, without any apparent emphasis.) They'd been there three, four days, you know, when they decided to take a ferry between somewhere and somewhere. Copenhagen and France . . . or Amsterdam and somewhere . . . I don't remember just where, and it doesn't matter . . . Comes time to get off the boat and the customs won't let them into France, you know, puts them right back on the ferry. Wolfman's girl then was a real pale blond, a white chick, real real pretty . . . and they told her she could get off, but he would have to stay, they weren't going to let him in . . . So she and Wolfman got back on. It was a bitter cold, damp night. They went back to Amsterdam or wherever the hell, and they wouldn't let him off! They just grinned at him, like "Fuck him!" and put him back on the boat. Now normally Wolfman when he's riled, he's a mean son of a bitch, but this time he's so heartsick and sad and cold and lost that he just starts crying, he cries the whole way back across . . . (Flynn pauses, considers.) I'm gonna finish this son of a bitch of a story, but I don't want you printing it unless the Wolfman says it's okay, right? You understand? The man's mad enough with me, already, I don't want to cross him, you dig?

I understand.

(Flynn nods once, and then once again. It isn't quite a threat, but it is making things clear, like setting a hook.) Man was like a brother to me once upon a time . . . (He nods again.) I don't want to cross him now, no matter what's gone on since . . .

I understand, Jack. It's a promise.

All right . . . So Wolf and his girl they cried together almost all night on the ferry, until finally Wolfman tells her they been jacked around too much and they got to get help, you know? So he tells her to get off and make a call to the team offices . . . But she won't! She won't leave him . . . They argue but she won't let him stay there alone like the man without a country . . . But by then there's people who know this crap that's going on, a friendly guy on the ferry crew, a coupla white American tourists, you know . . . Somebody calls the American consulate and a young, crewcut bureaucrat shows up on the ferry, somebody from the consulate . . . He doesn't say anything to Wolfman, you know, he just talks with the girlfriend, because he can see how Wolf is shook up and because he's a really sensitive guy . . . The ferry docks again. "Come on," the crewcut guy says. They walk to customs. The customs guys are smiling. They start shaking their heads at Wolfman, waving their hands like to stop him. The guy from the consulate steps in front of them and flashes his ID. "Let them in, you Frog fucks," he says, "or I'll blow you motherfuckers right out of the water . . ." They walked ashore and Wolfman hugged the dude and took a cab right to the airport. He and his girl came back that same morning . . .

(Flynn leans back and, surprisingly, takes a cigarette from my pack, lights it, and takes what seems an exploratory puff, holding it out sideways before him after taking the drag, examining the filter. It is shocking in a way to see him smoke, like seeing the good kid in your class toss an awkward spitball toward the teacher. I tell him this, and he laughs.)

Not me . . . (Laughs again, twirls the cigarette in his fingers) Spitball's not me, I never loaded 'em up much, couldn't get the hang of it. Now maybe Hamburg would scratch one up on his shinguard buckle now and then . . . (Laughs) Wolfman hit three homers in a game against the Mets that year behind me . . . Oh, he was angry that year . . . (The mood has returned after some lightness.) I remember, in Detroit, it was like a meteor hit, you know, a crater of cinders and burnt buildings . . . (Laughs sardonically) Grand Avenue . . . I think that's a street there . . . burnt. I went 13 and 16 that year and didn't finish ten games; it was a long slide into the seventies . . . I couldn't finish anything . . . I'm in my mid-twenties and starting to think of packing it in, you know. Saw two of my heroes finish it off, one the right way, one wrong . . .

Did it affect your marriage?

(Flynn's eyes flash, he stubs the mostly unsmoked cigarette out.) I don't want to talk about that.

Okay then, talk about your heroes. Who? Gibson and . . . ?

No . . . Koufax . . . Koufax and Bunning. I mean, Gibson was too special to be my hero, you know? I mean, I couldn't touch that, I couldn't see myself there. Koufax, I could see. Bunning . . . (He gives a cockeyed smile, the mood seeming to change again.) Time has a way of clipping itself into segments, you know, especially when you play this game . . . It's like fishing over a stretch of water, some good holes where it keeps coming, flat water where you watch the dragonflies, then a patch of chop water and weeds, where the brave can make out . . . where the survivors are . . .

So start with the good holes . . .

(Flynn laughs.) Went eight and four two straight years, that's a .667 winning percentage. Figured I kept up that pace I'd have it licked, get to put my locker stool in Cooperstown . . . (Laughs) Sadecki's two years older than me and he gets twenty, and the way I figure it I'm two years away from that . . .

You were right!

(Laughs) I was right . . . but it wasn't that easy, you know. There's a little matter of learning to pitch. I learned by watching, mostly. Got nineteen starts the World Series year, and learned by watching Hoot and Ray and listening to McCarver, every damn chance I got . . . watching Koufax too, and Bunning for that matter. Sandy got his third no-hitter, you know, and Bunning pitched a perfect game against the Mets, and I walked one man to close out my World Series record . . . (Laughs loudly.) It was a hell of a year when you think of it. I thought the world was a piece of cheesecake, you know . . . I mean Bing gets fired and it looks like the Skipper's going too and we're plain out of it, when Brock starts producing and Schultzie starts vulching for us, then Philly drops ten in a row, and there we are, the Series staring us in the face if we just take the Mets once and we drop two in a row . . . Shit, it's an exciting life when you're a kid and spot-starting and you don't know no better . . . The last day of the season and kapow! We win it of course! (Laughs) I got so drunk that night, I twisted all night at some disco—they called them that then too—and you woulda thought I was Bo Belinsky, or his boy,

Chance, though I didn't have Chancey's twenty wins, you know, and never did get near enough to win a Cy Young . . .

Restless Willard's voice sounded like Donald Duck's from behind the paper pollen mask. He sat perched on a nest of toilet paper on the tufted leather seat of the Maserati, gripping the padded dash before him.

"These here Mazeroski's a fast car, ain't they Flynn?"

"Speedometer tops out at 160, Willard."

"Never hit for average, though, do they?"

"Want to try, Willard?"

"Noosir," he huffed. "Nossir . . . you can dodge micro-organisms, Flynn, but don't have no luck with trees . . ."

Flynn laughed with Willard. They were heading toward Massena because Emma never came back.

"Tell me how it was, Jack," Willard asked. "Tell me 'bout the Worl' Series . . ."

Almost shit my pants, Willard, almost shit my pants. I was young and foolish and just sittin' there in the pen, wondering who the hell's gonna get us out of this kind of heavy trouble when the bullpen phone rings . . . "Get up, Flynn," they says and I damn near shit my pants . . . I was gonna be a World Series hero, Restless, and I didn't know Yankees from jackshit . . . After Schultzie gets knocked out, Gordie gives Mantle a double down the line that looks like a rocket shot; he's walking Howard when the phone rings . . . My first two warm-ups I overthrow and my arm hurts like a snake bit it. "Calm the hell down, pretty boy," Uecker says. "This here Yankee pretty boy ain't gonna touch Gordie anyway." Just then we hear the shouting rise up all around us, like the world's ending in a flood of noise, and Pepitone singles off the wall. "Better bear down, pretty boy," Ueck says, "looks like it's your day to shine." So I throw one over his head and it skips onto the field and the boys snicker, even though we're about to lose our ass . . .

"The new Rip Sewell," Ueck shouts as he settles back down, and Tresh settles back into the batters box miles away. "Yanks'll never touch this boy's eephus . . ."

"I should hope not, thweety," some wiseass lisps. "Flynn-boy, we tole you about the big thity," he says, still lisping like a queer. "Never let anyone touch your eephuth . . ."

I was starting to laugh myself when the roar comes up again and we all spot Tresh's high fly and then the Skipper walks out into the rain of boos and next thing I know he's waving his right arm.

"That's you, pud," Uecker says. "Don't frig up."

I throw one sweet fastball in on Boyer, just throwing strikes like the Skip ordered, you know, right into his kitchen. The whole damn park's cheering like I'm Hoot himself, you know, and they're getting on McKinley about every inside pitch anyway after Pepitone turned that foul tick of Gibby's into a hip-by-pitch, if you know what I mean.

Suddenly I feel this wet, cold river of sweat down my spine, and I lose it altogether, Restless. I start thinking: hell, I'm in the World Series and it's only my second year and everyone's watching me at home and I can end this rally, you know . . .

Then I realize I've already nodded to McCarver and I don't know what the hell I agreed to pitch . . . and I realize I haven't checked the base runners, and that I don't know for a fact who's on base at all . . . But instead of stopping, you know, like I would have later on in life, instead of settling down, I just try to figure out from Timmy's target what the hell he expects me to throw. It looks like outside, and that's a good bet after inside gas, so I throw a fast one on the outside and McCarver has to make like a long-armed monkey to keep it from going by, and he comes running out to tell me what kind of asshole I am, and how that wasn't no curve, and the river of sweat is running so bad that I think it's gotta show on my back, and my bowels are turning again, and I check each of Tim's signs carefully, and check the runners real careful, and play peek-a-boo with my stretch and I walk Boyer on three more pitches . . .

Keane comes out and takes the ball. Craig finishes it off as good as you can an 8-3 whitewash, and so ends my World Series career, and you can look it up in the register . . .

And Jack comes in, about two hours after the roast is done, with this scarecrow creature he calls his friend, the friend done up in a white paper surgical mask and carrying a little bottle of oxygen and a mask like some miniature scuba diver, and an old-fashioned leather satchel mostly filled with toilet paper, which he spreads out over the La-Z-Boy while I get the dinner on, and Jack whispers how this Willard fellow is going to stay with us—with "us" is what he says—for a while, and all the while the old coot is laughing at some game show and mocking the contestants in the foulest language you've ever heard, and he never stops laughing all night, just like some loon out on a lake, and I think the world's gone crazy, and besides that, Jack's done nothing yet about Esther.

Ah, Red, life isn't half so ugly when you give it a chance, not with dawn coming like a morning glory unfurling, and white gulls in from the river looking for scraps and shelter from the storm.

NINE

Emma drove southward into gathering rain on her way to Bing-hamton to gather her daughter, driving toward the place where, days before and—as they say—after all these years, she first met Flynn again. Flynn, the white knight, the protector of damsels by da road.

It seemed long ago and far away.

She had heard the awful ping and thud when the Charger threw a rod, seen the spray of oil and the single foul cumulus of exhaust, and pulled to the roadside, waiting off the shoulder of 81, just outside Syracuse.

Great, she had thought, no daughter and now no car. Having nothing to lose, she stepped out to the shoulder, waiving gaily to the passing traffic whooshing by. Whooshing back at them.

Flynn was not the first to stop for her, only the most obvious. First was a sleezo in an old Ford, who looked directly at her silicone tits, so leering and obvious she wanted to take out one of the floppy little prosthesis packets and hand it to him. Here's a tit, son.

He tinkered under the hood and brushed his bony hips against her skirt while she leaned next to him, then he slammed it down and promised to call a tow truck if she really wouldn't take a ride with him. He had a silver crown on a front tooth, very military-peniten-tiary and without any of the charm of the long-lost love with gold and emerald inlay.

Next was a harried man in another Ford, this one a suburban station wagon with a wood side manqué. He emerged babbling ner-vously that he knew nothing about motors, cars, or anything for that matter, and she wanted to give him a long hug and a warm, deep kiss full of tongue, and send him off home to Liverpool and his wife.

She didn't even bother to show him the oil-slathered motor, just asked him to promise to call a tow truck since she didn't trust the silver-toothed leerer.

The man nodded nervously and hurried back to his wagon, thankfully unGalahad, signaling carefully and rather endlessly as he ventured back onto the highway from the shoulder.

A girl could get lucky here, Emma had thought. End a life alone and settle down by the highway.

Just then what was to be Flynn slowed down in the opposite lanes, southbound to the city, the Maserati gearbox whining down in a fine low purr. She saw him negotiate the downward shamrock and emerge like a low grey cloud, a little low-slung bullet of polished metal coming toward her, gears meshing with awkward grace.

Molly, I think we've hit it now, she thought; and then out of the car came Flynn.

"God, I thought I'd died and gone to heaven," sayeth the white knight. "Seeing someone as beautiful as you are beside the road alone."

It was winningly fresh and uncomplicated, and she had to applaud.

"Don't you want to see my engine first, Flynn," she said and watched as his eyes popped at her naughty-girl voice.

He laughed, thank god, and asked how she knew his name.

"From ball?" he said.

"From life," she laughed back at him.

They went to have a drink at the Holiday Inn, calling the wrecker from there. It would conceivably be the third such call to random tow trucks, Emma knew, and she had visions of them tearing the Charger apart, like sharks caught on to a wounded dolphin.

"Tell me," he said, "it isn't fair to hold it against me . . ."

He was trolling little cauliflower heads through the awful herb dip, crunching them in his teeth and swallowing them down, tan even in candlelight.

Even so, Emma thought, this is a worried man.

She decided to seduce him, turned horny by a roadside stand.

"Your car smells now," she said, unanswering. "Christmas in July?"

She drew a little circle on the back of his hand, all very movie-ish, quite the coquette for a lady upon a dead charger. Flynn looked frantic. He wanted to know, he always wanted to know what she knew.

A game's a game, she thought he thought.

Play with me amid the salesman.

"Aw come on . . . ," he groaned.

"Botticelli!" she said.

"That's your name . . ."

"That's my game . . ."

All smiles, Emma essayed the dip with a curled carrot, making a "V" of prop wake on its green studded face.

Flynn made the sound conventionally spelled whew, and leaned back, expanding his lordly shoulders and fabled arms.

Settling in for the duration, she thought.

God Flynn I'll rub your muscles up, boy, if you give me the chance.

"What will happen?" she asked.

"To us?"

Now she had to laugh.

"I was thinking of the car . . ." She laughed again.

"They'll tow it in to the station and let it sit until you tell them what to do."

"To do?" she asked. "When I've got me a wandering boy with his own silver cloud?"

"Aw for chri'sakes," Flynn said, "a Silver Cloud's a Rolls Royce, and anyway I got too much on my mind for all this crap . . ."

Emma looked hurt. She was hurt.

"Ugly noun," she said and plunked a yellow fringed broccoli floweret in the middle of the pond. "You can take me to the station, Mr. Flynn," she said primly, "and I'll hold on to my name and my dignity both."

He caught her eyes, there was no denying that the boy had his hold on one. She could see him trying to put it all together.

It doesn't go together, Flynn, she thought, it just goes.

"I'm sorry," he muttered.

"No, I am."

"Really," he pleaded now, "I am sorry. I'm just under pressure."

So are we all, thought the mother alone, bereft of spawn, having left same with father. Her mood was returning.

Think of it as show and tell, Mr. Flynn. Mister Win. In the

morning, we'll have homecoming and I'll be your breathless prom queen.

"That's the one where you guess the initials?" he asked.

"What is?"

"Botticelli."

Aha, thought Emma, let's go to your room. Our revels are all ended.

A lonesome salesman danced with a bargirl. Emma's drink melted to a salty pool, little lime slice athwart on the bottom like a wounded greengill.

"Marguerita," she said.

He smiled, unfooled. Always under him there was this square-ness she liked, unexciting and excited.

This is the safest of all, she knew, knowing one unknown to one. A night with a white knight (she even thought this then), followed perhaps by a slow ride home on an unsilver cloud.

"E.L.C."

"What?"

"The Botticelli clue . . ."

He waved to the bunny-tailed waitress and a drink appeared on naked hips, low-slung cheeks peeking under the girl's fishnet hose. She made change from between her gold-lamé tits, a little nervous about all that green tucked into her flat floppers.

There was a team of fey go-go-boys played the North Coun-try bars, Flynn. Rumor is the ladies tucked similar green into silver codpieces.

"Thought you said TLC . . . ," he said.

Emma hummed. "Mmmm, I could of . . ."

He laughed square again. It was fun to play with one so fair, thinking of sliding palms over oiled muscles and rump.

What am I doing? Emma thought.

It's that bastard LaChaise, she thought, seeing him looking at my daughter like that sets the sap running.

She laughed and Flynn did not know why.

She choked upon the salty puddle of the drink.

Sap, she laughed. LaChaise was that. I loved him once.

I loved him twice . . .

"What is it?" square Flynn said.

"Thinking of a chair I used to sit upon," she said, and choked again, giggly now. Tia Maria gone to her head.

Oooo I'm quite drunk, low slunk, vegetable dunk, Flynn . . .

She was giggling crazy now, even to her.

"It is rather a clue of sorts," she said in her best British voice, gaining composure in her musculature if not in her giggly tummy.

She changed to a story-telling woo-woo tone, the one that scared Molly when she thought she saw bunny eyes.

"Once I was the chair, *en effet*, but I changed to Lady Luck on unmarriage day . . ."

She touched Flynn's nose!

He let her hand die there.

"You should get a room," he said.

And you get a womb, she did not say.

She woke, mostly naked, atop a gold brocade, untouched she knew, on one of two double beds. Flynn had set her down carefully there, she remembered, after a maze of spinning red walls and a sideways elevator. The room, too, spun and once when it whirled her stomach up, she'd run to the little tile bath, spewing a trail like a sour comet. She came out to find him, patient, cleaning her throw-up up. And this is true love, she thought, to clean up after Lady Luck.

It was after that she had felt him, gently gently, unbutton, unslip, unbra, unlove and cover her. Evidently some spew had soaked her; this boy was a saint.

And he'd seen what she didn't have, she knew. And he sat in a chair in the middle of the night in always unlovely Syracuse, light from a blue eye washing over his brown face. The all-night cable spinning a web of sports score shadows on the walls and him, Flynn, awake and almost unmoving, crying in a brocade chair.

She woke, like you do when you've been or are drunk, feeling a little below yourself, as if underwater. Above you there is haze, and then at a lower, heavier stratum, your body. Below haze and body you lie, an aura, momentarily clear-minded, yet afraid to swim up through body and haze, afraid to resume the mantle of all that has put you down here.

He cried in small, convulsive waves, like someone silently laughing, each wave of tears shaking those great, broad shoulders, head jerking with each wave like a wise man nodding.

He wore a Blue Jays tee shirt for chri'sakes.

She considered surfacing with a tough little joke. I couldn't have been that bad, could I, Flynn? But then she didn't.

Why would a man cry before a television in Syracuse?

Ha! she thought, that's reason enough.

She gathered herself enough to kneel on the bed, sitting back on her haunches, the brocade pulled around her, like an extravagant squaw. The first wave of dizziness nearly put her down again. A little gulp of sour bile rose and fell like a ball propelled by a carnival sledgehammer. It was just short of the bell. She cursed Mexico and drinks with salt upon them and sat there awhile, collecting her forces, watching the man cry.

Molly, I need you, she thought.

"Who the hell are you?"

So he had known she was there. He drew a large handkerchief from the pocket of his blue jeans. I am your daughter, she thought, for my father used to also use a great white cloth to wipe his tears.

"I'm your queen, Flynn," she said.

Little hammers bonged within her forehead like a vibraphone when she spoke.

He caught his breath in a great wheeze, and then cried a little despite his effort.

"Oh please . . . ," he moaned, "please cut that crap."

O, it wasn't crap, that ugly word, it was another clue. She had been a prom queen, he a prom king. Different proms, but a single past. If he remembered her, he would know.

Emma LaChaise had first met Jack Flynn eight years before, in 1971. She was no one then, a quiet wife in long skirts and long hair and bare feet, not bustling but moving slowly, sensuously, about, cooking great leaden gobs of bulgur and horrid greens for the vegetarian Yves, last of the French hippies and cabinetmaker deluxe of Westminster Park and other snooty islands and shores.

Yves of the flowing hair, the Guy LeFleur of jerks.

Yves of the bony ass, father of her child.

Yves the little boy, all wired because this famous baseball player no one ever heard of wanted him to do a job for him, a job that scared the shit out of him because he wasn't a boatwright and he didn't know a hull from a hatch and the boat was an antique, a St. Lawrence skiff, a secret gift for Flynn's father.

"But it's just the same, eh? It's a matter of joining wood, no? We make this one . . . ," he said, turning the *this* to *zis* more for effect than for heritage sake, "and we make a picture, no? Ever'one can see that Mr. Jack Flynn has Yves do *zis* skiff, and, voilà, we arrive on the gravy train, no?"

"No," Emma had said, but by then this response was too much an institutionalized joke between them, and also Yves was too wired to listen to reason.

He had danced around the shop in the way he had, tossing chisels carelessly into wooden boxes—doubtlessly chipping them irreparably, Emma thought, thus forcing him to leaf through his beloved, full-color catalogues of British steel tools and expensive Japanese saws—and swinging the giggly Molly in his arms.

Jack Flynn was number four hundred and eleven of Yves' versions of the promised land. Doubtlessly, Emma knew, the scenes in '71 had planted a subliminal time bomb which led to Molly's adolescent hero worship later.

Doubtlessly, Emma knew, she had grown a little fond of Flynn then.

She remembered the day Flynn was to come to Yves' workshop. It was Yves who was bustling then, putting cool jazz on the tape player, carefully setting out his newly purchased picture book of antique boats, shooing Emma out to the store to buy Brie and tinned pâté and wine beyond what they could afford.

He's like a big kid, Emma thought, and he probably never saw a baseball game in his life. It was not the job, she knew, not the SS Gravy Train, but the prospect of dealing with the Major League star.

"Zis is business entertaining, no?" he'd said as he urged her toward the stores, his Quebec accent growing each moment in anticipation of the pitcher.

"And when Molly gets back from her grandmother's, she can eat the scraps of Brie, no?" said Emma glumly.

Yves, the big goop, missed the sarcasm.

"*Mais oui, mais oui*, my Emma of the waters . . ."

He'd danced her about then and she had to laugh, and, for whatever reason, she'd changed into the long, lacy white gauze dress when she got back, carefully trying different undies to gauge their effect, before rejecting them all.

It was to be the honeymoon they never had, with Molly gone to

Grandmère's, and Emma wasn't quite ready to lose that, no matter who else's darling Yves might be on his long days on the islands.

Flynn arrived near sunset, hours late, the water and islands a lavender haze under the tangerine sun. Yves was a little sullen by then, drunk on jug wine and just short of opening the Châteauneuf they had been carefully saving for this client. One of the oblong cubes of pâté was already collapsed in a smear, with a rubble of bread shards dotting the Spammy-smelling surface.

Flynn arrived apologetic with a lean, silent black man in his attendance like a shadow.

"Wolfman had engine trouble outside Buffalo, we spent all afternoon in a hangar," Flynn said between the sorrys.

Hearing this impossibly romantic excuse, and seeing Flynn in company with what seemed a black bodyguard, threw Yves into animation and exaggerated versions of negritude. He cranked up the cool jazz and began to talk of Miles, he uncorked the Châteauneuf with a mighty whoop, and he wiped his hands repeatedly on the long leather apron, as if to assure the ballplayer that this hippy affectation was his everyday shop wear.

O, he wears the leather constantly now, Emma knew, Yves de la Binghamton, craftsperson extraordinaire, heartthrob of coeds and housewives. Including his zucchini bride, her potato-head kids.

Flynn declined the wine and bread and settled for Emma's Tab and Frito Lay ripples. Wolfman watered down his Châteauneuf with cold water from the tap, and he made the pâté into a fat sandwich. Emma began laughing then and hardly stopped all night. It became a lovely party.

Flynn talked hockey first.

"I play it in my dreams," he said. "Sometimes I'm out there skating alone on white, white ice, rushing down the left wing, my hair flowing behind me . . . Suddenly there's a goalie all dressed in black, head to toe. I know he's grinning behind his black mask . . . I shoot, and I never see if I score . . ."

Emma laughed and laughed then and Flynn broke into a little grin. He had announced the story as a fright, she thought it funny.

"'Tis death, little lady," Wolfman said quietly, but then he laughed too. Yves gave her the look that said she was a fool, and she laughed more.

He kept trying to turn the conversation back to baseball, to "*dee*

Ezpo" as he called them, and Flynn always talked about Les Canadiens. It was very funny really.

Finally, when they were all good and drunk except him, Flynn took out the Polaroid pictures of the boat. It looked like someone had stepped through the bottom of it, springing the boards, and Emma laughed then too.

Wolfman laughed in a low ho-ho-ho. Emma had her head on his lap, having placed herself there shortly after Yves passed the hash pipe and glared at her for hanging so closely on the black man.

She liked the way the white gauze looked against him.

And she hated also how Yves and Flynn had talked about her like she was a pet poodle.

And she was high, so high she needed a jet-man, a wolf-man, to get her down.

She was hanging on Wolfman to tease Flynn, she knew.

Flynn and Yves discussed the boat.

"I know you've never done this work," Flynn said, and Yves waved instinctively toward the fat and expensive coffee table picture book. "But I want someone who knows good wood and how to use it. I figure you can learn the rest . . . I want this to be a beautiful thing, you know, for my father . . . I want him to have the most beautiful boat in the world . . ."

Emma raised her eyebrows at him. If he had been drunk, it might have been less extraordinary a thing to say.

She wanted to cry then. It was such a hopeless thing for a man to say. Didn't we all want that for our parents? Beautiful boats to convey them along the dark river?

Instead she spoke.

"You should have him build it new then."

Yves was surprised, and Wolfman grunted beneath her. She meant it though, say what you wanted about Yves, he loved wood and the ways it could form itself into things.

He made her a tulipwood thing once, a little gewgaw, no more than a polished curve, a sculpture. It was a beautiful thing, it made you happy to hold it.

"It's a dildo for a goddess, no?" he had said when she asked him what it was.

It gave her thought, though she never tried it, thinking that, like Cinderella's slipper, it did not do to test yourself against perfection.

Yves was a slunk, but he knew how to do what he did.

Flynn had taken a long time responding to her suggestion.

"I thought of that, ma'am," he said, "but my dad has the river right up in his bone marrow, you see, and I want him to feel it in the wood under him, if you know what I mean. Anything less and he'd know . . . you know?"

"I know," she had said.

"I know," she said to Flynn as he cried before the Syracuse television.

She had risen up, her forehead booming, and moved to touch him, the brocade wrapped about her like a cape. He shuddered at the touch and pulled away. It was awful to see a man crying like this. I know, she said, but she did not know, it was something you learned to say when you taught high school girls. Always they wept over something unknowable and it was a comfort to say you knew. It was not a lie.

She sat with her legs under her on the matching chair before the television, the two of them sitting there as before a fire, watching the newswire type and lift each line of meaningless woe.

She had sat similarly across from him in Yves workshop, while Yves and Wolfman patrolled in search of more wine years before. She was aware of her body then, curves and flats under the gauze and muggy air. She had stroked her foot as she sat there, daring the all-American boy to take her goopy husband up on his queerly nervous jokes.

"You're welcome to her, if you can tame her," Yves had said before he and the black man left, "but do be careful, Jacques, she bites . . ."

Wolfman had met her eyes, sounding her to see if she had the stomach for this foolishness. Flynn had only laughed.

"No thanks," he said. "I already have one that stings, don't I, Wolfman?"

Wolfman had slowly nodded. The deal was done, the night was old, and they were about to leave her alone with Flynn for what could be hours until they found someone to sell them wine.

She had teased Flynn then, got him talking about himself. When he said he had been prom king, he was embarrassed, and he was more so when she had said she was his queen.

She still had breasts then and she had let them show themselves in the décolletage. She couldn't remember why Flynn hadn't gone with the two other men, but she had the vague feeling always that he stayed to protect her, and, too, that he had seen she was willing to tease.

She wasn't teasing any longer. She was only trying to get him to stop crying.

"I'm sorry," she muttered, and he waved the large handkerchief before him, acknowledging. "Do you want to tell me?" she asked.

"No," he said, and cried again.

"You cleaned me up, Flynn. It's the least I can do to clean you up too," she said. He gaped at her. She had gotten through to him.

"The Wild Geese," he said.

"What?"

He gestured toward the bottle on the lamp table next to him, Hennessey's cognac, fairly drained.

"Five Star's a product of the noble Hennessey," he said. "Ran away years ago to fight for France, the Irish did. My Dad told me that . . ."

Emma nodded benignly, thankful for talk of any type.

Was there a point to this, she wondered.

Flynn lifted the bottle to look, the gesture was a cliché among men as far as Emma knew. The next step was to pour off the last drink in noble sadness.

Flynn did not.

"Jeez," he said. "That shit disappeared, didn't it?"

"Why are you crying?"

Flynn looked at her. "Do you know who I am?" he asked. "Really?"

"Card-carrying member of your fan club," she said.

"Ha!" he laughed. "You're no Baseball Annie . . ."

No, she thought, but I do have a card, thanks to my darling daughter. She considered whether to show him, but decided not to. The thing was to keep him talking.

"No Annie at all, actually," she said. "Do you want to know my name?"

He waved his hand, back and fro. This meant no; this meant I don't know.

"Flynn's a French name," he said. "Originally. Peel any Irish and you find a Frog or a Dane . . ."

Was he remembering her? Her Yves?

"Like a hard-boiled egg," she said. "The sun within a cloud . . ."

"What?"

"Peeling," she said. It was something Molly said.

"Someone told me once that inside a baseball is the moon," he said. "When we were kids, we'd peel them down and then milk them, you know?"

"No," she said.

"No," he said, "that was golf balls gave milk." He laughed. "Remember that. If you're ever stranded on a desert island, milk in golf balls and . . . ," he laughed, "rabbit's in a baseball."

He laughed again. There was evidently a joke in this comment.

"Why are you crying?" she asked.

"I don't know really," he said. "Because I'm drunk, I suppose, and you were so hopeless . . . I mean, helpless . . ."

Ah, Flynn, she thought, you may be right at that. Hopeless is more like it. She nodded at the electronic campfire. The newswire said that President Carter was fishing somewhere.

Sometimes Emma longed for news of Margaret Trudeau.

"Because . . . ," Flynn said, and he paused for a long time, more thinking to himself than for effect, "because I must consider whether there is life after baseball . . ."

He laughed aloud. He was slowly regaining himself.

"What is it your comedian says?" she asked. "Is there life after sex?"

Why should she play the Canadian with him, she wondered. She was as much an American as he, born by pure error in Albany, New York, and thus holding joint citizenship.

My natural homeland is the river, she thought, out off Wellesley Island where the imaginary border curves like a floating line.

Perhaps it suits me to be foreign to him, just as it suited me to be American for Yves.

Meanwhile Flynn looked anguished again.

"I'm sorry if I disappointed you . . . ," he said.

My God, she thought, the poor boy's anguished that he didn't plank me whilst I was puking.

"I didn't mean that," she said.

He was mewing his face up again, and about to reach for the bottle of geese.

"Don't go weepy on me again, okay Flynn?"

He nodded vigorously, trying to hold it together.

"I'm a wild goose myself," he muttered. "We are dying, the Flynns . . ."

Oh Christ, we are all dying, Flynn. I have within me the seed of a jellyfish, a transparent little glop looking to adhere to something fresh and full of blood. Cancer never leaves you, Flynn, it just swims in the dim.

"Are you sick?" she asked, politely.

It made her laugh, the tea-time tone of her question, but then the laughing got away from her, out of control, like a line running fast from a reel, hot and crazily spinning down to the gleaming spool. It was all so sordid, the whole affair. From dropping Molly off with the grinning Yves, and some chickie with bobbing tits moving about in the back of the shop, staring at Emma with her supercilious, kept smile; down to the trip back upstate, the lust like a hot flash at the side of the road, gulping salty Margaritas like a sorority girl intent on losing her cherry, spinning her way upstairs to sit, half naked, under a bedspread by a forlorn television, her clothing vomit-stained and damp in the bathtub.

She went crazy on him and she saw him stiffen with panic. She was one weight too much for him and she saw him brace himself against her and then lose it, slowly, weeping like a boy who had lost some bright thing.

She kept trying to swim up from it, the awful flood of loss. You are one sad woman, Emma, she thought, to burden this tanned man with your little losses.

But each time she surfaced, she fell down again. It was nearly morning after a long decade, a long night.

When she had exhausted herself, he began talking. Some of the things he said she already knew from talk or mutual acquaintances. What she did not know was how utterly bereft he was, how helpless before the loss. It had seemed to her as if he had seen a handful of bright coins fall into the water, watching helpless and fascinated as they tumbled through the dark depths beyond his grasp.

It was her fault. She had lost it herself and triggered him. He told the whole woe in a monotone, as if answering the questions of an unseen interviewer.

Brother, mother, father and friend lost, sister nearly gone; arm like a wet rag, a sopping towel, sent out into a world without the bright lights and the dazzling lime fields.

He had talked himself into a stupor, unraveling as if following her example. They were orphans in a motel dawn.

Emma had slept again, and woke in front of the dimming camp-fire, the television in morning glare, alone in the chair, cramped and sad and mascara-stained.

By the time she had washed out her things, he was back and surprised to see her there. He said he didn't know her; and she tried to joke him from it. He gazed upon her calmly and leaden-eyed, seemed unsurprised and unmoved when she said she was accompanying him north.

He said he didn't know her.

It was panic, she knew, no more than that. He would wake from it as if from a dream, for she would accompany him.

It wasn't amnesia, she knew and told him, just a sort of mental glitch, a blown fuse, the result of too much cognac and stress.

He had nodded complacently, looking terribly fresh for some-one who had spent little of the night asleep.

He had handed her a package, a blouse and skirt in her size.

"So you remember some things," she had said.

He looked confused.

"I guess so," he had said, and then asked in a puzzled, puzzling tone, "Didn't you ask for these?"

"I would have if I thought you would have gotten them," she said.

"We'll go when you are ready," he had said.

They had gone north then, to Clayton and onward, just as now she went southward, retrieving Molly from the French fool, her father. Things would change, Emma thought. No more will I drop her there for him, I'll only go halfway. If he was so frantic to see her, he could get one of his chippies to drive up to Syracuse to pick her up.

Emma would do that much, she would go halfway. Things would change.

Molly would somehow know how to draw Flynn the rest of the way out. Things would change.

Molly had looked into the blank eye of the universe. She would guide Flynn out of the depths, just as she had drawn Emma out of the endless shadows.

Emma shot southward in the rented car, thinking things would change.

TEN

Emma was so sick she could just drive you nuts sometimes. First of all she shows up at Papa's bruised under the eye and all bent out of shape—I mean just raving nuts—like there's cat shit on the bedspread again or something—and it turns out she has this plan, you know, another one of her plans for how they're going to handle visitation. It's like that's all she has been thinking about for a week, and so she comes flouncing into the workshop, first thing, just raving away about it, how things're gonna change.

And the bizarre thing is she's all done up in this new outfit that's the first thing she's bought in years that doesn't look just weird . . . I mean this poplin straight skirt that's perfect for her and a blue oxford cloth button-down blouse that makes her look so cool, and she blows it right away, just when he and Bethany had been arguing and there really seemed a chance that maybe it wasn't too late after all.

Then she calls Airhead a concubine! I mean . . . first of all, she thinks she's so damn smart that nobody's going to know what the word means because nobody's ever read half her dippy books or even seen a Walt Disney movie, you know? And then to say that about Airhead . . . It made Papa nearly puke. I mean, all Airhead's good for is sweeping up the sawdust on the shop floor anyway, that and wasting good cherrywood, which is practically all he ever talked about at the house, until it drove Bethany and the vegetable eaters as crazy as me. Airhead's this, and Airhead's that, you know, and in comes weird Emma with her fancy secret word . . . and even that's not the beginning of her latest crap.

Her big plan is from now on Papa's got to bring me up to Syracuse on his own, and he's got to get me there or else I can't have visitation, or he can't, or whoever it belongs to . . .

I mean, I can just imagine it! Me and the vegetable eaters in the back of this rust bucket pick-up truck that can hardly get out to McDonalds, let alone to Syracuse, while he and Bethany sit up there and nag at each other in the front seat, catching their butts on the springs in the seat and choking on the exhaust from the broken muffler.

Meanwhile Emma's got this rented Buick that's boss, sitting out in front of the shop, and she's wearing new clothes, and she's still raving like the same old weirdo about child support and lawyers and concubines, the shiner under her eye making her look like she's winking.

So I started crying, you know, halfway cuz I couldn't help it, but mostly to get them to stop acting wired and weird. So he grabs me and calls me his little pickle or something in French, and she's tugging at my arms and saying we can talk this out later by phone, and Airhead's still pushing her broom around the shop because she can't get anything else to dance with her, like Papa says.

It was bizarre.

And it got worse . . .

We're halfway to Syracuse, and I'm finally getting most the wood chips out of my hair and stuff from Papa's crazy hugs, and Emma's calming down enough to relax her fingers on the steering wheel—although she's still smoking cigarettes one after another like she's daring me to say something about why she started again, when out of nowhere she tells me she's been spending time with Flynn!

Fucking Christ! Can you imagine! I mean that's how she tells me something as important as that! After a hundred goddamn miles or so, and in her teacher-teacher tone, all la-di-dah and serious like someone's having a baby, you know, "Molly dearest, I just feel that I must tell you, darling, that your mother has been spending the whole goddamn week with about the most important person in the world . . ."

Something like that, you know.

I mean, I'm almost creaming my jeans and there's Emma talking like Flynn died or something, and she just has to wait until now when we're hanging over the side of a cliff on a ratty highway to tell me.

I mean, I almost wanted to grab the wheel and make her turn around and tell that to Papa Yves and the vegetables, you know.

But then she's crying!

Emma is so positively weird you just never know with her. She's crying and getting real heavy about how I have to help her, and then how I have to help him, can you dig that? Me help him and she's crying so strange and sad that I wish she never told me and I only just overheard it staying up all night sometime when she didn't know it, because I just don't know what to do, or how she thinks I'm ever gonna help anybody. And beside that I'm starting to feel icky about it, you know, like when you get something for a present that you've been pushing for for months and then it doesn't seem right anymore, you know.

I mean, what if Flynn was fat or dumb? or a faggot?

What if he was like some uncle you never met? Or worse, what if he loved her, and he wanted to marry her, and she already screwed it up by acting so weird without anybody there to keep her straight?

Probably got a black eye walking into a wall . . .

So I asked her what I'm supposed to do to help him, and she says I don't know honey, I don't know, just like that, biting her lip to stop crying and right then she gets a ticket for speeding on radar, I swear! Right then.

"How dern long does it take to do a person's fortune anyways?" Restless complained, but the girl just kept mumbling and dealing her cards.

Ah, but the world had changed, Restless thought. What with a bed to sleep in where the old fussbudget boiled the sheets sanitary-like; and meals; and a teevee where you didn't have to touch no dial, only push a button on the control, which, too, kept things clean as a baby's farts.

And now there was the little princess around to keep things interesting. Willard was sure she was the same kid came to visit once and he touched her hand so's to see if he could; and, what's more, he was sure she was the same kid he's seen on the diamond outside the nuthouse window.

She denied it all, or rather let it sorta wash off her like he was just an old man talking, but she was a real prospect nonetheless and now it turns out she can tell fortunes from baseball cards, though she takes her sweet time.

Molly had eighteen cards in all, including the two Kellogg's which told you the most about Flynn, but she was only working with seventeen because of the World Series-year card that Emma had in her wallet, wherever she was now with Flynn.

She had to go over the cards to remember how they worked, because mostly she had done this for herself before, herself and Emma and strange Julie at school. The vegetable eaters weren't interested even though Bethany made a big deal about how creative it was and how it was just like Tarot cards, which it wasn't at all.

So when the old weirdo in the paper mask asked her about what she was doing, she told him, and then he got all excited about it and Aunt Bertie turned the teevee up so she could hear and Molly agreed to do it so she could shut Willard up.

There were four suits, two red, a brown and a blue: St. Louis, Philadelphia, San Diego, and Toronto. There were two special cards, the Kellogg's, and only two cards in the blue suit, which was good because the blue suit didn't always mean good news.

The shorter of the red suits was only three cards with the World Series gone, and it meant change and growth.

The first card was number 538 and it had two pictures of Flynn, in the big one throwing, and the little circle picture shows him standing in his stretch. It was a rare card and so it meant great fortune was coming. Flynn said they rushed and took it at spring training because he was in the college league the year before when they usually took them.

It looks like the Cards will have to find a place for the sensation prospect, Flynn, who tore up the Rookie and PONY leagues with his blazing fastball. Jack could round off the Cards' potent staff.

Next to the story part there was a cartoon that was supposed to be Flynn, pitching in a mortarboard, with a caption that read, "Jack brought Iowa to the College World Series for the first time." Under the cartoon and the story was his minor league record. This card meant sudden success.

The missing 1964 card Molly knew by heart. It just said, "Flynn had a very impressive winning percentage in his rookie year. The hard-throwing right-hander gives St. Louis at least a double threat for years to come."

Willard said Flynn wasn't wearing his hat because the Topps

people thought he would be traded, but Willard didn't know much anyway.

If she had the card in the pack, it would have meant success will come soon.

The 1965 card was the dumbest-looking photograph. Flynn looked like a fish or something with his jaw dropped. The cartoon on the back was dippy too. "Flynn's pitching helped the Cards in their fantastic pennant stretch," it said under it.

The card meant waiting when you used it for a fortune.

1966 was a great card, and it meant good luck because the little caption on the cartoon said "Jack looks to be a 20 game winner," and he did win twenty that year, even though he only got seventeen the year before. Plus his picture was pretty foxy for those days and they didn't have that dumb team pennant across his chest like the year before.

The next year started the second red suit. These were the hardest cards to read because they had real mixed meanings, and they depended a lot on what cards were next to them when you read your fortune. Like the first one, for instance, which usually was a good card because it had a great picture and an autograph, plus two cartoons on the back. But sometimes it could mean unexpected changes when it was next to the wrong card, because unexpected changes were what happened to Flynn.

"A real fireballer," the first cartoon panel said, "Jack struck out over 200 for the 2nd straight year." But the little story told the unexpected changes: "Jack's trade to the Phil's rocked the baseball world. This 20 game winner should be the perfect complement to veteran right-hander Jim Bunning. Together they may just get the Phils on track."

Willard had snorted when he saw this card. "Naw," he said, "stupid-ass Cards trade Flynn and first thing you know Clee-minty breaks Gibson's leg. They was lucky to get to the series after that trade, sweety . . . Was a bad year for injrees all round, this fellow Conigliah or something damn near got his head knocked off . . ."

"Don't swear to the child!" Bertie said.

"She's gotta get used to life around baseball," Willard snapped back.

It was that kind of card, the '67, it got people riled because it was so weird, even if it was the year she was born.

1968 was just plain bad news. First of all the card had this stupid border around the picture, and then the picture showed Flynn with some machine behind him. It was all junked up and blurry. Then the little story on the back just seemed like the Topps people didn't know what to say. "Flynn paid-off the Phil's investment with a second straight 20 game season and a third straight 200 strikeouts, earning him an All-Star appearance."

This card meant that things were not what they seemed and the next year's card proved it. "One of the premiere fireballers in baseball, Jack managed to pick up thirteen wins despite arm troubles and an uneven performance. The Phillies know he can finish games for them and they look for him to come back to his All-Star form after a minor dip."

A minor dip sounded dumb. Flynn looked worried and hurt in his picture on the front. This card meant that someone was going to die, or something real bad would happen.

"Fellah could be dead or something before you got to his fortune," Restless said.

"You want it right? Or do you just want me to make up something for you?"

He laughed his funny stairstep laugh: hee hee hee, his voice cracking into a cough.

1970 was a mysterious card, you had to really think about what it meant, especially since it was one of the two years she had Kelloggs cards for, and they were good. The Topps card from the red suit showed Flynn looking kind of grim but handsome, like some sort of wise, sad prince. The little story under his name and stuff showed that he was serious: "Jack improved his winning percentage by 70 points last year, and seems to be regaining his strike-out form. He's known as a loner and serious thinker."

Molly hadn't seen all that many baseball cards, but she was sure there weren't many that said something like that. The cartoon was also fairly serious. "Jack K'D 18 batters in his first start with the Phils in '67."

The card meant something like you had to think and make up your mind, but success could come if you worked at it.

The Kellogg's card for that year was a wild card, because it was 3-D and because it told so much about Flynn. If it turned up in the right place, it meant really good news or great changes even though Flynn didn't do so well for a few years after that, and Kellogg's didn't put him on a card until 1973. The picture showed him on his follow-through, looking really determined and strong. There was a little circle in the form of a baseball with his name across the center, and his autograph was written sideways down his uniform. It was the new autograph, which she didn't like as much as the simple one on his early card.

The back of the Kellogg's card was boss! Besides all the usual stuff about right hand, height, and weight, it listed hobbies as "Fishing, Antique boats, and star gazing." Molly figured the last one was a joke, but she knew that her Papa had fixed an old boat once for Flynn.

The little story on the back was maybe the best one of all. "One of the most consistent performers among NL pitchers," it said, "Jack is an articulate and careful young man. Many feel he has a career ahead of him in broadcasting. Although he has had some consistency problems, he has one of the strongest arms and best heads among veteran pitchers. Never a league leader, he is nonetheless always among the best. A really steady performer with real velocity, he once struck out 271 in a season."

Something about that story made her want to cry sometimes; she liked the card almost best of all.

The '71 card had an autograph again and a picture of Flynn smiling kind of goofy-like but nice. That year they put a copy of the picture on the back instead of the cartoon. The story made the card mean a reverse in fortunes.

"Flynn had some strong outings toward the end of last season after suffering arm troubles and family tragedy. It was a year in which some other fine young pitchers also suffered set-backs, and Flynn looks to regain his 20 game winning form this season. FIRST YEAR IN PRO BALL: 1962 FIRST GAME IN MAJORS: 1963"

Under the story they only gave the last year's season record and Life. '70 was the worst year of all, 6 & 7, a 4.22 ERA, but his Life ERA was 3.13, which was still real good.

The San Diego cards were what Molly called the brown suit, and they were cards that told you about people around the person whose fortune you were telling, because Molly was sure that Flynn didn't really like California, though she didn't ask him yet.

The first one was the only other one without a hat, and she was pretty sure that Mr. Willard was right about that meaning a trade in this case because you could see that Flynn was wearing a Philadelphia shirt even though the letters around the top said PADRES.

There was only a one-line story, "Jack will give the young Padres a proven performer," and the cartoon was a little quiz, "How many times has Jack K'D 200 batters in a season?" The upside-down answer said three, but it was a mistake, since he struck out 200 for Philadelphia before he was traded and the numbers below showed it.

Willard said that meant the card was probably worth a hundred dollars; Molly knew he was nuts.

The card meant that someone new would enter your life.

'73 was a great card, it meant someone would bring you good fortune or good news, because it was the year after Flynn had his no-hitter, and another 20-game-winning season. "Flynn did it all last year," the story said, "No-hitting the Reds, leading the SD staff with 23 complete games, and setting a club record for SOs and shutouts."

The cartoon showed Flynn with a microphone. "Jack works as a broadcaster in off-seasons," it said.

"Hah, he did the danged weather!" Willard said. He was looking over her shoulder now, impatient for something to happen.

He swiped the Kellogg's card from her hand and touched her in the process. Molly waited for him to say something about that, but he let it go without saying anything.

"Just look at this thing," Willard said, "shining like a three buck whore."

"Mr. Walker!" Aunt Bertie shouted. "I insist . . ."

She had ears for stuff like that.

"Beg yer pardon, ma'am," Restless said, "but just look'it this picture, will you? Is that the way a man's supposed to look? I ask you."

Bertie was in the middle of a long set of commercials, so she did come over. Molly was sure she was surrounded by nuts.

What was the big deal about the picture? It wasn't 3-D but it was some special sort of picture and it had a kind of sparkle to it. Flynn was shown laughing inside a crest shape, with his last name under him like a little banner. He looked like a real California movie star.

"Jack was so handsome then," Bertie said, and although it was kind of weird that she said it just then, Molly wanted to tell her that he was still handsome now.

"It ain't that," Willard said. "It's the whole she-bang! Ball players now act like a bunch of sweet asses, you ask me, and it's stuff like this makes 'em that way."

"Mr. Walker," Bertie snapped, "I insist!"

"You can't argue with histr'y!" Willard said.

"Why ever are you here in this house, Mr. Walker?"

Why are any of us here, Molly thought, but then Willard said it, and it made her laugh. Aunt Bertie scowled at them both, and it made Molly feel bad, but then Bertie's show came back on and she just sort of slid away from them.

The next three brown cards, '74, '75, and '76, were kind of blah, and they meant things like "Someone will keep you waiting for news" or "Someone will disappoint you," and they didn't interest Molly, even to read.

The '74 had a little cartoon of Flynn in a boat and it said he was a fishing guide in off-season, which wasn't quite true. The story did tell you that Flynn had won a big salary in arbitration, but that only meant that the card was about money. The '75 had a quiz instead of the cartoon, and it was about this guy VanderMeer who pitched two no-hitters once. And the '76 didn't even have a story or autograph, only a cartoon fact about Red Schoendienst hitting a 14th-inning home run to win an All-Star game. Because Schoendienst was once Flynn's manager, the card could mean that someone from your past would do something.

That left only the blue suit, both cards from when Flynn went to Toronto and changed leagues. The '77 was the better of the two of them, even though it didn't have any story or a cartoon about Flynn. It was better because it came after he pitched another 20-game season, which they should have said something about, because he always did it after he was traded. Since the blue cards really decided your future, this one meant that you could expect continued success.

The '78 meant that the future would bring trouble, but also mixed blessings, if that made sense. It was Flynn's last year, and the year that he got into all the trouble about fighting with that guy, even though he won twenty again. The card had a little game on the back instead of a cartoon, and you were supposed to play pretend base-ball with them or something. Flynn's card had an "X" and some half-circles for the diamond, and it said "Ground Out" on the bottom, which wasn't very good.

And that was Flynn's whole life.

"All right," she told Willard, "shuffle the cards while you think of your question . . ."

"What question?"

"Your fortune question!" she said. This really was going to be a drag, and she wondered why she ever started.

"Why I gotta have a question to have my fortune told?"

She sighed and Bertie cleared her throat and glared, so Willard did what he was told.

He slapped the cards together so hard she thought he would bend one and ruin it.

"Now what?" he said.

She took the cards from him without answering and dealt them into the three rows that gave you past, present, and future.

It was so weird. She'd never seen the cards like this before. She felt the tears coming to her eyes, and she didn't want to tell him.

Bertie wasn't watching her show. She gazed from the La-Z-Boy like she was watching the school play or something. Willard sat there and looked at Flynn's different faces, his eyes bugging out from over the top of his paper germ-mask. Nobody talked. A lady on the television said, "I suppose I should weep for him, but I don't feel a thing. He's dead, that's all."

Molly felt one of the little headaches starting in the space behind her eye, like someone stuffed cotton in there and you couldn't itch it.

There would be more rain this afternoon. Already the sun had been snuffed by the grey clouds in off the river. Emma had said she didn't know when they would be back.

Molly tried to think of a way to say it so it didn't sound so bad. She wished they weren't watching her, it was only a girl's game, something you did when you were lonesome, not some big fancy deal with hangmen and the Queen of Cups.

You were loved in the past, but someone brought you bad luck. Now there is change coming into your life. You may come into some wealth, but there is death in your future, rapid change, a trip by water, a sad-eyed lady with dark hair.

ELEVEN

Like lifting a frog, the legs dangling limp, the blunt, smooth skull upright and alert, unseen heart pulsing, then letting it gently down again, folding, liquid, to its element, it was all one gesture. The woman had been unconcerned about it, matter of fact. She had come around to the passenger side of the station wagon with a determined, graceful stride, opening the back door first to pull out the chair, extending then locking the accordion supports of the seat, adjusting the footrests, wheeling it into position just beyond the swing of the passenger door. The boy waited as if in a trance. She gripped him in a bear hug at his waist and then, inconceivably, pulled him up into the air, swinging him over toward the wheelchair. For an instant he hung there, expressionless and calm as a statue, the pressure of her grip bunching the jacket about his chest, the legs dangling gently, nobly, until her momentum shifted and she was able to let him down, arranging his arms along the armrests, lifting each heavy leg in turn until the feet were parallel and composed, each on the flat of its own footrest.

Only then did she allow herself a deep breath, a moment to compose herself and rest, before closing the car door and wheeling him up the incline toward the cream-colored building. Never once did the boy change his expression or give any indication of curiosity about what she was doing just beyond his sight. Even as she wheeled him away, he seemed placid and self-possessed and as graceful and weightless as he had been for that brief moment careening in air.

Flynn sat in the car until they entered the building, the silver spokes of the wheelchair flickering then disappearing into the tinted glass of the entryway. He would have to go this same way, and he wanted, if at all possible, to keep from seeing them within the building. He wanted to know that they were safely on their way before him, for he knew they had more business here than he did, and knew also that some kindnesses deserved to be unwitnessed, remaining in a soundless and empty orbit of their own.

Emma would have told him this was nonsense. She might even have pointed out the obvious: this was no special occurrence, no laden moment arranged by fate for the benefit of Flynn. These people lived their lives this way. Day after day, this mother—surely she was the boy's mother—moved him through space with the same determination, and, most likely, with not just a little boredom and weariness.

"Life takes these shapes, Flynn," she might have said.

But at the last moment he had made her stay behind.

He had driven up to the hospital with her silent beside him, silent even at his indecision. He swung back out of the lot almost immediately, taking the turn toward the bridge and exiting at the ballfields, bringing the car to a stop in the middle of the empty gravel lot.

There was no one on the fields, twelve noon of a brilliant sunlit day and the diamonds were empty.

"Why?" he said.

"It's a hard thing," she said, "I couldn't face it myself."

She had said it too easily, with a woeful little shrug, a yawn, to let him know she understood.

"So . . . are you supposed to be a test for me?" he snapped. "Is that how you think I should see it? Even Emma finds this hard, so I shouldn't feel bad myself . . ."

"I'm sorry," she said. "I know I put it badly."

He knew the remark had hurt her, he knew she meant what she said, but there was something in the prissiness of her apology, the schoolgirl diction, the social worker's care, that made him want to press his advantage.

Just the fact that he had an advantage at all made him want to press it.

"You're goddamn right, you put it badly," he said.

The phrase sounded idiotic to him, leaden and muffled within the car. It was a foolish thing to say, part of a script, husband's talk. He laughed.

"I'm sorry," he said. "I wasn't even talking about that at all. I meant the ballfields. I was wondering why they were empty."

She was crying softly. She cared about him.

"I don't know why I'd want to punish you," he said, "after . . . after . . ."

After what? It was all the same thing now, just talk. It was what he dreaded about the afternoon ahead, it was what it always all came down to, empty talk, a car all alone in an empty lot.

For more than a year now, from the one cold afternoon in April in Exhibition Stadium, when somewhere along in the twenty-third or so pitch in the damp and ugly bullpen, something happened, a hitch or tear or a calcification—something like that—along the margin of the muscle, and he had pitched through it, thrown another ten or twelve before he told them to tell Roy he couldn't go that afternoon; it had been all talk. Talking to the writers in the clubhouse, talking to Roy, talking to the trainer, the doctors, the specialists, the therapist, even the hypnotist; talking lines from imaginary scripts. And even a real script or two, for a restaurant in Buffalo that wanted him to attest to the goodness of their steaks and their whorehouse decor, for a Toronto haberdasher that wanted him to praise their imported fabrics and Old World tailors.

And it took fifteen lousy takes to do the haberdasher spot, each time lifting the arm up to show the richness of the wool, pecking at the seams to display the wondrous alterations, each take the arm screaming in pain. And yet he had smiled through them, smiling even as the shoulder began to stiffen from holding the dead weight of the arm.

Finally, in August, on the way to an eight and six season, and, even so, nearly leading the staff, talking to the sportswriters again, he found himself saying it, then repeating it to the skipper, to the front office.

Retiring.

Done, boys.

Hangin' 'em up.

The boy swinging through air, his body dead weight and yet so unbound it seemed buoyant, weightless.

At the end of September it was on the newswires, and in the *Sporting News*, and in the magazines, and it was done. Even then there was talk left to be done, a life sentence of talk, together with a nagging, mistaken feeling that it was just something that could be shaken out, like a cinder in a shoe, a hardened ball of lint in the bottom of a pocket.

"I was so sure," he said, "So sure that it would just roll out of there, like some hard little thing, and the arm would be back, you know? Free and supple, and smooth as silk . . ."

He had been daydreaming on her again, and he was sorry and afraid he would make her think that he would not be able to handle the day ahead and what had to be done.

The sun had reflected from the white gravel of the lot at the Little League field in a single, blinding sheet. It was cool and silent within the air-conditioned cockpit of the car, dim but for the sheer light through the untinted portion of the windshield. It was as if they had descended there, floated downward without effort or mark, like some flying saucer, like the boy dangling, held in the air in his mother's careful arms.

But Emma had spoken then.

"I know," she said softly, almost bitterly. "Believe me, Jack, that is one thing I really do know. I know exactly how you could feel that, even long after it is possible at all."

And Flynn remembered the bare, frail chest, the smooth sheen of skin pulled tight over her birdlike breastbone, the twin slashes of lavender scars where they had mined something from her, something more than muscle and tissue or the small, stony tumor. Driving away, he had given the engine too much gas pedal, spinning foolishly in the empty lot, leaving a roostertail of smoky dust, a contrail behind them, as they skidded out of the lot, turning, not toward the hospital again, but to the bridge, to Canada.

He could see the small cloud of dust behind him from the bridge, dissipating in the clear sky, sailing off.

She wanted to know why. They were waiting in the modest line of cars at customs, and she asked him why.

"I have to do this alone," he said. "She would be frightened seeing someone she doesn't know."

"She won't know anything, Flynn. She's no one now, she's no more than a breathing body without a mind. Like a frog with its head cut off, you have to understand that."

Emma put it brutally, but he knew it was only because she cared for him, she wanted to make sure he understood.

"I know." he said, "I do know. Really, it is something I have to do this way."

"Then take me home, take me back to Molly . . ."

The customs agent was a young, Irish-looking woman in a green skirt and a crisp white blouse and wide, sensible shoes. She was waving them forward into the booth, but Flynn would not move until he knew that Emma understood. He knew the customs agent could not see them through the tinted glass. She was warm from the sun, and mildly exasperated, and her pale skin was flushed, and she waved at them, waved them forward, then wiped at the perspiration on her forehead.

"Please," he said. "Please wait for me on the other side. Have lunch or something and wait for me. I want to know that I can go away when it is done. I want to know that you are over here, waiting for me. I want to know I can run."

Emma nodded and Flynn pulled into the booth. The woman agent had been prepared to scold them, he knew, you could see the impatience in her eyes. But she had not been able to see them through the windows, and when she saw Emma there, and the man crying, she had asked them the questions and waved them off.

Some intimacies deserved to be unwitnessed. Emma had waited outside the tea room in Johnstown, watching until he drove off back toward the bridge. At the care facility, Flynn had not been able to see whether the mother and the boy were gone before he entered the building; had not been able to see the cool and burnished tiles of the corridor leading to the reception desk. It was unlike other hospitals he had been in, and he had been in many.

For a long time, for too long, life for him had been what you could see. Or could not. Pitch 'em where they ain't, take away the good eye. Year after year there was little more than that. That and the numbers: balls, strikes, wins, losses, strikeouts, shutouts, innings pitched, pitches per inning, complete games, earned runs, numbers on numbers, a whole trail of them behind you like the icy tail of a comet.

And behind the comet, out at the edge of a shrinking universe, was the shadow, the ever increasing awareness that the body eventually betrays you and all you are left with is talk. For a time however, for a number of years, it was possible to stay out in front of the shadow, to stay in the sun. In the sun, you blinked away the shadow, you blinked away the talk. It was like Satchel Paige said, "Don't look back, something may be gaining on you."

Atrophy of the flexor, rotator cuff, the count, the talk: something always was gaining on you. Weariness, batters, or memory, like blips on the horizon of a videogame screen, it always came. Satchel, for one, had stayed ahead of it, like a great heron flying out ahead of the shadow on slow wings.

As a kid, Flynn had seen him, without really knowing what it was he saw. They had gone down to Syracuse to see an International League game, Satchel throwing smoke with an easy kick, a slow unfolding arm. It had seemed so easy, without any of the dazzle he had expected from all his father said on the drive down, without the quality of awe that fed the talk around them in the stands. Just a skinny, sad-eyed man throwing smoke and strolling to the dugout.

But he was young then, Flynn was, and as the years went by he began to understand how hard it was to be easy, how hard it was to stay ahead. Even so, the sad-eyed man kept the same place in his memory. A June afternoon and the sun-baked circle of the mound, the sea of jade grass, pitcher in grey and batter in white. It was that simple when all was done and said. You pitched to stay ahead, you stayed ahead as long as you pitched. It was a simple game, and it ended.

Pitching was often no more than a matter of what a batter could or could not see. The flickering white, or—depending how you pitched it—the blurry red, dot of the slider gives a fraction of a second, a number, to pick the rotation up before it's gone. In that instant a lapsed reflex is a betrayal, and the batter lunges at where the ball was, swinging through an empty orbit with a sad grace. It was something to see.

With the good hitters, however, with the best of them, the most you could ever see was little more than a vestige of animal decision, a momentary twitch in the upper body and a switch of the hips signaling either a failure of will, or, more likely, a pure and savage discipline. They were nothing but will, waiting on you, looking for something else and willing to wait you out until you gave them their pitch. The best gave you nothing but eyes, no check swing, no measuring stride, not even a blink at the call of the pitch.

You could see them wait you out, every pitch was a number, a flick of the catcher's fingers then the number of the count. Your numbers against theirs. With the best, you'd see them run through it as they stepped from the box and positioned themselves before stepping back in; with the best, if you'd faced them a hundred times before, they would be remembering a hundred pitches corresponding to the one you were about to throw now. Meanwhile you'd be running through the numbers on your own.

Last time threw him on the fists, last month threw him three-quarter speed, yesterday he hit so-and-so's slider, last year he hit everything with two strikes. You'd feel your own twitching start up, fight to keep it from showing.

The idea was to keep from letting the body betray you, keep breathing, keep loose, find the groove; keep from opening up throwing the curve; keep square, drive through; keep changing the pace, keep him thinking, keep an edge; keep it up and in then down and away, keep it down again and keep him honest; keep letting them know what belongs to you.

Gibson would say that, you could hear him curse them from the mound in that strangely high, shrieky voice.

"That belongs to me, dammit! That's my part of the plate!"

They might have thought he was nuts, but he made them believe.

Seaver claimed he could move it to all four corners of the strike zone, each pitch starting in the same space at the middle of the plate. Most times Flynn settled for two rather than four places, with maybe an occasional riser, lifting up and away. Four speeds in the good years, three still at the end. A garbage curve and a sweet one, three moves to first, two ways of pitching from the stretch, and one sweet groove for everything else, so much a part of him he could do it now if the arm would move through.

Numbers.

It was Wolfman told him what batters see. Some say you ain't a good pitcher unless you had a great batter tell you what he can see in you.

"The curveball, man, he's smilin' the moment he leave your hand, jus' layin' over there on hes side and smilin'. But the fastball is angry lookin' up and down . . . she jus' spin straight-op, man, you know? And she always buzzin' there like some wasp. Real nasty lookin' for all you see of her . . ."

"The slider?"

"Ho, man! The slider! Ha . . ."

Wolfman treated the slider as a great joke, a fluke of nature, an occasion for showing teeth and laughing, for shuffling in the dirt in a gleeful little dance.

"Yes, man, the slider . . ." He exhaled a long breath of admiration for its voodoo self. "Now the slider sometimes she give you this fat white face, you know? Sometimes you can slap him up!"

Whap! He clapped his hands then grinned.

"But sometimes that same white one, she jus' zip off there when you think she hangin' . . ." He laughed and scuffed the dirt again in a little hop. "But the red one, man, she always, al-waays, zippin'! You see that red dot, man, with two strikes and you jus' try to fight him off . . . yeah, man, you jus' try to fight him off . . ."

They were young then, both of them, and Wolfman still talked a kind of island talk, but they were old men—at least within the game as it was played now that Sachel's gone—when they ended it at two strikes. It ended between them in the sun-baked circle and by then Wolfman talked like an angry lord, and Flynn was already nearing the end of his reign as one of the crown princes.

They had come to find themselves in the wrong league and on opposite sides, with the numbers against them and under a bad sign. It was how history happened, how friendships ended.

Flynn could still see it like it just happened, still see the pitch and see him take it, see him running for the mound with the bat in his hand, still hear the Wolfman lecture him as they wrestled.

"You won't have me like this, Flynn! Goddammit, you won't have me owing you! Do you understand me, you honkie son of a bitch! I won't be owing you!"

He had still shouted it as they dragged him off, arms pinned back behind him as if manacled, the bat still in his grip.

"You won't have me owing you, Flynn! You won't have me owing you!"

People misunderstood. Some thought he said "oh and two," and some "owning you." It was a great mystery for everyone but Flynn and the Wolfman, but they both knew what they had seen; they knew both the numbers and the talk, but they had been friends for a long time and, even when it ended, they neither of them would tell all the world. Or so Flynn thought; Wolfman had never really said.

But Flynn had seen the anger in the eyes, the burning, as they hauled Wolfman off. Flynn had seen it through the blur of his own eyes, the bleary red dot of the blood. He had felt the syrupy warmth flowing from his forehead after the initial blow, was aware of the blood as they wrestled together, remembered some spattering in the tangle of bodies. The blood seemed another taunt, like the words about owing. Only later had there been the pain, the searing bone-pain of the fracture, the blue vision of the, for a time, constant head-aches. Only later had he seen the now-famous photograph.

In it Wolfman's eyes were white circles of rage, the pupils lost to the contrast of the film, the sun, his dark black skin. The shutter had clicked at the instant of what showed on the videotape as the second of two blows to the skull, before Ashby pulled him off, before the last glancing blow to the arm with which Flynn fended Wolfman off. The photo seemed truer than the tape because the events on the tape took place in greater warmth, and with more color and swiftness than Flynn's memory held them. On the tape it was a petty event, a sort of circus, while the film disclosed the elemental slowness, the dignity, and the sadness of it all.

The photo was like a wall painting, a tableau. It slowed the moment to the time in which it really had seemed to occur, and it gave to the scene the importance which such brutal intimacy required. There were the two men, black and white, one in white and one in grey. The great black club was lifted over the bloody skull, Flynn looked placid and helpless. But he was not moving away, even in the photo you could see he was coming toward the Wolfman, he was trying to talk.

The newspapers and the television all wanted it to be Marichal and Roseboro all over again. There was always what you saw, base-ball was full of these instances of repetition, the numbers, the words that recalled other words. But this was complicated by the color of the men, and by the fact that it had happened in Canada. There was a young attorney, a solicitor general or something, and he pressed charges. They were making a point, he said, it was the same point they were making in prosecuting hockey incidents, he said.

"A free society cannot tolerate barbaric practices in the name of sport," he said. He had misunderstood. They all did, but it was the end of something. Wolfman was put on waivers, no one claimed him. The charges were dropped.

People misunderstood. Oh-and-two was commonly thought a pitcher's pitch; it wasn't, not always, not even usually with the good ones. Just like three and two is supposed to be a batter's pitch. Not always, not even usually, not when you have two or four pitches, two or four slices of space, which belong to you.

There is always only what you see, and what the talk says. People misunderstand how it is when you know the numbers, when you live them through for ten, twelve, sixteen years. When you know the man there, what he's likely looking for, what he's been chasing, what he's been hitting. There's a world in numbers. Each set of numbers has a different face. One-and-oh, for instance, can be behind or ahead, up or down, depending on what you got going, what you let him see, what you're setting up. Oh-and-one, on the other hand, can be hell when you know what he almost got, when you know how much it cost you, when you know how little you have left, when you see him waiting for another and know you've eventually got to throw it because it's all you have.

One and one is almost always yours. Two and one almost always his. One and two widens the window of the world, gives you three more pitches at least, sometimes more. If you think you can stand to give him a chance to fight off the cut fastball on the fists, or if you have the rising heat sailing away and you know he can chase and touch it but he'll never catch up to it, never straighten it out, for a time the world is yours.

One and two you can throw him rainbows, hang a half-hearted curveball that gets the elbows twisted. You can smile at his contortions, whisper and tell yourself that the world is a wide and wise place. You can take so much time that you begin to get the infield, and sometimes even your catcher, sure your gonna lose him if you toy with him, then come in and hear them laughing when it's over, hear them say you had them going for a while.

As long as you get out of it, that is. As long as it all don't go wrong, and the world shift faces on you, the looping fly sail out, the ground ball skip off your glove and catch the shortstop going the wrong way.

Even the behind counts leave you room sometimes, even three-and-oh can give you an edge.

"I'm afraid not," the young doctor said.

He blinked against the light. They were standing in the room where the burnished tile corridors led. Flynn had not seen the woman and the boy in the wheelchair. He had not seen anyone or anything he knew until they came to this room and saw Esther.

But it was not Esther he saw there, it was his father all over again. The tubes into each nostril, the IV slung from the shiny stand, the Foley bag on the bedrails below. Even the bank of green screens, the monitor with the craggy heights and valleys of the heartbeat, the numbers of her respiration, the blip-blip-blip of another, flatter set of waves along the horizon of another screen.

The doctor pointed at the flat wave as it crawled across the screen. It was called a crawl, Flynn knew, he had worked in television. The doctor blinked against the light. Esther had their father's face now, she was old in her illness and balding through patches of her great, once-swollen skull. She had turned into an old man, and the young doctor was saying it wasn't possible that she could live.

". . . massive paramedial infarction," he said. "Considering the history . . . despite the CSF shunt . . . prognosis of further myocardial infarction or outright cardiac failure . . ."

Flynn watched the lines crawl the screens. Esther, I am here; I too not clear-headed.

"To put it in plain language . . ."

"I understand the complicated language," Flynn said, then— more gently, "Thank you, you've explained it very well. I have a friend who has explained these things to me . . . I've been in many hospitals . . . I . . ."

"I'm not much of a baseball fan, myself," the doctor said, "but I understand you were among the best . . ."

"Thank you," Flynn said. For a time they watched the monitors shift through their cycle. It was like the fish finders, Flynn thought, these machines hunt what moves through the depths. They illuminate and print it here, but you still have to draw them up through the water, you still have to land the fish.

"Couldn't we keep feeding it quarters?"

"How's that?" the doctor asked.

"Give it another play?" Flynn said. "You know, Space Invaders . . . ?"

The doctor wasn't sure if he should laugh. Neither was Flynn.

The young doctor fiddled with a dial on the monitor, adjusting the contrast, the waves suddenly more intense. These boys learned serious, Flynn knew. He knew what was coming.

"You may not be able to stop the quarters from coming, Mr.

Flynn," the doctor said. "I am of the impression that we are discussing this aspect of the custodial relationship provided by this state."

This one was a healthy boy, a control pitcher, Flynn thought. They are all joggers these days, bean sprout and avocado eaters, low cal and high fiber, never tainted by tobacco. The doctor was signaling him with this talk; they would have to play it his way, some fancy dancing with the ethics involved.

"The state has a sacred obligation to maintain life," the doctor continued, bearing down now, "as I do . . . ," he said, catching Flynn's eye. "Our mutual burden is mitigated by the health care review process, wherein professional committees weigh the patient's rights against the medical realities and the institutional capabilities."

"How many quarters, right?"

"As you will," the doctor said. For a moment he became human again, dropping the careful tone. "Usually it works pretty well, Mr. Flynn. An attending physician has a good deal of latitude, but . . ." He was ready to pitch again, feeling his way. ". . . but," he said, "when a public figure is involved, such as yourself, there is inevitably a more careful scrutiny."

They might decide to keep her alive forever. You want to know what I'll do, Flynn thought. Everyone does. The doctor stared through him; this boy had staying power, Flynn thought, he was a real careful worker.

"With the level of nursing care and life support services we have available—even here—we can maintain life for an indefinite period," he said, "a rather long, indefinite period, but . . ." He paused because she moved. He and Flynn both stared into her lifeless, open eyes.

When she moved like that—her heavy arm flailing lightly, as if pushing up through water, as if, like another woman her age, she were parting the gauze of a kitchen curtain, staring out at a morning where children played and the earth crawled on toward lonely death—you doubted all talk, all the earnest and burdened percentages which the young doctor could quote. She seemed alive. The eyes were alive and unmoving. Perhaps she wants to die, Flynn thought, perhaps she has turned the singleness of her gentle mind to this charade.

"Why?" he asked the doctor.

"Akinetic mutism, I know it's disturbing, coma vigil they call it. I can close them if you like . . . the eyes . . ."

I wouldn't like that, Flynn thought. Life is what you can see. The clear eyes of fish turning cloudy on the cleaning table. But further strokes will come, the doctor said, or cardiac failures, one after another like . . . Like thunder off the river, Flynn thought, as Emma shuddered in her sleep. They were all inside and safe from the storm, a whole mad crew of them. Willard and Bertie, Emma and Molly, and Flynn with his waking dreams, light flashing from the windows with each crack of the storm.

"Sometimes they even display a sleepwalking cycle," the young doctor said. "Though not your sister, not in the shape she's in . . ."

Wide-eyed and breathing, eyes like bottomless springs, not as Emma had described at all, not headless, not no one.

"Let me see if I have this right," Flynn said. "You think the state will keep pumping quarters into the machine because of who I am. If it came to that, or if it fell the other way, I could probably sue for custody and the whole thing would drag on as long as the machines worked . . ."

The doctor had dug into the batter's box and wasn't giving any ground, not even a nod. Flynn continued through the options, it was an old habit with him.

"Meanwhile she could die on her own, but, if I believe you . . ." The doctor looked up. Caught him, Flynn thought. ". . . you say she cannot live."

The doctor nodded. Esther's eyes watched him.

"That's my medical judgment," the doctor said.

"And if I asked you to turn the machines off?"

"That would be my medical judgment also."

"But you'd do it?"

"I can't say that to you, Mr. Flynn. The case is scheduled for review soon. I cannot say that."

But you would, Flynn thought, as the thunder rumbled.

Flynn didn't know what to do, so he tried Wolfman's number again.

TWELVE

Wolfman, he had an enterprise, you dig, a regular satisfaction, an amazing grace. Wasn't no man could touch that, you see, for he was a long time paying dues and he be where he was now because he been where he was before.

Where he was now was in the high silence, in the cool dome, the smooth air, the high pressure. The sweet rocking, low buzzing, endless blue juju eye of duh god-dam worl', man.

Flying alone, aha, yes.

Yes.

It was the best kind of flight. Twenty-three thou' and without turbulence, seamless air. Jus' you and da view . . .

Winston Romulus Hunt could—did perforce—exist on several planes, you dig, pun—truly—intended. Airplanes and metaphysical planes, time frames and mind games, woofin' and rappin' and signifyin', mystifyin', almos' dyin'.

He felt good, he had to admit. Righteous even. Reconciled.

"Mr. Jack Flynn, a former associate and adversary, has requested my assistance, baby, and you know how the Wolfman be of assistance . . ."

He had had to laugh. That woman she knew from nothing about assistance. All she knew was she was sleepy-eyed and mean-minded, and it was five a.m. and the brother he was duded-up and talking of flyin', man.

He knew she just wanted to put that pillow over her head and roll over again and dream of sugar, Sugar, dream of sugar and 'cain and lazy afternoons. But Wolfman had to be flying. The low-pressure system had gone through, pounding up along the Great Lakes and into Canada, rattling the roofs of Montreal and the roofless field of ratty Olympic Stadium, raining out Les Expo, and rolling on out to sea.

Rollin' on out to sea, leavin' smooth air fo' me . . .

It amused him to talk so, to hum them bluesy lines like some baadass bro' in the hood. It was truly another plane, like the ladder of altitudes coming out of O'Hare, lifted from one life to another—height to height—like some ol' croaking bullfrog all legs and throat. And when you reached the top, when they gave you over to Great Lakes control, there you was on top of the air —on top of yo' airs, you dig?—high flyin' and unafraid of dyin'.

And everything below was still yours, you dig. Every level, every plane, there to be had, a whole ladder of attitudes and altitudes.

For enterprise sake one could be the redoubtable Mr. Hunt, former ath-e-lete and now entrepreneur, based in Cleveland but citizen of the world, responsible spokesman, leading citizen, force for change, of assistance to all and sundry, yet still able to talk on the square, my man, still able to lay a rap down.

For amazing grace one could resume the island attitude, calypso cadence and aristocrat eyes, gentle manners but purposeful stride. Yes, mon, he com' a long way home, yes he do . . .

Yes he do.

But what could one be for Flynn?

Flynn, he was mostly a lame sucker, that be fo' sure. Given to booshit, blue-eyed, bogue-ass sentimentality. Verily a prince, but a prince of lames, a place-bet all the way, a certified second-place finisher, born under a bad sign an' deaf to the blues, half-assed, raggedy-assed an' blameless, but goin' back a long way.

And a gamer. Yeah, baby, a gamer an' carryin' a heavy burden an' goin' back a long, long way. Yes ma'am, a long, long way.

And I owe him, Wolfman thought. If the truth be told, I owe him more than one.

He sighted the worn mountains ahead of him, the abraded hills of the Adirondacks far ahead, some sad mounds filled with little round eyes of blue water, the hills themselves blue from this height. To the left was the silver band of the river, the shed skin of an eyeless serpent. Off farther to the left and about three thousand feet up was the C-1-whatever the hell, all army-green like some flying hill and full of weekend soldiers about to jump on Drum. The air was full of traffic here, rickety farmer-built general aviation and military junk, Hueys and low screamers from the Canadian forces, swooping down over the horizon and supposed to be laying down ground fire and rolling fires for the weekend warriors out there playing their games. It made the Wolfman nervous to think of it, him and the farmers circling there, held in their patterns for fifteen minutes while the game went on, seeing the smoke roll up from the ground of the military reservation far off ahead, seeing all them dumb, damn surplus bombers and transports painted green.

Not even sense enough to make 'em grey like the Air Force do so as to disappear in air. Brother could shoot him down a plane or two if he fitted himself up with a nose gun or a few heat-seeking rockets. Alien attack, Jack.

Oughta put up some motherfuckin' balloon on a cable with traffic lights if the motherfuckers gonna close down the damn sky for chri'sake.

Wolfman, he went to rocking his wings, oh so gently, holding there and circling in a wide arc waiting for the light to change, waiting for da life to change. Nigger show them farmers a thing or two, yes he do. Put himself to rockin' and singin'.

Amazing grace, how sweet thou art . . .

She was sweet, Lord knows. Esther, a sweet star, that's what it meant. But she wasn't meant to live, not like most folks live, Bertie knew.

There had been something like this on All My Children, many of the same questions. It was about the time that that sweet girl, the Quinlan, was in a coma in Boston or wherever it was. If you had any kind of mind, and watched closely, you could see when they did that on teevee. It was interesting in a way, to see that there was something real behind a story like that. It made you think.

She would never bloom. Like the Chinese hibiscus in the parlor, its main cane clipped mistakenly to an eyeless stump, a smooth scar, she would leaf but never bloom. It wasn't easy for Jack to see that, a whole canopy of dark green leaves and all the family he had left.

It wasn't easy.

But that didn't excuse him. The old man snored in the wing chair, his snout covered with the paper mask, the chair bedecked with toilet tissue bunting. Little fibers from the paper remained in the velvet each time, the chair had already begun to look like it was in a fog.

And now a negro coming. It didn't excuse Jack, what Esther's state was.

The girl and Emma weren't so bad, women in a house were never so bad. They knew silence and where to stand or sit. Even a woman like Emma with all her notions, she knew what to do with a soggy tea bag, how to make a bed in the morning.

She had slept there. It was a modern thing to do, though it ended innocently enough, with Jack on the sofa where the girl, Molly, had been, and Molly with her mother, where, Bertie assumed, Jack had begun.

It wasn't half as scandalous as she'd thought it would be. You got used to things, television and the changing times made you used to things. She had even had to confess to a certain excitement about it. After all they were two adults, and Jack had lived in a fast-paced world. Even Karen, the first time Bertie saw her, looked like nothing else but an expensive whore, all done up in silver eye shadow and neon tangerine lips and frosted nails, tanned to the roots of her hair.

Lying out in the yard of a morning, the discarded bikini top in her outstretched fingers like a gaudy hankie, and Jack standing guard over her like she was an expensive china cup. He had tried to explain to Bertie that, in Arizona, Karen had gotten used to being able to do that. That people thought nothing of it there.

Jackie would always be a North Country boy.

You could see then that Karen would never give him children. Her body was too hard for that, the wishbone of her pelvis too narrow, and you could never be certain when a woman had those little nipples. Children don't feed on rosebuds, they used to say. Still, Karen had sadness in her eyes and Bertie had come to like her.

She liked Emma too, don't mistake. It was just that she was trouble. You could see it in her. Skittishness and temper, hardness of the will rather than of the body, and all those fears submerged there, like weeds along the shallows of a channel.

Emma gave the fears to the girl. It was the storm that made Molly move in with them, a girl her age going in to sleep with her mother on account of some rolling thunder off the river!

And she wept at the sight of the china doll, whined for her mother to take it away. She feared its eyes, Emma had explained, and Bertie didn't mind, not even after pawing through the whole camphor-smelling attic to find the trunk with the old toys. Bertie didn't mind the child's fears. For young girls were given fears by nature; fears gave a glimpse into the nameless changes, the emptiness, to come.

A child born with empty eyes and swollen head. They had wanted to take it away right away but Nell wouldn't let them. She wouldn't ever bloom, you could see it then, but Nell had a willfulness of her own. She made them bring it to her, each day, fed it at her breast, called it Esther. A china doll.

And who would've thought it could have lived all these years? Born into the emptiness, and never quite, really, to experience the nameless changes.

Even so, that had been the fright of it. Esther's body had gone through all the changes, blood flowing and growing heavy-chested, desires budding in her gleeful eyes, though no flowers to come. And they weren't always careful, the attendants. In the years after Nell had given the girl up to the state, you would sometimes go to see her and her backside would be hanging out of the gown, or she'd sit with her legs spread wide. Back then the old hospital was a dark and closed place, there used to be rumors now and again of misuse of the women patients. And you could never tell, Esther could tell you nothing sensible. They would walk her into the dayroom for visits and leave her there, bright-eyed and large-browed, a swollen brainless creature, no different from a slug, despite the simple things they taught her to do. It could break your heart.

There was something monstrous about her sweetness, no less monstrous than the sight of Joey at the end, shrunken like a beanpod, his bones screaming at the weight of the breezes in the room. Or Red, beautiful pale-skinned Red ashen and blue at the lips, unable to swallow air.

Nell herself had died beautiful. The pneumonia made her birdlike and pale porcelain. No different really than poor Esther looked in her waking sleep, even Esther had a beauty to her, Nell's beauty. Every day the nurses came in and washed her all over, combed the dark, beautiful strands of her China-black hair. It was a crew of negro nurses from Ogdensburg in their white Dacron dresses, a skinny girl and a plump one like The Jeffersons. The plump one was always talking to her, talking soft to Esther and combing her black hair. There had been changes. The retarded were cared for now.

Now they married. There was a teevee show where these two retarded married and lived in an apartment. That nice young Cassidy boy from The Brady Bunch had played the part, and very convincingly too. It was brave of him to do that, being a teen idol as he was, and instructive for the kids who watched him, Bert supposed.

She'd have to ask Molly about David Cassidy.

She missed her really. Already she missed her. It was nice to have a young girl moving around the house, even if she argued and cussed with old Walker, even with all those fears in her sad, little eyes.

Fears could fade. Even so, it wasn't right for a mother to give them to her daughter, for they came naturally enough, and, though they faded, they remained always in some dim portion of the mind. Like a china doll in a steamer trunk.

Like buttons. Bertie had feared buttons as a girl. She still felt faint when someone ran their fingers through a tin of buttons hunting among them. On and off for years now she had begun to suspect that there was some connection to sex in that. She looked for mention of it in the quizzes in magazines and the Sunday supplement. You didn't have to be one of these psychologists to think there was something to that.

Maybe a girl can see what she hasn't a name for. Maybe she gives it the name of something else.

Bertie feared the arrival of the black man. It wasn't right. She would, for instance, never give Mr. Willard the satisfaction of knowing her fear. A lot that's ugly went under the name of prejudice. But this man was no more than a common thug. Despite what he had become, he had still nearly bludgeoned Jackie to death on a baseball field.

Wolfman. They all had names. There was a man called Wolfman on teevee who talked down in his throat and laughed all the time, he was popular with the teenagers. Bertie could not help but like that one, there was something soft and childish about him. But Jack's Wolfman she had only seen in the team photographs and in the films of the assault.

It was a brutal attack, now and again they showed the tape of it on some sort of sports show on teevee. He had struck Jack again and again, and if you looked closely you could see that all the while Jackie was trying to help him, all the while Jackie whispered to the black man, trying to get him to stop.

It was a dream you had. Black men and they will not stop. She was ashamed to think it, but it was a sort of dream.

"I know what he's up to," she said aloud.

Damn this weather, she thought, it is what has left me irritable. Electricity lingers in the air after storms like these. Though the air be clear as a bell jar, you can see the clouds of electricity which linger and slant the light.

She knew what Jackie was up to. Flynns and their ideas! The whole family died of ideas. The brown screamer and Jack's anger drove Jim to the river. Nell wasted away with some idea that it would save them all. Joey's innards were consumed by ideas, by his own cells hating themselves—that was a fact, there was a report on the news said cancer was caused by the nerves—it was like the old story, how the eagles came down and gnawed at the liver of the chained man.

Esther's death was the inevitable result of the idea that she could have a life that would flower. She would die. Whether Jackie told them to take her off the machines or not, Esther would die. The idea of life would kill her. Jackie could not stop that. Let him fill the house with strangers and madmen, witchdoctors, children, and blessed ladies, he could not save her.

It was clear what he wanted to do, it was nothing more than to save himself from whatever idea pursued him. It wasn't even his to choose, the young doctor had told him as much. Esther was a ward of the state and the responsibility was with the doctors and the nurses. They did what they did only because Jackie had been who he was. Even that was over.

She was very tired she knew. She had been awake half the night. Jets screamed over the house, flying loud and low, coming from Canada. It wasn't good to think at times like these, when life seemed monstrous.

Once an eel washed on shore down near Clayton with a penis as big as a man's.

They embalmed it and put it on exhibit until the preachers stopped them.

The paper snout flapped whenever old Willard snored. Drool covered his stubbled chin.

The girl feared china dolls and buttons. Children have come near to drowning when the water became electrified, only the eyes of their grandmothers held them from death. Esther's eyes were ever open.

Alberta Flynn's eyes closed slowly into uneasy sleep, pursued by ideas no more monstrous than most, untouched by the fantastic colors of the silent screen before her, the remote control in her hand, thinking she was no more than daydreaming, remembering a performance of The Emperor Jones in a white-sided pine building somewhere up along the river, an island place where city women put on summer theatricals and couples strolled out afterward into the fine summer air, yet confusing it all maddeningly with some other production in which the black men played harps and laughed and reclined on cotton clouds with great flappy wings, aware the dream would not let her go back to recapture the title, forcing herself to think on it, staying off sleep, thinking of Green Mansions and of the coming darkness, of being lost and being found, of the blind now seeing.

THIRTEEN

In time Emma faded from view, a woman waving, a dot, then gone and the river turned. The child tired of waving long before her mother, and settled against the plastic seatback, feigning calm, trailing a scooped hand in the water as children in boats invariably did, while the other hand gripped the gunnel, knuckles white.

She smiled at him, he smiled at her. They had nothing to say as yet.

Flynn attended to the dull slap of the chop against the aluminum hull. It was calm and clear and a bad day to fish with the river at a high stage after the rain. He was heading to Atlantis, and thence along Oak Island and up to Goose Bay, to Marsh Island and the inlet of Cranberry Creek, thinking to fish there and then work around Point Marguerite.

"No day's a bad day if you know where the fish are."

It was what his father said, he would not say it.

The silence was a gift. Molly wore tight corduroy Levi's and a denim shirt, stylish rose-framed and rose-tinted sunglasses; she seemed a copy of her mother, a miniature, as she watched her hand trail through the water.

He opened the throttle up a notch and she viewed him with abstract eyes. She wants to see if I am trying to frighten her.

He waved a hand toward the gingerbread houses, and she settled back again. A stretch of river to cover, something had made him come down to the landing at Chippewa Bay, rent there rather than the more familiar places upriver. Thinking no one here would remember Joe Flynn, thinking once I saw children here, a pedalboat along the near channel, a coil of yellow rope.

The rental was an unwieldy thing, squared off like a jonboat but with a severe little crimp for the keel running below them like a gutter, curving up into a blunt hatchet, high prow. Foolproof, touristproof, a good boat for a scared girl on a clear day.

Maybe run up to Fisher's Landing and show her the skiff.

No.

Four jets, tan and green Canadian Forces camouflage, screamed over low, the noise trailing behind them like Molly's hand through the water, arriving in a roar, popping behind them. They were heading south-south-east; Wolfman, east.

She pressed her hands against her ears, screamed into the roar. Shouted it again as they trailed off into silence.

"ASSHOLES!"

Flynn viewed her wryly, one eyebrow cocked high, nodded. It was not a shock really, not after years of hearing them in the stands, even the teenyboppers shrill. "Hey faggot! You're washed up, faggot!"

"Fucking assholes," she amended it, again testing.

He viewed her likewise.

"It's so goddamn bogue," she sighed. "Don't you just detest the fact that all our lives will end that way?"

"What way?" asked Flynn.

"Nukes . . . the bomb . . . whatever." She yawned, as if weary of her own sophistication. There was a hint of pink lipstick on her mouth, she had snuck it back on sometime during the loading and embarkation. It surprised him, not that she had successfully spited her mother, but that she had been so deft with it that he had not noticed.

For one reason or another things had not gone well between Emma and daughter this day. They were either weary from the sleepless night of the storm, or wary of each other on their first time out together with him. Neither really wanted to fish, but when Emma so obviously did not, Molly accepted the invitation to press an advantage.

They had arrived at Chippewa Bay glumly. Flynn aware that each of the two of them saw him as patronizing Molly with this outing. Emma and daughter each aware of his obvious excitement about the project. Emma noticed the lipstick as soon as they crawled out in the sun of the lot by the boat rental.

"No," she said.

Flynn hadn't an eye for the subtleties of this sort of standoff, he hadn't an idea what Emma was saying.

"You want to go somewhere else?" he asked.

The two ignored him.

"Oh crap, mom," Molly complained.

"No."

It was small-minded and sulking, Flynn thought, whatever the dispute. Molly spit into a tissue and rubbed off the lipstick with exaggerated gestures.

"Maybe if you did something with the circles under your eyes, you could keep a boyfriend . . ."

Emma grabbed the girl's wrist overly hard.

"Listen," she hissed, "I have nothing to prove to Jack, and I won't have you exploit his kindness."

Flynn had said he would go in and see about the boat. When he returned they were overly courteous and simmering with tensions.

Emma did have tired rings under her eyes, like the hazy halo of ice around the moon that portends rain. She didn't tell him until they had the boat loaded and Molly had clambered aboard. Flynn was bent steadying the boat against the dock, straining against the girl's shifting weight with his nearly useless right arm, and waiting for Emma to get in.

"I'm staying here."

"Shit," he muttered and Molly smiled. He straightened up and the boat drifted out on the rubber-covered painter chain. Molly shrieked. She was afraid of floating away.

"Damn," he said and pulled the painter in. His back hurt terribly. "You could have told me," he said, "before . . ."

"Go ahead, darling," she said. "I have reading to catch up on. I'll sit and watch the water."

Bitch, he thought, that "darling" wasn't fair. It was a first usage, and used against Molly. So he got into the boat. The hell with her, the hell with both of them.

He unlatched the painter from the pipe of the dock and pushed the boat outward. They floated in a slow half-circle out six feet from the dock, Flynn not yet putting his hand to the starting cord.

He missed her, six feet away and floating in a circle, and he missed her.

"Emma?"

"Yes, Flynn?"

"I miss you."

They laughed so hard he thought they would each fall into the water, one from the dock, the other over the side. He grinned foolishly and started the motor, if only to drown out their hysterical laughter. Emma shouted something into the noise. He nodded to her, as if he had heard.

"She said she loves you."

Flynn nodded to the girl.

They nosed out of the inner channel and into the river. Molly was waving mechanically, mockingly.

"Actually she said she would clean the fish if you cook them," she said.

"Do I need this grief?" he teased her.

"Do you?" she had said more seriously.

They skirted Oak Island at something more than trolling speed, bouncing in the slight, constant chop from all the boats out on this crystal day. The 35-horse Evinrude on the rental had a pleasant, pedestrian growl to it; a smell of gas and an iridescent trail of oil in the churn of the wake betrayed the overly rich mix. It was a nice boat, really, you could imagine children in it, warily studying their father as he checked himself against his memory of operating these things on vacations past, see them sitting there bundled in their orange rental life jackets like waifs in a storm. The rods would be jammed under the thwarts, bobbers flailing madly as he made the first unsuccessful pulls on the starter cord before remembering to move the throttle grip to the start position. One last pull of the cord and this motor would hum, sending off a spew of waste oil, then settling in as he engaged the gear and they abruptly jolted off, the children holding on for dear life.

The river was full of such families today, each of them collecting memories and photographs. "We rented a boat and went fishing one or two days." The other days we spent in the accordion folds of the camper, or bobbing between the floats at the roped-off beach, or driving into Clayton or Alex Bay for ice cream and souvenir daggers with huge plastic rubies at the hilt.

"You really think it will end that way?" he asked her.

"What?"

She had tired of swirling her hand in the water. He upped the throttle two more notches.

"The world."

She laughed brightly, her mother's laugh.

"I thought you meant you and Emma," she said. "I thought you were asking me how I thought that would end."

He nodded. A fool in an inboard with a loud chrome engine cut a broad swath across their bow, sending up a half-hearted rooster-tail, setting them rocking in his wake as he sped back upriver. Asshole, Flynn thought.

"Don't you?" she asked.

He hadn't thought of it in a long time. Some things you learned not to think of. He said this.

She looked at him blankly. "Everyone I know figures there will be one," she said. "Sometimes I even dream how it will be."

"How?" he asked.

"First a blinding light, like thunder, but lasting a real long time, then everybody screaming because of the blood and all that yuk. And the houses melting, you know, and then . . ."

She shrugged her shoulders. It was a precise and gentle gesture, the world slipping off her in a tired heap. Flynn thought of the memorial at Hiroshima. When he was playing the exhibition tour in Japan, they had taken them there on a huge air-conditioned Mercedes bus with plush grey seats and earphone jacks. Inside the memorial there were the photographs: a blinded woman wailing in the midst of the rubble, one hand tearing at her hair, the other outstretched in a gesture of inconsolable grief, as if she were begging for something; and the one he remembered most, the dark silhouette of another woman, folded between a wall and the street, the silhouette itself actually a part of the two surfaces, printed there by the heat of the blast. She had been blown into thin air, her shadow remaining as an endless witness.

Esther also witnessed now.

"Are you afraid of dying, Flynn?"

You could read the depth of the water in the differing slaps and pings and low tom-tom bongs of the water against the hull. You could map the surface of the bottom with a jig at the end of a long line. You could see where fish were likely to be by reading the weed beds and the holes.

"Yes," he said, "I suppose I am. Everybody is, in a way."

"But why?" she asked, "You did a lot already. You were famous once."

It was charming to see how she wished now to protect him from what she had said. She literally snatched at the air as if to take the remark back, then covered over her mouth in embarrassment, giggling helplessly while her dark eyes studied him for hurt.

"Like Ulysses at the ships," he said, then, "It's alright, really, I know what you meant, I do. Anyway it's true. It was once."

Once.

(Flynn seems jittery, and mumbles the response.)
Did you say once?
Yes.
When?
When everything happened, in 1970, I really considered hanging 'em up then. It looked like a long, long tunnel then, with little light at the end. (His voice catches, for an amazing moment it seems as if he will cry.) My brother . . . (He clears his throat, starts again.) My brother had his accident that year. When they found him the lights were still working, you know. I mean, the car was upside-down in the river and the lights were still shining. Somebody said that the firemen, when they were trying to get him out of the seat, they could see all these little crappies swimming in and out of the lights . . .
I'm sorry. Maybe we should shift to . . .
I remember times with my father, out at night, he'd hold a lantern over the side of the boat, down near the surface of the water, and you could see them there, sliding in and out of the glow. Sometimes there'd be a big one, you know, a northern or muskie or some damn thing, like a big dark bullet, a shadow . . . I remember another time, just a few years ago, I was up at a camp in Northern Michigan, you know, it was this grand old place some clients of mine had, a corporation. They kept it for their executives, only no one went there. This grand lodge built of pine logs—even the door latches were pine dowels, the size of a kid's arm, you know—it was like the old camps up in the Adirondacks, what do they call them? I think they call them that, Adirondack Rustic or something. The whole place was hand-built, in other words, and I show up there with this woman, and it's like we're the only people to ever use it for twenty years or so. I mean the folks who were the caretakers, this couple from Ishpeming—I'll never forget the name of that town—they are

so happy to see us they can hardly stay away, you know. (*Laughs*) And, well, I didn't exactly go there for company, you know. I mean, I took the invitation thinking this lady and I could be alone, if you know what I'm saying.

Yes. Go on.

Anyway, there's this incredible lodge, and a boathouse, and a great dining hall, and little cottages out on the islands in this lake. And the lodge and cottage have all the beds made up, you know, in crisp linen sheets. And there's birch canoes, for chri'sake, and golf clubs! Wooden nibbies or nubbies or whatever the hell they call them! Wooden-shaft golf clubs! And fly rods and wicker creels, and god knows what else, a whole paradise there, fully furnished, and no one goes there except these two people from Ishpeming, who keep the beds made and polish the golf clubs and all . . . And so we're out there on this little island, skinny-dipping, you know—this is after we've convinced the two caretakers they don't need to baby-sit us, they don't need to cook, although they insist on bringing picnic baskets out each day—and this lake is so isolated, so ignored, that the fish don't pay you any mind. I mean there's five, six, and seven-pound trout just swimming around your legs, you know, pecking at your pecker. (Laughs) I thought of my Dad and the lanterns then too, swimming in this emerald water, watching golden bubbles shoot from the nude body of this woman, knifing through the water from the dock, and swimming toward me in slow strokes, you know, all honey flesh and tan and leaving a golden trail that the trout swim after . . .

(All the time Flynn has been telling this story, his eyes have the well-known intelligence, the searching quality, about them. There is the feeling that he is toying with his listener as in other times he toyed with batters, setting them up for the pitch he wants to make. It is marvelous theater, in its way, the work of an intelligent, connective man; and yet it follows so quickly upon his almost breaking that you can't help wonder if the theater isn't for his own benefit.)

I thought of my Dad and all he wanted for me, for each of us . . . It was one of those times, you know, when the world seems a simple and golden place—like certain games I remember, in real baseball weather, when you're out there on the mound under a high sky, feeling the sun warm you, and hearing the noise. (Without warning, his tone turns again; this is theater.) Not five minutes after, we're standing on this dock, toweling off, you know, when this jet comes SCREAMING over the trees, not more than ten, fifteen feet up from the treetops, screaming over us and then gone in an instant, flash!, the noise trailing behind it like a bloody scarf, and the whole sky exploding with the boom. (Pauses) Without knowing it, I hit the deck, I mean I threw myself down on the actual deck. It was the goddamnedest thing! Here we were in the middle of nowhere, in an impossible magic place, and this machine comes over! It rips right through us, and there was no way of knowing that it wouldn't take off your head, you know, that it wouldn't crash right there. I thought maybe that was it, you know. I thought the war had started and the bomb was coming and we were going to find out this way, away from radios and teevee, away from everything in creation . . .

What did she do, your friend?

(Flynn ignores the question, he has come to a place he set out for some time before.) My brother, see, he had these jets in his ears all the time. They were always flying low for him, always right behind him. Screaming after him . . . It took me that long, you see, it was three, four years after he had died, and I finally understood that it wasn't just me that drove him into the water. I told him he had death on his brain, and he ended up trapped upside-down with the lights still on and the radio playing and the crappies swimming in and out of the glare, and it wasn't just me that sent him there . . .

(Again his voice cracks, but this time there is no question of him breaking. The vehemence in his eyes, the pure, cold fixation of them, makes it clear that he has seen some horror and he will not break. It seems certain that the interview, if not over, is in his hands. He knows this also, and obligingly, typically, he changes mood again, laughs, although even this laughter is laden and chilling.)

It was funny in a way, but also very scary, what she did . . . She pissed on herself . . . While I was hitting the deck, she was having her bladder let go, you know, it was an hysterical reaction. She pissed on herself and she swallowed her tongue. I had to literally save her life, you know, reach down to her tonsils and pull it up and out so she could breathe . . . . Needless to say, the goddamn jet spoiled the weekend, but the Ishpemingers said it happened all the time, you know . . . These planes came down across the wilderness screaming.

1970 I was six and seven, twenty-seven years old, finished only one game all year and that a loss. My brother died that year, Nixon was in the White House surrounded by busses and bombing Cambodia while a half a million of us walked the streets . . . I mean just add it up, I bottomed out, you know. It's funny in a way. It wasn't Jimmy drowning that got me—like I told you, that took a couple years to really hit me—and it wasn't even when Wolfman got shot . . . What it was was a combination of things. McClain's troubles, Bouton's book, and Gibson winning the Cy Young. Isn't that bullshit, though? Your real life doesn't touch you, but a game does?

Explain. How did that combination . . . ?

(Laughs) Nothing made sense, you see. It was all meaningless. Bouton made that clear in a way you couldn't deny inside, no matter what the clubhouse philosophers and the commissioner had to say. McClain proved that, you know, someone that good getting done in by an absurd set of circumstances. It was a Watergate in a way. (Laughs loudly) But with real water, a bucket of it, and a real smoking pistol . . . And meanwhile there's Gibson, thirty-four years old, and he goes 23 and 7 . . . And there was Bunning back with us . . . (Flynn fixes his eyes again in the testing stare.) I really started to think about death then, you know. I mean, I had seen Bunning three years before, at 35, tear up the world, and a year after that seen him fade and get traded away, and then seen him come back again that year and damn near lead us with ten wins; and so I knew the pain, you know, I knew the possibilities, but I was damned if I could tell if it was worth it. Not unless you were Gibson, you know, one of the gods—not unless you could just keep on daring them, and mowing them down. It was either that or what Jim did—Bunning, I mean—making the rounds, pushing yourself up that hill again and again and always aching afterward. And I didn't know if it was worth it, you see, to find yourself always on the edge of your life ending—seeing it end!—at thirty-five or so. Or earlier . . . like in the case of Koufax, at 30, pitching down the stretch with no rest, the elbow going, a World Series game lost to errors, and then gone, retired, an old man at thirty, arthritis. I couldn't see it . . . I had three years to thirty and the game didn't make any more sense than the world did, you know? A radio playing underwater made more sense . . . I thought a lot about death. Life seemed all shallows, full of crappies in the dying light . . .

And does it seem any different now? Now that you are giving it up? Are you an old man at 35?

Once.

Flynn dug through the tackle box and found an old wooden bobber, shellac peeling, the green paint of the stripes chipped away in places. It looked like an antique toy.

"My father made this."

Molly hummed a kind of assent.

"My father makes wooden things too. But I bet she already told you weird things about him, didn't she?"

"Didn't have to, he did some work for me."

Molly ignored the ambiguity of his remark and settled in on the impression he had intended.

"Well, fuck-a-duck!" she said. "My whole damn family knows you and I'm the last one to know . . . Figures."

"I wish you wouldn't talk like that," he said. "I'm afraid I'm old enough to be embarrassed by it, even if I know everybody talks like that. It's just that . . ."

"I'm a girl," she said. "That's it, isn't it? You want me to wear a nylon dress and anklets?"

"Horseshit," he said.

He'd show her the skiff, he thought. The bobber was his father's, the tackle box was Jim's. Bertie had known that when she told him where to find it; the rods and the tackle box were Jim's, his initials were scratched into the inside of the metal cover, a schoolboy's cursive "J. J. F." Jim detested the river all his life, and yet there was a sheath knife at the bottom of the box, an oriental knife with a straight chrome blade and bamboo hilt, the leather of the sheath elaborately engraved with dragons and the single word "Vietnam."

"You have a mind full of death, and you're killing her, you bastard. You're the reason she's sick, you junkie motherfucker!"

It wasn't true. He must have put the knife in the box after he came back from Nam, and so it wasn't true. You couldn't keep death in your mind and go out fishing on the river. You couldn't . . .

And for a moment Flynn felt him there, under everything, like a lost self, a naked and golden presence swimming under them on this gentle afternoon, swimming through the dying light and the submerged music.

They were all there, a family given to water, each there on a different plane. Above them his mother, a creature of air; and below them Jim—a grunt, whose element was mud—freed now. His father was the membrane between them, a man of surfaces, the guide.

It was a foolish thought, he knew, something too simple.

The girl squealed delightedly as he pulled the crappie from the water at the end of her line. She wouldn't let him throw it back, she wanted to show her mother.

The crappie's eyes had a milky clarity. Esther's eyes. This was the fourth plane, neither depth nor surface nor sky. The plane he shared with her. It thrashed for a moment on the bottom of the boat, sliding down into the scum of the keel gutter, until he snared it, slipped the stringer through it's gill and let it slide back into the water, tethered but momentarily free to range its small circle.

FOURTEEN

For the old woman was to sleep, Restless he went to see who was at the door, and there's this big buck, a mulatto-looking nigger in a dark green, fancy silk suit with a satchel at his feet. Restless tol' him they don't need nothing through the door, and turned tail on him there and went back into the parlor where she's napping on the La-Z-Boy, her plump and pretty legs up in the air, hands tucked up under her big pillowy boobs holding the switcher thing for the teevee. Then the bell rings again but he ignores it and sets down to watch the soundless screen, which is just as well since the Game of the Week is on and in late innings and he don't need no wop and polack to tell him what's goin' on in no baseball game.

His eyes stray to her again and you can see she is dreaming on account of the eyeballs working away behind the window shades of the lids, and her breath catches some, then revs up real good and there's a little bubble of spittle starting to form at her lips, the bubble honey golden from the way the light strikes it.

The bell rings again, except this time it's the back door, and she stirs a little in her sleep, the bubble collapsing as she works her lips. She's near to deaf, which you can tell from how she cranks up the sound on the teevee when she's got it up.

Another ring and Restless knows he's got to do something about the goddamn uppity jig or else the old woman will be awake and probably invite him in to have tea or some damn thing, maybe give him a chance to convert them all to Gee-ho-vah's Witnesses or sell them Fuller Brushes or tie them up in the telephone cords while he loots the house.

So he goes to the back door but the jig ain't there but no sooner does he set himself down again than the front bell rings.

He wishes he had a pistol, put a fright into the big buck.

"Yessir," he says, careful to swallow the urge to call him boy, because they get real riled about that anymore. "What can we do for you, champ?"

"Mr. Flynn?" asks the buck in a how-do-ye-do voice, and Willard knows for certain this one's a Gee-ho-vah or some damn missionary Baptist on account of his eddicated tone and gentleman ways.

And so he answers, "Yes, what's it to you?" to take some of the heat off the old woman.

"May I come in, sir?" asks the buck, pointing to the screen door as if Willard ain't knowed it was latched.

"No," says Restless.

"Is Alberta—Mrs. Flynn—at home? I believe Jack told her to expect me . . ."

Kee-rye-st! Wouldn't you just know it was Flynn sent him here. Probably going to turn the place into some damn commune.

Willard fingers the latch, making up his mind. The buck coulda just knowed it was Flynn's aunt's place.

"Winston Hunt," says Mr. Greenjeans out on the porch. "Wolfman Hunt?"

Oh horseshit! thinks Willard, and he pops the latch and shuffles back to the parlor, waving the buck in behind him. Might as well face it, Flynn's gonna fill up the house with every damn fool crackpot and pisspot kid he ever run into until it'll be no damn different than livin' at the Care Facility excepting there won't be a chance to step out and see a ball game or have a room properly disinfected.

Hunt come down the hallway on quiet feet, nosing into the room right the moment Willard set down. Restless he let him have a shot right away, straight between the eyes.

"What you couldn't handle no fastball up your kitchen, boy? Had to bust him with a bat? In my day a ballplayer stood in there, and if he had to fight for himself, he used his dukes!"

I'll be damned if he didn't laugh aloud, real nice and easy, and stretch out his big pink palm and manicured nails for a handshake.

Nossir, Willard shook it off, stuffed his own palms under his arms, folded up in the chair. They'd track you down like death, if you didn't watch 'em, passing on the diseases with their baby pink hands.

Still, he didn't back off, this one.

"I don't recall you bein' there . . ." the black man said, "with Mrs. Flynn at her sister's funeral . . ." He made a gesture toward Bertie; the old bag would sleep through anything but Wheel of Fortune.

Bertie had no sister; he was talking about Flynn's mother. He and Flynn was still roomies then, big compadres.

"Answer my question, Hunt!"

"Shut you face, old man!"

Restless burst into a cackle. The buck had heart anyway.

Wolfman smiled with them ivory teeth they all have.

Bertie moaned in her sleep, and got to breathin' to beat sixty again. They watched her. She moaned again and uncrossed her ankles, crossed them back the other way, and her breathing eased. The Game of the Week had a close-up of that weirdo with the orange hair leading cheers in the stands, the kind of dandelion puff of hair all them blacks used to wear for awhile, but this orange and on a white boy.

"Should we step into another room and let her sleep?" Wolfman said in a low tone.

"Step where you like," Willard said. "Ain't no one can stop you anymore, can they?"

"No," said Wolfman, "not anymore." And the way he looked at Restless he just had to follow after him, it was like he knew it all.

They went out on the screen porch, out on the shaded side of the house overlooking the rosebushes and the plastic birdbath where a sparrow was just splashing off, and cocked his head, hearing them, and flew away.

Fine, thought Restless, ain't no better place for a showdown, what with the cleansing breezes through the screens and the lawn furniture with the webs where no germs can settle.

Wolfman carefully removed and folded his green silk suit jacket—the inner lining blue as lapis lazuli—before stretching out on the one lounge chair.

"Who are you, my man?" he asked gently, then laughed in a loud and musical voice. "Who was that masked man?" he said, and whooped laughing at his own damn joke.

"Name's Willard Walker—Restless Walker to some, Mr. Walker to you—managed the Washington Senators in 1943, 4, and 5, and damn near won a pennant. Got fifteen votes in the Vet'rans Committee of the Hall of Fame last time out—which is a damn sight closer than you ever gonna get, buck—and got a lifetime winning percentage of seven hundred pitching in the Nationals and the Federals back before the Great War when the mustard gas got me and I had to hang 'em up and start wearing this thing on my puss. I'm Mrs. Flynn's fiancé and that damn fool Jack's financial advisor and the man responsible for him making it to the bigs in the first place. I got a forty-five caliber in my room upstairs and a half a hundred thousand clams in the bank, and I don't need no lip from you, or no leave to speak. You take all that in, or you want me to repeat it slow so's you can understand it?"

Wolfman folded his arms slowly up behind him, resting his neck against the huge hands.

"You ain't that old, asshole. You ain't old enough to have pitched in no Federal League. What's a matter, really, you got asthma? Or rose fever or sumthin'?"

"Something like that."

"Where's Flynn?"

"Out fishin' with his girlfriend. You plan to answer my question?"

The big buck was enjoying him, he let out a slow smile, and stared right at him.

"You plan to listen if I do?"

Willard nodded helplessly. This feller had a way of commanding a person.

"You know baseball, Restless? I mean, really? More than you' sad-sap story about pitching in some Federal League?"

Willard wouldn't answer him nothing. The big buck was just toying with him now, so he just looked out at the rosebuds and the shadows of the leaves across the lawn, waiting him out.

"Walter O. Dropo," says the Wolfman.

"What about him?"

"That name mean anything to you, old man?"

"Hell yes!" Restless said. "You gonna chaw or spit?"

Wolfman he just lay back there smiling, his eyes glinting, his long legs stretched out on the lounger, a toothpick between his teeth. The bottoms of his eyetalian shoes splayed out like peacock fans, the leather on them hardly worn. They was gold on his fingers and at his wrist. Restless he felt the urge for a chaw coming on—whether it was on account of the saying he'd tossed at the buck, or seeing as they was setting out to talk the game, he couldn't say—but it was a powerful urge, all the more so because the old woman she wouldn't let none of that in the house. He would even of asked Wolfman for some chaw if he hadn't of begun talking just then, still laying back there dreaming and twiddling that damn toothpick between his plum-colored lips.

"Nineteen and fifty two, old man, middle of July, Mr. Walter O. Dropo was playing first base for the Dee-troit Tigers, having just come over a month or so before from Boston. In the course of two days, a single game and a double-header, Mr. Dropo managed to accomplish something quite against the odds in that, for twelve consecutive appearances at the plate, he managed to hit safely twelve times. This feat established, or some would say matched, an American League record which had stood for some fourteen years. I, for one, consider it distinctly a record, since Mr. Dropo hadn't the advantage of an intervening walk within his streak, something his predecessor, one Michael "Pinky" Higgins—himself later a manager of the selfsame Boston Red Sox—had enjoyed twice . . ."

"You don't have to explain the damn game to me!" Willard complained. "I knowed what you meant when you said twelve plate appearances." He softened his tone then, his tastebuds now aching for a chaw. "Fact is I knowed Pinky Higgins and Moose Dropo both. The Moose I managed in the Mountain League, and Pinky I knowed for he played against the Senators when they was mine . . ."

Wolfman viewed him coolly, with an expanding grin and calm, clear eyes. Restless was getting restless without a chaw, and he wanted to swap stories. The sparrow was back at the birdbath, dousing his brown-black crown in the green water. The day was still heating up even as the afternoon began its slow collapse, but there was an occasional fresh breeze from the northwest, and a promise of cooling in the gathering shadows. It was silent here, some edge of the world. The only sounds were from the birds, and distant traffic, and the old woman snoring delicately within the house.

"I think you are a liar, Mr. Walker, but an interesting one. You know something about baseball, don't you?"

"Thing or two," Restless allowed. "Say," he prompted, "you wouldn't happen to have a chaw, would you?"

"'Fraid not . . . Snuff?"

"Any port in a storm," Restless said.

He reached carefully to extricate the snuff from the gold lozenge which the black man proffered, avoiding contact with the germ-laden metal of the snuff box, and yet grasping a healthy pinch. He flicked the paper dust mask upward, tucked the snuff to the right of his left lower molar, and replaced the mask, the whole loading process accomplished in a bird swift flash.

Dadgum minty shit burned the lip! Let the juices flow and the sweet, weedy flavor of tobacco met his tongue. He then wanted to spit.

The black gentleman continued his highfalutin' story.

"Nonetheless," he said, "nonetheless, it is important to contextualize this, to understand for instance that Mr. Dropo's accomplishment not only surpassed that of Mr. Higgins in the manner which I've suggested, but, what's more, also surpassed by two hits the existing record, held by eight men in the other league, only two of whom had done so without a walk, only one of those in this century."

The Wolfman was fairly working up to something, but Restless had to spit. He flipped the mask up and back in an instant, squit-squitting a fine spray on the old woman's jade plant sitting on a wicker plant stand to his right.

The tobacco stains dotted the dusty thick leaves. The snuff didn't behave like no chaw, it kept washing up and over and getting swallowed.

"You followin' me, old man?"

Willard grunted. He was drowning in the damn gritty juice, and the mint had the effect of some foul weed, clogging his sinuses, making the whole process of breathing a pretty shaky proposition overall.

"Well then . . ." The black man brought his hands out before him and placed them longwise against his face, the tips of the long, slender index fingers resting at the bridge of his not terribly predominate and relatively fine-boned nose. The hand was fragile for a hitter's, the fingers delicate and long, and, with the fingertips pressed against each other, and the large hands flexed, the fingers made a little bell-shaped cage with accordion struts, the soft, pale palms blinking through the open spaces.

"Well . . ."

Willard spit and left the mask up on his nose.

". . . we come to the subject at hand, the 1977 season. I was goin' pretty good, y'know, old man, flirting with .280 and looking to pulling it up to .290 or so, which was damn fair for me coming over, like your boy Jackie, into the other league. If you know half you seem to think you know, you can see how it was different for me. Jack, he had the advantage, you dig? A leg up being as the hitters they don' know what a pitcher's got when he comes over free agent, but a hitter, y'know, has to adjust to it. I mean wasn't no big surprise for Jack to go twenty that year, throwing like he was; but for me to be up there with the old-time American Leaguers, now that was something . . ."

Willard was just a-chewing the damn little wad of snuff now, it was like having a tea bag bust in your mouth; and Wolfman he seen that, and he bends way forward, sliding his legs down over either side of the lounge, folding up his little bird cage, and he puts the snuff out for Willard to take another hit, but just then remembers something, and reaches back to the green silk jacket, the dark cloth the color of the dark leaves on the weedy-looking hibiscus the old lady kept in the parlor, and he fishes in the pocket of the lining, the lapis-blue cloth rustling, and comes up with a cigar in a tube, that he breaks loose and offers to Willard, saying, "Hey mon, you wanna give this a chew, mon?"

And Restless he takes it from the long fingers, careful not to touch, and he opens the thing, a damn Havana for chri'sake, like the old days of the International League, when them Havana spics played and you could get them things by the box for a buck a throw, and Luke Easter he used to show up at the hotel in Syracuse and sit in the lobby smoking 'em.

Now Luke Easter, he was a damn good boy, and a hitter to beat all. Thirty-some years old by the time he went up and he still could hit! Damn . . . !

Damn there were good days then!

"And I come up against him in July, on a day as pretty as this, him and me on the top of our forms, you dig, and after all that messin' around they be doing with me, all that jive-shit desig-nated hitter do, and wanderin' from pasture to pasture in the outfield while the man try to decide whether he gonna play me regular, whether he gonna let me hit, you dig! Finally! Finally, I was getting regular swings and really beginning to read them cats, and suddenly like some damn miracle, like being born in the waters, I'm at the top of my game and ready for fame, thirty-three years old and pushing

.285, on a tear and loaded for bear . . . And we come into Toronto, which is as bag-ass a city as you ever gonna see, old man, and I gone four for four comin' in, and I scratch out three more while we losin' the opener against them, but I got Flynn coming up against me, you dig, and I ain't ever really hit against him nohow, which isn't surprising seeing as how I went and tol' him everything he ever knew about how hitters think years back, back when we both be boys and I was an island dude and still thinking he was some charm for me, you dig? Thinking he be gris-gris fo' me . . ."

There was a film of silvery sweat along the black man's brow, the delicate hands flew before him like blackbirds pecking at each other in the air. The cigar was a rich chaw, but juicier'n hell, and Willard he slipped the jade plant from out of its outer bucket and used that to spit into.

"First time up he make a mistake, you know, trying for to set me up with a wasted curve but let it hang out there a little closer than he wanted to on the first pitch, and by then I gone seven straight and I know I'm close to something but don't know about no Pinky or Moose, I just know I want to keep it goin', you know, maybe end my life like Joe DiMaggio sellin' coffee and lovin' honeys, and so I swing real fine with it, just goin' with the pitch and driving it through, and bam! she's down the goddamn gap for a double. And he leaves me still standing there when the inning's over, and he turns and just sort of nods at me, real mean and sappy like he always is, before he trots in.

"Still it's eight straight, and I be damned if I don't luck out and outguess him next time up, catch the ass end of one of his fine, motherfucking sliders when he's got me oh-and-two and all twisted in my head . . . hit one of them damn red dot specials and pull the sucker clean for a single and a ribbie to break his shutout, and make it nine for me. And I hit him again when we're all hitting him in the seventh, and he's watching the damn floodgate open, my man, the Watergate, you dig, and still they keep him in there cause they ain't got much else since Vuckovich went in relief the day before and they ain't seen that much from Clancy yet . . . And then he finds it somewhere like he always do, you know, and we get set down with the bases full and only up by two. And he keep finding it through the eighth, and suddenly it be like he's starting over again with all his shit together, and they get one for him in the home half, and we's up there looking at him strong again in the last inning and with only a damn run in our pockets. And I be on a tear, gone ten straight, and some asshole motherjumper's got to tell me all about Walter O. Dropo then, sitting in the dugout and watching the illustrious Mr. John Flynn in the midst of one of his fabled resurrections . . . and the two of us only claim jumpers, really, come over to the Americans on account of the money, and finding ourselves on different sides, engaged in a battle for nothing more than the first seat on the plane home in September, that and pride, old man, who can hit who, who can git who . . .

"And some sucker's got to tell me about old Walt Dropo, you dig. There be them kind of cats all around, try to spoil it for you, you dig, try to break your juju . . . Bastards hated me! Tha's why they put me out so fast, weren't nothing about Jack or no bat alongside the head . . . nothin' about no Lord High Justice gonna show me how they do up in Toronto . . ."

Mr. Winston Hunt reclined again, having come to the center of the story. He stretched himself out and recalled, you understand, recalled and recollected, hands behind his head, great white eyes wide and looking out beyond the garden, beyond the birdbath, to the very edge of the green that makes all the world a baseball pasture, an Alpine meadow, the source of rivers, the low-pressure center of God's green earth and silver water.

And Mr. Willard Walker sat intent and chewing, poised to catch the black and careful creature in the web of whatever lies he might dare, poised to snatch him if he faltered, to stun him and weave around him, bind him there until Jack returned.

"And it come down to oh-and-two, just like that. And he knew out there, he could hear them yelling from the bench, he knew I was on the edge of something and that he could spoil it. He knew he could! He carved me up with two straight pitches, two flashing silver knives I couldn't touch. Suddenly, man, I was so goddamn weary, you know, I been such a long time coming and I knew it was done, you know, I knew he had me. I was weary inside and kind of sad, and trying to get myself back on key, you dig, trying to find the line. I was psyching myself and getting madder than hell, not at him and not even at me, mad at Time itself, you dig, mad 'cause of all the people getting older and how the afternoon was slipping into shadow. And the shadow was out there on the edge of the horizon, Restless, like some black dot of a ship out at the edge of where you can see on a lake. And I was mad at the changes, boy, mad at the changes . . . So I stepped out and I thought myself what he would do, you know, I analyzed the whole damn show while I fiddled with a shoestring . . .

"Then I straightened back up, you know, and pumped myself up. Pumped up my arms and took a few slow rips at the approaching shadows. Oh-and-two he'd throw me high and inside, throw that rising fastball that ain't got no more rise on it than if it got caught in a gust of wind, but which rises in an instant, like a hawk climbing up a little updraft; he'd throw it so it started off just high but on the edge, you dig, close enough you had to look it through or commit before it lifted that last little gust. But . . ."

"But you been hittin' 'em high," Willard said, and spit, "you been hitting 'em high and so you knowed he won't throw you that."

"Yessir, tha's right, I hope to die if that ain't it," Wolfman said quietly.

The two of them studied the advancing shadows on the lawn. It was suddenly getting cool on the porch, a smell of the river coming in, and moistness in the air. Almost too chilly to keep sitting, but the story had to be told.

"I figured he would know I knowed he was going to give me the high inside pitch. I figured he knew I would anticipate it, if only because I had no other realistic choice. I figured he'd come after me, sure enough. I knew he wouldn't really waste one now, not unless it was something close enough, as close as the high inside. And so I figured he'd come down the pipe at me, you know, that he'd trust to my expectations, and trust to how I'd never be looking for it right down the center, not when I was going for a record, not when he knew he had me thinking. I thought he'd throw straight at me, so I decided to look for it high and inside after all. I figured I could catch up to him and protect the plate if he come down the pipe, but I'd be damned if he'd suckered me high and inside. So I sets myself up a little back in the box . . . you know, old man, jes enough to be able to get the hands extended but not so much I can't foul off no outside pitch . . .

"I picked up the spin the moment he released. It was coming high and tight and sweet as shit. It was a goddamn gopher ball, coming high and tight and fat as an old hot air balloon. And I felt it click—I knew I could wail that sucker from here to kingdom come, catch it on the updraft and pull it while she was still rising—and I wasn't about to have Mr. Jack Flynn sucker me with no owe-you-one, wasn't going to have him sully my record now, and so I headed for the mound before it even went past my head. Headed out there with my blood rising and the shadow in my eyes . . . Next thing I remember they pulled me away, dragged me off yelling down the dirty wooden stairs into the piss-smelling clubhouse. It was over then."

"You thought he give you one?"

"Tha's a fact, Restless! That's a genuine fact . . ."

Restless, he worked the chaw over so's it was set right in his cheek, tucked it there and considered. If what the buck say be true, there's a justice in it, you know. Somethin' that never come out at the time, but that explains Flynn's danged fancy quiet about the episode. I mean, you think a man givin' you something for nothing, and spoiling your record for all time in your heart, that could anger you up. Could explain.

"So why's it they shoot you, Wolfman? Explain that!"

Restless moved the chaw back out of the pocket with his tongue, chewing it over good while he watched to see if the buck was telling the truth after all. It's one thing to rush the mound when you think you been had, but another when a lady's husband shoot you at a motel.

Wolfman didn't blink. He stared the old man down with them angry eyes and Willard he felt the weariness coming upon him then, sure as night.

"You don' know nothin, old man," Wolfman said. "You like all them dudes, you think you know but you don't know nothing . . . All that sappy talk of forty-five's in you room, and all that shit, and you don't know . . ."

It was hurting him, Restless knew, he saw it in his eyes. Hurting him but the weariness was coming . . .

"Black folk know," Wolfman said, "motherfuckin' guns are real, Jack, for black folk . . . Eight, ten years ago, old man, it was a strange time, a very strange time. Dude could walk out of a lounge and a lady comes up to him, rap a bit, maybe she know him, you dig, maybe she seen his face in the papers, seen him around. You be talkin', real quiet like in a dim parking lot, just runnin' a little number, you dig, and smiling some and feeling good after a coupla rums, and someone show up in the light, you know, the lady scream something about no, baby, you got it wrong, you got it wrong, honey, he just come out of the bar and we said hello . . . You see the blood's angry eyes, you see that he all coked up or some damn thing, and the gun just glitter there in the damn sad parking lot light . . . feel the bone crack, old man, feel that lead slam into you leg like some damn freight train . . . hear everybody screaming and crying—o baby, o baby, no!—and you know, old man, you know . . . You read about you'self in the papers and you know it don't matter what you say 'cause people be knowing better than you, no matter what you say, it happen that way."

Wolfman, he watched the old man nodding, watch his jaw work and see him nod, and nod again, the damn fool paper mask setting up there on top his nose like a white hump on the forehead, the rheumy eyes gathering in the shadows, weakening, beginning to fall shut in a sad-ass tremor, real gentle like, like most old men do, how they be like babies sometimes, falling off. And then, when he seen him off, you know, see the old man settle into it, the muscles on his scrawny arm trembling just a little from the cooling air—the faded, bad-ass tattoo, this here "Live Free or Die," looking like the pale blue stamps on a side of beef—or no, not no side of beef, but some scrawny, butchered goat, some mutton; when he seen him go, Wolfman he knew he take him a nap soon too, waiting on Mr. Jack Flynn out on the river, waiting on what come next, whatever he bring him here for along the river of air.

For a time he studied the lines of the yard, playing an old game in his head as he settled into sleep. If you took the shadowy area around the birdbath as home, then the right foul line would run down toward the roses and the garage. It was a short porch out there in right field, maybe three hundred, three twenty-five down the line, but scooping out real quick toward right center, a long alley out past the lilacs, all of deep center still bathed in light, like a pool of gold, bright and silent and a sky high enough to hang a ball up forever, get it lost there in the glare, maybe even catch on a breeze and carry out on over the next yard, the town, the river itself. Canada even . . . an international blast if it carried right, if that old black ash got enough of the moisture in it, if it sweaty enough to make it a hammer, pound that sucker like a thumbtack into the sky.

But left field, man, that was another story. Left field, she just stretched on forever into the light. Out there it ain't no pool of gold, out there it's bright, Jack, you dig? I means bright! Bright as electric light, forty miles away from night, out of sight, right and tight . . .

Ain't nobody could pull one out there today, my man. Nossir! Left field stretch til the end of time, left field got men on horseback patrolling there, jet planes, you dig, I mean room to spare, my man, time to set you'self up a picnic lunch and still be able to mosey over under a long fly ball. Left feel here's a ocean, you dig? Don' take no jujuman to know they be no pullin' the ball out of here there.

Issa way wif ev'ry park, you know, they's always somewhere's too far to fly, Jack. No matter how tough you be, my man, they's always some part o' the park gonna gather you in. You fly sometime, you see what I mean, my man! You see them parks from the air! They be goin' on forever, they do. Always got a deep side sliding off into the horizon. Don't do to be figurin' on beating them odds, my man, it's a space time continuum, you understand, an arena of instantaneity and infinity.

And the shadows be comin' there soon, Jack, the ocean turning dark, the sun setting there. Ain't no one beats them odds. It over then. That the game, my man, it over when it over and that's God's truth, no lie.

FIFTEEN

Emma watched them out into the channel, saw them nose around the islands, then disappear, the boat low in the water, the two of them sitting at some distance from each other and waving to her as she waved to them, removed by layers of formalities: man and girl, hero and adolescent fan, and—she supposed—whatever formalities described their feelings and fears about her. The boat rode so low that the wake from the inadequate motor lapsed behind them like soiled lace, a swath of barely frothing white.

Goodbye, my daughter, she thought; goodbye, my . . . what?

She laughed at herself. My what, indeed. It was too easy to think so of Flynn, too terribly adolescent of her. My ride, she supposed, summed it up. A ride back from Syracuse repaid by some few days understanding. Women have paid much, much more for a ride in a fancy car.

My friend, she thought, then literally turned heel and walked up from the dock, leaving them to the particular formalities of the river.

Behind her the boats screeched at their mooring, and a low murmur hung above the water like a haze, the whole river humming. Ahead the road rose slowly past the rental cottages and the combined office-store. The monarchs were back, dusty orange and slowed by the sun, landing in a fold of wings then flitting on in corkscrew flights. She walked toward them.

It felt like skipping school, the sun some constant force upon the mud and gravel here, upon her arms and shoulders, the back of the sundress she was naked under. Cool, Emma thought, not seductive or suggestive, only cool.

But there was some license to it, she knew. Like the low and subtle breeze in off the water, like skipping school or skipping off, especially to one raised in a Canadian convent school. She remembered the French nuns as motionless, their woolen habits the color of Concord grapes, starched wimples about the skull and down in a stiff half circle across the impossible breasts, the fabric of the wimples as dazzling white, as wheaten, as communion wafers.

Nonsense, she thought, there is no connection save in books. The same nuns had dark lisle stockings and Irish linen handkerchiefs, they shared wine on name-day celebrations and whispered secrets to one another daily under the stone arches of the cloistered gardens. Even in classes you could see they had other lives, for they read in French of Eloise and Abelard, the consonants sighing, dark eyes alive behind the white bibs. You grow to know you are beyond the illusions you have of your own early innocence. There are simply choices to be made. A girl from Trois Rivières goes off to Paris and becomes a nun in blue, returns to teach a younger version of herself in the guise of a girl with a name from a romance novel.

Molly too, Emma thought, and Esther. Bertie also. Each of us naked under ourselves. Even so, she did not, as she had planned, go back to the car, but continued up along the dirt road through the cottages. Looking for something, she thought, courage or grace or whatever was lost. Or merely sustaining the feeling of skipping free.

We came here the first day and so he comes back here now. He skipped stones and seemed Ulysses by his ships. Regained his senses, went to sea. I am, she thought, whatever is the opposite of Circe, the un-enchanter.

And a nun of sorts, she could not deny. Even officially, the Lay Healing Order of Saint Luke, a blue scapular in my purse ready for healing visits.

Is it this I've done, Flynn, healed you?

Ha, she thought, healed myself as well.

There was—had been from the shore—a pebble in her sandal. A small, grey bean of stone there like a penance, a reminder of what she had before her, what she had planned. She turned back toward the car, but was stopped by the roses.

They were in the yard of the only cottage with both a yard and a different façade, this one alone cedar shake not clapboard, painted not cottage white but barn red some years back. The red paint was powdering now, chalky except where the shingles met. Behind the cottage a split rail fence surrounded a green square of lawn which seemed to float there uneasily, as if there was not thatch enough to grip the clay here where only broad fescue and crabgrass thrived. The rose bed was just outside this compound, an island of its own, a bare trench holding off the ground ivy, the bushes carefully pruned and high and lush.

She had seen them from the rear on her way up the sloping road, as if coming upon a stage set, only a few blooms bending obstinately back, toward her and opposite the natural westward exposure. There were no more than five bushes across the twelve-foot bed, their canes strong and green at the tops, but bent forward and heavily laden, the root stock thick and dark, woody arms holding all this up. From this aspect it had seemed more a hedge than a garden, the bushes trimmed flat, the flowers intended elsewhere.

If they were remarkable, she had not sensed it, only noting that this was surely the cottage of the proprietors of this small non-village. The red shake, the floating lawn, the established roses all said this. Emma imagined a woman left here, making something home here while her husband tended to the rental cottages, the broad and low rental boats with their swaths of dull lace trailing behind them, the bait shop and grocery, its shelves stocked with overpriced and miniature cans of soup and chili, family-style loaves of airy, substanceless bread, charcoal lighter.

She had paid more attention to the window boxes with their jarring marigolds, the rust orange making the cedar shakes seem even duller; and to the rowboat planter out in front, swamped in dark potting soil up to the seats, daisies and columbine and whatever else sprouting through as if from under the whole hull of the world.

On the starboard side of the bow she had carefully lettered the words S.S. Primrose in periwinkle paint, the hand showing some talent, perhaps even some art training, the letters proportional and with serifs.

Emma had told herself a little story and just as promptly forgotten it: a life led here, a woman with dreams, some perhaps fulfilled. But now, coming back down upon the roses, the story suddenly frightened her. It had substance in the awful weight of the cabbage-like blooms, unwound by the sun, and in the floribunda spreading like panicked mouths, all of them screaming. It was all too much, abloom like this and untrimmed, it was the trouble with roses. You could never keep up with them. If blackspot and aphid and fungus and mite did not get them or demoralize you, then there was the constant cutting, the trim and cut and cut back to the cinquefoil eyes, the tilling and watering and spraying, all to keep them coming. There was a wall of them now, in all possible stages of bloom, blast, and decay; a few tight, long-stemmed buds buried in the greenery like forlorn and doomed virgins about to fade into the wilt and spoilage, the cabbage fullness of the surrounding matrons. The wall of them—the steaming, pungent and invisible fog of their fragrance hanging over the road—was momentarily too much for her. It was a stupid story, and she had told it to herself, had herself to blame. It was no way to ready for what she had to do this afternoon while they were out there on the river.

She willed herself away from the roses and the story both, hurrying down the road to the car, slipping into its anonymous odor, popping the small grey bean, the stone, under her tongue, keeping it there not as a penance but as a reminder of what persists, feeling the saliva rise to wash it and turning it sweet there, smooth, solid and immutable, knowing that this too heals.

The stone was still there when she entered the tile room.

"Hello Esther!"

The woman did not stir, nor had Emma expected her to. It was a habit, the greeting, come of years now in a healing order. "Reality orientation" was the fancy term for it, a simple courtesy really, an invocation. The dying and the failing alike suffer a disorientation not unlike that which strikes the living who come to see them. Any illness first assails the concept of self, the body floats off above, as if in a dream or accident. This cannot be happening to me, one thinks, or—because it is—I am no longer who I was. It is as if the old self gives birth to a new at the end; it was not uncommon to find dying women thinking, a delirium, they were again giving birth.

Before Emma had known any fancy terms, she had known that the first step in healing was to invoke the self.

Yes, it is you who this is happening to. Not fate, but the beginning of a last achievement. The illness is not outside you, nor has it taken you over; you are simply who you are, living the life you have been led to live.

Emma shortened the invocation for Esther. Normally, she would say what day it was, tell the time of day, and then perhaps mention the prevailing weather, or the number of days the patient had been here.

A quiz: what previous meeting did Jack Flynn not remember?

Answer: who was the anonymous "nurse" who told them the trick of using Styrofoam cups to keep the sheets from pressing on the pain-wracked flesh of his father?

It was the occasion had blinded him, Emma knew. And the scapular. It was an effective blazon, a badge of office, keeping the living focused on the healing and not the healer. At certain times the whole healing task was little more than persuading the living to let the dying one pass. Sometimes you could see the patient linger for days until she or he was certain that the awkward, frightened family would let go. They would be ready to die, but hold back, denying themselves what by that time they were certain was rapture, arguing by their silent presence that what was to come was not unlonged for and not lasting.

Ein Augenblick, a blink of the eye, the last two words of an old dairy farmer she had attended to once. He was smiling when he whispered the words, trying to console her even as he died alone. Sometimes the healing is letting oneself be healed.

She wet her thumb with spittle and blessed the forehead and the eyelids of Flynn's sister, careful to open the lids again after she had blessed them.

There was no established rubric for Emma's office, and so she made do, sometimes improvising sacrament and ceremony as the occasion called for. A patient would want to confess when there was no priest on call or no hope of his making it there on time. Emma heard their sins and asked their prayers for her sins. One of the delirious women begged that Emma baptize what she imagined to be her newly born child; Emma performed the rite as well as she could remember, using the bloody spittle at the woman's lips for unguentum and the sweat from her brow for holy salts, leaving out the part about denying Satan and his works.

Sacrilege? Perhaps. But each woman makes her own priesthood, and Emma had come to this whole process sacrilegiously enough anyway.

The first death had been her own mother's, and she had discovered her calling then. In what turned out to be the last twenty-four hours, the devout woman had suddenly, perplexingly, turned doubter. She could not understand why she hated the idea of nothingness, the simple fact that one morning would dawn without her.

"Look," her mother had said. "You see these chocolates he puts here?"

It was a satin box with satin roses on her bedside table. Their father had put them there as if a ransom against death; in the last weeks, when her appetite failed her, late one night she had craved chocolate, and now at the end he sought anything that would detain her.

"Yes, Mama, you want one?" Emma's sister asked.

"He loves you," Emma said. "He gives you roses."

But their mother ignored her, focusing on the foolish Ann.

"I'll be gone before they melt," she said. "Put them in the sun and see what I say."

"She's lost her mind," Ann said, turning oddly hysterical. "The cancer has gone to her brain, don't you see, Emma?"

"A casket," their mother said. "A casket of roses . . ."

Ann fled the room weeping. Emma stayed.

"Would you like me to sing a sad song?" she asked.

It was new ground for her, the nearest she had ever come to inspiration. She merely knew that it was she who would have to be here for Mama, and that there was no guidance, no precedent, and so she resolved to say whatever came to her, and to pray for grace that it be right.

Her mother nodded and Emma knew she had spoken well. It was an exhilaration to know this, she felt an unaccustomed strength pour through her marrow. She was excited about what would come next. She began to hum, crooning low and waiting. And in time the song came, the fool's song from Twelfth Night, the least-known one.

Not a flower, not a flower sweet,
On my black coffin let there be strown;
Not a friend, not a friend greet
My poor corpse, where my bones shall be thrown.
A thousand thousand sighs to save,
Lay me, O, where
Sad true lover never find my grave,
To weep there.

Her mother's eyes had closed, but Emma knew she was there. The song had come from school, a Shakespeare course once, something she had never even hummed before. It was a calling.

"Is that it?" she asked. "You are afraid for him?"

"He has to know he'll lose me."

It was desperate and loving to say this, and Emma told the truth, even though they had been made, absurdly, to agree not to.

"He knows, Mama . . . He knows. The doctor told him you don't have long. We all know."

And then, without knowing why, she added, "You can go now, you can leave when you are ready."

At first instinct it felt to her like treason, but as soon as it was out she knew it was right. Her mother's eyes opened.

"I'm afraid there is no heaven, my Emma."

"There is."

"Ha! How easily you all can say that." There was some spite in her voice, a testing. "You are not where I am now."

"I can only tell you what I feel, Mama, and promise you that I believe it enough that I will always think that you are there."

"If there is one, I will be there for you," her mother said, and for a time she stared toward the ceiling watching nothing.

"I just don't know," she sighed, and then turned toward Emma. "I am very tired and I need to think. You can leave me now, I promise, there's no need yet."

"Sleep," Emma whispered. "I want to stay. When you wake, I will wash you and change your gown."

"I will wake."

"I know," Emma said.

And it was cast then, without her knowing. She sat there for another hour, washed her, changed her, went down to tell them not to worry, to tell them that she had told her. They understood and seemed relieved, despite the agreement not to say. The next morning she had washed her again, sponging over the cooling flesh, already feeling the warmth receding from her mother's arms and legs. She went down to tell them and they came up. Emma had hummed a tune and held her hand and then closed her eyes for the last time when no one else moved to do so.

It was a calling, but there wasn't much call for it. There was Molly and Yves to use her time and anyway people didn't really ask you to come and help them die. It's like they say about some stories, funny stories, you really had to be there.

She had laughed.

"You really had to be there . . . ha . . ."

"You lied," Flynn had said.

"No," she said.

"You came out to find me. It was all a lie, the motel and the road back. You lied."

"No."

"They sent you to find me."

"Who?"

"Bertie, that doctor, Lenny . . . everyone."

There was an awful storm out on the river, moving in. They could hear the thunder, like giant's boots. Molly was whimpering in the next room, whether waking or sleeping Emma did not know. They were all in the house and Wolfman would be coming in. Flynn had seen Esther, and now he had to do whatever he would do. Emma's only lie was saying Esther was no one; she *was* someone, she was herself, but not who Flynn wanted her to be. It had been necessary to use this lie so he could see. It, too, was a healing.

"I have to know the truth, Emma."

"Yes," she said, "you do."

There was a sudden crack, a flare, a rolling cannonade of thunder, echoing off the nearby houses and then far away on the river. All the house had been a hum of different fans, but now the humming slowed and died, the pale eye of the bedside clock dimmed. The lightning had been near, the crack was a tree splintering, the electricity had died away. They could hear the thump of Molly's feet across the bedroom carpet, the slap as her feet reached the wooden floor of the hall. As she pushed in with them, the fans resumed and the light from the clock washed across her face. The rain came in a great sigh and a rush of cool air, the rainfall rattling against the roof and open windows. Flynn rose to shut the windows, switch off the fans. Molly pressed against Emma.

"Love me, Mama," she whispered.

"I do," Emma said. "I will."

Flynn was sitting on the edge of the bed. The rain came in clattering waves against the house, hard knots of rain, hail perhaps. The house was breathing on its own again, without the fans.

"There are two places where you can lose a game," he said, "the first innings when you haven't yet found your rhythm, and the middle innings when, if you're not careful, it can leave you without warning. You tire all of a sudden and it's gone. Maybe it's a ground ball too sharply hit, it looks like an error on the books, but you know he got to you, hit something too hot to handle. It opens the floodgates, next there's a clean shot, or maybe a squibber, a walk, then a long fly. You're on your way out . . . Someone else wins or loses it for you.

"The early innings you maybe can or can't survive on your own. I been in games where I let them get three, then the other guy lets us get four, or two, or tie it up. Then it's like the heat is off. We both settle down and it's a pitcher's duel . . . until the middle innings anyway, when either one of you loses it. It's funny, but in a game like that it's never both of you, always one of you stays in his form, you know . . ."

Why are you telling me this she thought he knew.

Molly made a big deal of pulling the pillow down over her head. She could still be an unreasonable girl in the night, in a storm.

"I'm feeling like the one who goes out in the middle," he said. "I'm feeling like I lost it both ways, Emma."

Molly flopped over on her other side, groaning slightly, pulling the pillow back over her head. Flynn picked the pillow up and dropped it back against her, he was teasing her.

"What do you say we all go fishing tomorrow?" he said.

"In the rain . . . ?" Molly groaned.

"It won't be raining. It's moving off already. What do you say?"

Molly sat up straight. "Really?" she said, then "Mom . . . ?"

"Sleep," Emma said. "Go back to your bed and sleep . . ."

"No," Flynn said, "I'm going to get up for a while anyway."

"I'll come . . . ," Emma said.

"No."

And the rain had moved off then, moving with him, the cool air sliding back in behind it with the wind shift.

She watched now for a shift in Esther's eyes. There was no sign of acknowledgement and yet the eyes were deceptively lively. Emma could not recall the details of the story. Had Sleeping Beauty pricked herself with a sewing needle, or bit into a poison apple?

It was a calling, and of the places to practice it, this was among the better. The little ICU was not designed to do any more than stabilize someone who had coded, keeping them alive long enough to be able to ship them out to somewhere else. It was among the unusual privileges that Esther enjoyed that she could stay here.

Enjoyed? Hardly. And yet there was a special status. The facility wasn't set up for this kind of maintenance. The young doctor ran the risk of having to do some explaining to the review committee and the auditors in coming months. Already he was feeling the pressure for staffing the ICU. Flynn had to act before the doctor could not help. There wouldn't have been the ICU here at all if it hadn't been for the largesse of the federal government in the boom years past; when the title grants went out, institutions like this got all that they could possibly get, right down to the monitors and crash carts and dark brown tiles.

"I remember your father," Emma said to Esther. "He was a very tired man at the end, he had come a long way and he was enough of a guide—he had lived long enough in his body, to know how close he had come."

Emma glanced away from the wide eyes to the sinusoidal wave of the monitor. There was no alteration, no radical swing in the digital read-outs of the vitals. Esther watched innocently mute. Her life was in Emma's hands now, not because of the healing, but because Emma had persuaded the duty nurse to take a break from the station.

They knew her here. She had been a regular visitor to the care center for years now, sometimes bringing Molly, leaving her to play baseball alone on the empty diamonds.

It had begun as a mistake, a foolish notion stolen from the pages of women's magazines. Yves left her for a summer woman, someone from New Rochelle who wanted new cupboards on her island. Each weekend her husband would fly up from his brokerage in a small jet, spend the weekend prowling for fish, tanning on his boat. Each Monday the Frenchman would return. It became a likeable arrangement, but ended when the summer did. By then, however, Yves was gone from Emma, she would not have him back.

She went back to teach in the fall, a single mother with a custody agreement and fictional child-support payments scheduled. Yves made little money after autumn.

"I went quite mad," she said simply. "You'll understand what I mean, I think, Esther, when I say I was someone else despite myself. You've seen enough of that in your time here, haven't you darling?"

No response. The sinusoidal marched across the screen in the up-down hills of television cartoons. The IV drip kept time.

"Everyone had suggestions. Sister Therese was the principal then, and she advised putting my soul in the hands of the Blessed Mother . . . She meant it well, it wasn't so silly as it sounds. Another teacher, a friend until then, suggesting putting other things in his hands . . ."

The monitors told her that she had only imagined laughter, still Emma smiled, felt the blushing. She was always surprised by any humor in herself.

There was someone there. Despite the machine waves, the dripping fluid, the soft rush of the air into the nostrils, Emma knew that Esther was there.

"You're hiding, aren't you?" she said. "I suppose you've spent a whole life like that, always taking in . . . Jack tells me you used to be quite girlish, he says you always liked to laugh."

She patted the hand strapped to the IV board, warm. Took the stone bean from under her tongue, put it in Esther's other palm, folded the fingers around it.

"The world," she said. "I've given you the world to hold."

The words had come, it would have been an embarrassing thing to say otherwise. You trust yourself to your guiding, Flynn's father knew this. To him at the end she had said: "It is a beautiful, sunny day outside. Jack has gone to eat, the fish have moved off the spawning beds to deeper water. Esther is near, your son and your wife await you."

His breath had caught in the way she recognized as the end. Something in what she said was enough to satisfy him, he had committed to the tunnel of light. She pressed the nurse-call and shouted out, but she could not leave. It was important to maintain human contact at the end. She held the guide's hand in hers. The breath caught again.

When his father died, Jack had been an instant late. Emma was humming and still holding the hand, the nurse held the other hand.

"It was very peaceful," the nurse was saying as Emma silently excused herself and left the room, removing the scapular as she went.

"I know," Flynn had said. "I could feel it when I came back in. He is still here . . ."

Only then had his voice cracked and the weeping come. Oh Dad, he sobbed, and folded himself across his father's body. He hadn't really seen Emma, the scapular had hidden her.

"It was a mistake, you see," Emma told Esther. "This article said you should immerse yourself, do volunteer work, whatever. I was raised a good Catholic girl, and so I took the advice. I began to visit patients. In time, I found there were courses, medical social work. I had no plan. They paid you more money at the high school if you had graduate credits. I was only doing it for that I thought, and to help me be a good volunteer . . ."

She laughed. Oh Esther, I have needed someone to talk to.

You know, don't you? You have been a woman longer than most of us, taking it all in, always taking it all in, your huge skull filled with the buzz of it.

You want to know what kind of girl I was? A giant, I was a big, hulking giant, five-foot-eight at sixteen, frightening to them and yet afraid of everything. It was my mind, you see, I hated my mind. You have that blessing—it is one, you know, for you, it is—but I always saw something. I always was the great good girl with good grades, handsome and homely behind wire rims, ratty hair pinned up in a snarled nest, my whole self all unfurled like roses in the heat. When we graduated I had all the honors, all the honors except maybe the home economics prize. When I was coming off the platform with my diploma, Mother Superior raised her hand for silence and called me back. I was afraid she was going to take my diploma back, afraid they had discovered it was all a mistake and I was a fraud. She said some words about my accomplishments and my face stung with the blushing. I was mortified. I stood there, even then not knowing what to do as the applause lapsed. She had to gesture for me to continue down the stairs from the platform. When we marched out, I ran off to the bushes and cried. My parents couldn't find me for a full half an hour, by then everybody was gone. I am used to hiding too, you see.

I was always off crying in the bushes. I remember the tea dances. For some reason I always wanted to go to them, I was always excited for days before. Always it was the same disappointment. Standing there in the dim light at the edge of the grand parlor, not even near the punch table, the usual station for girls of my type, towering above them, blinking out at them, and feeling so, so alone, Esther. So alone . . .

Sooner or later, I'd give up on it and run off to the bushes and cry, damning God and everyone for my graceless body, my awful mind . . .

Can I tell you something awful? Can I tell you what a woman my mother was, what awful love she had for us? The senior dance she made my brother take me to, she insisted that I go and that he take me, and that we tell no one who he was. She made a dress of drab lace, with ribbons strung through the waist and bodice, and she bought him a new blue suit. We posed for pictures beforehand, both of us grim and frightened.

If you knew the world, Esther, you would know this is not an unusual story, you would know this happens more than people know. What makes it unusual, however, is what happened when we came home that night. We alone it seemed not joining anyone else for breakfast, or swimming, or carriage rides through the park afterward . . . She sat us down and brought out a board of meat and cheese she had fixed for us, all sorts of meats and cheeses and pickles and different breads and small rolls and vegetables and dip in a fancy bowl, just like you would do for a girl and her date. She sat with us while we ate, asking questions about the decorations, the music, the other girls' dresses.

"I have never stopped crying about this, Esther, the awful love my mother had for us, a love that wouldn't believe anything but that life can be beautiful, that her daughter was a special woman. A meat and cheese platter, for god's sake . . ."

And so when in later years the beauty came, when the ugly duckling became the swan which the impossible story had promised, it was not a blessing but another weight upon me. I knew who I had been and was. Yves, the dashing Frenchman with sex in his fingers and mad songs on his lips, could not fool me. When he left, when he was gone, I understood. I am not saying that I was a victim, Esther, I am only saying I understood that there was more to it than it seemed.

She felt a coolness drifting through the corridor and in the door. The ICU was air-conditioned, but the suite outside was not. The coolness entered from outside as if a shadow passed over the buildings or the weather had turned with the coming twilight. Down the corridor in the staff dayroom, someone had been watching the Game of the Week on television; now the television was off, the

corridor silent. Only the hissing oxygen, the rubber valve of the res-
pirator working up and down on its chrome harness.

"So, when he left, you can imagine the hunger . . . For a time, I
took all offers, do you see, Esther? Even the man with the hands . . ."

She laughed again, the laughing echoing against the tiles.

"How is it the song goes? 'O the married men, makes me feel
like a girl again, to run with the married men . . . '"

Again. Laughed. Her eyes were a great cavern, a great calm.

I wasn't sure, you see, when they offered me the job through
Catholic Services. By that time I was what you would call a satisfied
sinner. Or mostly satisfied, anyway.

But then I just couldn't see why I should abandon God to the
non-sinners, can you understand that, Esther? I had a calling, do
you see?

Will Jack?

I had a daughter to raise and the pay was good and the hours
were flexible, and so I took it. Later I even entered a healing order.

That's what it is, she thought, what we each of us are seeking now.
The secret of the roses is that they require constancy and patience,
otherwise they frighten. Old women know this, you see them move
through the gardens in the dying light of evening. Flynn gave a life
to patience, and now he wants it all at once in his new life. Molly too
wants too much.

Order heals. We enter into it, we women. Not the orderliness
of what commonly goes by that name, but the order of change. The
patience of a watching woman, the sinusoidal wave, dark eyes, and
the world in her hand.

The nurse was coming back from the dayroom, squeaking down
the corridor on foam soles. Emma kissed the open eyes.

"God love you, my sister," she said. "We will know soon, Esther
darling."

When she got back to Chippewa Bay it was nearing dusk and
they were nowhere to be seen, although the boat was back and had
been for more than a hour, according to the lovely small woman
with the roses.

SIXTEEN

Big people were mostly alike, men anyway. All of Emma's men acted mostly the same way. At first they'd be kinda far away like you knew something they didn't and you made them nervous anyway. Then they'd ask you a million questions like they were your best friend or long-lost stepfather or someone, then finally they'd get this lame, jokey tone in their voices and every time they talked their eyes would be pulled way up in their foreheads like some frog or something. It was supposed to be cool, Molly guessed.

It's because of incest. Emma had a book that said that adults are threatened by the intense sexuality of adolescents, and so they turn them into objects of ridicule or targets of aggression.

"You want to make fun of me, Flynn?"

"What?" He was pulling in the fish for her, and she thought she'd test his psychological stability. It was another one of those flat, spiny things that he said had all kinds of names. When he gave her her choice, she decided they would call them pumpkin seeds cause that was an asshole name for a fish, but she figured he would think it was cute enough for her.

He got it in his hand, his pitching hand, and slid the hook back out from under the gickey transparent lip, then he flopped it back on the water. You could see it screw itself down through the light and then disappear in the darker water down below. Dumb shit would still bite the next hook you dropped. Already she had seen that happen, Flynn threw one down and it bit her damn hook and made the bobber sink. Pumpkin seeds sucked, as far as fish go.

"Make fun of what?"

"You feel like you want to beat me up or something . . . ?"

"Jesus!" he said. "What the hell are you talking about? Look out, damn it! Your bobber's a foot under. Hook him!"

"Aha!" Molly said. "You do feel anger."

She purposely let the pumpkin shit swim away with the bait.

It was calm in the bay, real smooth and hot after the flop flop trip down the channel. She kind of liked it better, even though there were bugs and all these crappy little fish. At least Flynn was starting to get a little less hyper. For the first hour or so you would of thought he was that geek Jim or whatever his name was from Wild Kingdom, the guy Marlin Perkins is always getting to go into the pen with the wild pigs or wrestle alligators.

And he was sad. You could tell that even in the middle of all the cool talk. Maybe the big sap did miss Emma like he said.

Though she couldn't see who would.

What was Emma doing right now? Probably sitting on some big rock by the river, getting real daring and pulling her skirt up and tucking it under her like a diaper so she could tan her thighs. Maybe even letting her straps slide down over her shoulder to get some sun there while she read some book about sad women and dinosaurs or any of that crap she read. Actually Emma hadn't worn any underwear at all except for the tube top thing that held her prostheses in place. She was getting daring.

"Can I take my shirt off, Flynn?"

"Christ!" he said. "Spare me from pre-pubes . . ."

Molly laughed. It was a great word, pre-pubes, it made you think of something growing on you, like yeast infection or something completely gross. But when she laughed, she banged against the bottom of the boat and made a big noise, just like he warned her against.

"Oops," she said and stuffed her hand into her mouth like it was what made the noise. It made her laugh again.

"What do you want to take your shirt off for?"

"Tan."

"What you got on under it?"

"A bra."

"Ha," he said and pissed her off.

When your breasts got cut off, did that part of your body just go away? I mean, was it something that didn't count anymore, like your knee or something?

"Answer a question?"

"No," he said, "fishing's not talking. Anyway, I'm getting tired of the twenty-questions routine."

"You and Emma make love?"

"Shit!" he said and banged the boat himself. "I swear I'll run us right back if you don't cut that flirty-gurty crap!"

Flirty-gurty! Jesus, Flynn was a hundred years old sometimes.

Actually she already asked Emma once, not about Flynn, the operation. You could ask Emma anything.

"No . . ." she had said. "It's still part of me . . . I mean, I still like to be caressed there, you know . . . Oh shit, you know Molly, it feels good but I don't . . . I don't trust everyone with the scars."

"Why?"

"They're mine, darling. I earned them. It takes a special man to be understanding about some things . . ."

She had let it go at that, Emma would only tell you anything up to a point, and that point probably didn't include telling which of them were understanding men. It was just like when she had asked about how it felt to make love. Emma would go far enough to say it was warm and close and it built to something that took you over, but she wouldn't say exactly what it felt like to have that thing stuck there. And she absolutely threw a shit fit about calling it fucking.

Or calling it "it" for that matter.

In fact, Emma had a whole set of careful words about it. Not making love to, but making love with; not rubbing, but caressing; not frenching, but another kind of kiss, a deeper kiss.

"Let's do it?"

"What?" Flynn had the same scaredy pre-pube tone.

"Twenty questions."

He pulled the rope on the motor, nosed the boat back out toward the channel. Bye Cranberry Creek.

Little packets of spray bounced up from the floppy front of the boat and went shooting back over their heads. Molly ducked them, one by one. When you got going the wind sort of made you grin all the time, the way it pushed down your throat and pressed against your eyes and face. That's why people on boats always look happy, Molly thought, they're bored to shit but the wind gets them grinning.

"Prostheses," she said.

Flynn shouted back to her through the wind and the grumbling sound of the motor. "What? I can't hear you . . ." He throttled it down so it sounded like a blender and the boat kinda just dropped in the water, real satisfied like. She liked that, how the boat would respond.

"I was only talking," she said. "It's the name of a guy in one of those old-time Greek stories."

Flynn nodded, and sort of set his jaw, looking along the river like he expected to see something there. Rhinos crossing maybe. It was surprising what he would believe. She moved back in the boat to be nearer to him, crouching real low as she moved, stretched way out to hold the two sides.

"Careful," he said, but he didn't try to help her. He could be okay when he wasn't hyper.

"A hero," she explained, still running a game on him about prostheses.

He nodded again, keeping a careful eye on the dreaded rhinos while Marlin took a moment to say a few things about Mutual of Omaha.

"What are you grinning about, girl?"

"Sex and violence and drugs," she said. "Don't call me girl."

All he did was nod. She started to think of his head like the bobber, a round wooden thing with a stick through it.

There was something she didn't want to talk about. Something she wasn't sure if she understood at all. The more time went by, the more Flynn just started to become somebody like anybody else, and that was okay—in fact it was good, now that he wasn't being the good guy or hyperspace freak—but it made her feel weird about herself. I mean, you find out that someone who was always your hero knows your whole goddamn family, and that's kind of exciting. Then you spend a few days around him, and that's weird but not so bad. You even know that your mother is probably making love with, caressing, and giving another kind of kiss to him, a deeper kiss, and that's okay too, even if it doesn't quite make sense. (I mean, he was around for years and they never saw him and you go away and come back and he's there and "confused" according to Emma and it's like he's one of her patients, except he's not dying.)

Is he?

"You're not dying, are you, Flynn?"

He turned the throttle way down now, so it was like an egg-beater sound. She expected him to say Jesus again and give her that pre-pube look. Instead he just looked at her, and suddenly it was much worse about how he wasn't really a hero anymore but only somebody, and she felt like she wanted to cry but she didn't know why and it was a stupid thing to rhyme like that and it only made her feel worse and why the shit didn't he say something!

She was a strange girl, Flynn knew. From the moment they had cleared Chippewa and put Emma out of sight it had been all questions, all keeping him off.

"Who was the best pitcher ever, Flynn? Except you, I mean . . ."

"Henry Schmidt," he had said without pausing.

"Who?"

"Henry Schmidt. Went 22 and 13 for Brooklyn in 1903 or so. One year up and never pitched again."

She had turned her whole head cockeyed to look at him, as if hunting for a hint that he was putting her on. She lifted her hand from where it trailed in the water, let it trickle down upon the bottom of the boat in a pattern. She let herself be convinced that he was serious.

"Why?"

In the beginning of the trip, before she tired of the effort and got a little bored, all their talk had really been shouting, across the length of the boat. It was an odd feeling, strangely reminiscent of being interviewed on the field after a game. The announcer with a finger pressed against the little earphone, the microphone thrust in your face like a grey cloth ice cream cone, and all the fans shouting from the stands, all the noise of people making their way out of the park. You talked through a wall of noise then too, and only the announcers face and your own little earphone told you what you or he had said; and even then you would have to pick your voice out through the noise of the director in the truck, whispering on a track that only you and the announcer could hear that there was twenty seconds to go, get ready camera three, ready to roll the credits, one more Brian.

And how do you view your career now, Jack?

In twenty seconds.

"Because," Flynn shouted through the noise, then he throttled down so she would understand, "because he measured himself, or so I guess. I don't know a damn thing about him except the stats, but he had to have measured himself. Added it up and decided to go back home. It takes courage to do that at any time, but once you've seen the heights . . . well, he must have been a special man. I mean, the game was different then, a guy named Happy Jack Chesbro won forty games back then, but still . . . you win twenty-some games, you get a decision in thirty games, you've seen the heights then. You've been to the mountain. Takes a whole lot to walk away when there's games to be won, a whole lot . . ."

He had expected her to say something. Expected praise, really: you've been there too, Jack, or something like that. You walked away from the heights, you did, Flynn.

They were just coming up on the Summerland Group, about to cut back inward and fish the inlet. They were just short of wonderland, turning away just before the river broadened out into a magical expanse. He felt himself an enchanter, convinced himself that he was giving this lovely girl something of his own, his father's river, a boy's eyes, visions. There was that feeling of wanting to do something for someone so badly that you only dimly perceive that you are doing it for yourself. A great cloud of seemingly undifferentiated love all falling down on yourself. Team spirit and all . . .

She annoyed him with her silent acceptance of the truth. In the moment of telling her the story, Henry Schmidt was himself, Jack Flynn. It wasn't true, she saw that and said nothing. In the shallows the water formed itself into floating saucers, pockets of blue rocking into one another in an easy rhythm, smoothing into silver sheets. Now and again there was a little eddy, a miniature water whirl, circling down. She watched him watch the water. He taught her to fish.

It was a lie, he had brought her here to ask her terrible questions, not to give her things. There were matters which he had to understand and she could clear them for him, tell him things that Emma wouldn't.

I wish I were my father, he had thought, and I could summon her a great fish, a walleye with onyx eyes, an ancient pike with rainbow patches along its flanks and gills of crimson.

I wish I were her father, Henry Schmidt, Yves of the flashing eyes, with magic in his fingers.

Now she asked if he was dying. It was too neatly done, too coincidental. He had to ask the things he did not really want to ask her.

They were playing games with him, and he knew how to play games.

She looked stricken by his silence, and so he smiled to ease her, slipped the throttle down another notch to choke the motor off, and reached forward to slide the oars into the water. He let them sit in the locks, rocking up and down on the pins, while he stripped his tee shirt off for the rowing.

"Yuk," she said.

"What?"

"Those scars," she said. "They go all around your shoulder. Didn't it hurt?"

He had retrieved the oars and begun pulling them, reaching way forward on the retrieve, extending his whole back and legs on the pull, feathering lightly at the end of each stroke, the oarlocks pinging as he let the water go and brought the oars back to row again. It was hard going in this bastardized boat. He hadn't wanted to make her shift around while he changed benches to row properly, hadn't wanted to paddle-wheel her like the guides do, so he pulled them backward, plowing the water against the flat stern and the heavy motor.

Oh for a double-ender, he thought, his arm already limp with the rowing.

"Hurt, yes . . . but not as much as it hurt before they operated . . ."

Nor as much as it hurt at the end, he thought, like part of you has died away. For the last few years it had been that way with every start. For the first inning or so it was as if something caught there, a great hump of bone, a knobby scar of muscle. It was a grinding ache, deep, not something present. You could feel it release with the pitch, literally feel the muscle mass begin to warm with the blood flow, the ache receding but never disappearing, gone like a boat to the horizon of a lake. Now and again you'd come from the side, just to let it ease, to feel the arm swing through like it had years before, move the batters back to let your arm breathe.

The numbness spread from the shoulders and forearms both, a radiating, gentle pain meeting at the elbow and bicep, occasionally surprising you with jolts of electrical shock you felt in the bone like thin hot wires. Sometimes these would come so strong you could feel them in your teeth, but none lasted beyond the time it took for the nerve to fire and then scream along the hot wires. Then, when you had learned again to ignore the oncoming numbness, the bone chips would start to ache, the pain gradually piercing the dull throb of the elbow joint, until you could locate them exactly as an x-ray in your consciousness. You were sure you could cut them out if you could somehow get in there, operating on yourself as if opening clams with a knife, picking out the stones, flipping them off with the spring tip of the blade.

Then, almost without knowing it, you'd be there. The smooth water, the mindless place, the pain nothing more than a yoke across the shoulders, a cable of muscle, and the dim and borderless hurting low in the back. Tuck the chin, pull up and kick in the high leglift, power through from the legs, rotating the hips, opening them slowly out, rolling as the arm came over effortlessly unwinding in one long reach for the target, releasing right, feeling the stitches themselves as the fingertips ticked them at the last contact, setting it spinning, spinning, hearing it crack into the mitt as the formless pain caught up on the follow through, catching you up like a vacuum, the tail of a comet, as you straightened and waited for the ball to be returned.

By the middle innings the pain would begin to chisel down through the shoulder. Dull and narrow at first, it would open out through your core like an awl through a block of ice. It would grow as the game went on, establishing links, circuits, with the low back pain, the ache in the thighs, the numb arm, the white hot wires, until there were buzzers and momentary flares in distant, seemingly disconnected places. The bone along the arch of the right foot ringing with pain, a rib throbbing as if ripped from its covering, or your throat raw when you cleared it and bunching when you swallowed.

If you measured yourself before and after a game you'd see that you lost a half inch to an inch from the jolting of your vertebrae, driving yourself down into the mound like driving log pilings into river muck. Meanwhile the pitching arm would shrink and swell both. No matter what you did after the game, the muscles in the arm would begin to convulse, shuddering away like an eel hit by a ball-peen hammer. Little electric flares of pain sparked here and there in your body like fireworks. You couldn't lift your arm, couldn't stand to sit for long because of the constant aching of the lower back.

But you really never began to hurt until the following morning. In the morning the knives ripped against the shoulder, the back was stiff and heavy as concrete, in the morning the fingers stung and tingled with a constant shocking like a permanent case of pins and needles, in the morning your mind hurt and your arm was a rag and your head ached and your legs would not stand the weight. You just hoped you'd be happy, happy you hadn't let it get away on you in the eighth, happy they hadn't taken it away.

It was beautiful pain, startling as light.

"There's a lot of hurt in life, kid. Life is hurt . . ."

"No," she said. "No, it isn't, is it?"

First she spoke bravely, then she bit her lip and questioned. It was wrong, he was browbeating her. He pulled and the boat crawled up into the water, eased itself down. She was a child in designer clothes, a girl with a fearful man.

The river traffic spun in and around them. A big cruiser slowed to hail them, the man at the wheel tight with muscle, his stomach two columns of knotted muscles, slathered with oil.

Flynn waved him on. "Exercise!" he shouted, and the knotted man nodded, fired the cruiser back up, the water itself roaring with the inboard.

"I'm sorry," he said to her. "No, I'm not dying. Of course I'm not, it's my sister who is, you know that."

She stared toward the islands, all sophistication again, but wary nonetheless.

"You rowing us backwards on purpose?" she asked.

"You mind?"

She shrugged, Emma's shrug.

"Bet you didn't think this would take so long," he said. "I mean your mother and me . . ."

"God, Flynn, you are weird!" she said. "I don't care what you and Emma do with each other."

He laughed. "No, I mean you probably didn't think she'd have to spend as long on my case. I mean, she must have told you, you know . . ."

She didn't know. She thought for a minute he was seasick, what with the damn boat climbing up and down in the rocking water, and Flynn pulling away at the oars like Charles Antlas or whatever his name was, all the while they're getting nowhere. Just when she figured he was mellowed out, he suddenly has to get hyper again. Definite big person move on his part, but she figured there was no choice but to go with it and hope he didn't get them hit by any of the million motorboats that started to show up as soon as they cleared the mucky bay with the pumpkin shits.

"Emma doesn't have cases," she told him. "She calls them friends or patients, mostly friends . . . except for her real cases, you know, the people she drags in and tries to change their lives. But the dying people are her friends. I'm surprised she hasn't given you that crap about the air being filled with friends. Emma's a real card, she is, it's all Casper the Friendly Ghost with her."

Flynn was really working away his brain cells trying to come up with what to ask next. He even forgot to row for a while, just when she spotted this big-ass freighter starting to make its way down the channel off in front of them a mile or so she guessed.

"I am real sorry about your sister," she said, figuring that might help him out.

It was turning out all wrong, she knew, and it was her fault for trying to live through it all before it happened, like Emma would say. She forgot about the river, how it could get all jammed with tourists and assholes, how the stupid big houses could get boring after a while, how it took you forever to get anywhere even if you had a good boat, which this tub definitely was not. She had imagined something neat, a quiet place where there were ducks and reeds sticking up and flowers on the water. She imagined Flynn like he was on teevee, all in control of himself and careful looking. Now here he was sweating and rowing assbackwards, with a steamer bearing down on him and some cloud passing by turning the air cold and the water dark and purple under it.

She just had to figure it was Emma who had messed him up and turned him crazy.

"But what did she say about me?" he asked out of nowhere.

Molly thought he meant his sister.

"I never heard her say anything. I never saw her really, although Emma says we met once on one of her famous visits."

"I mean Emma. What did she say when she was coming down to meet me in Syracuse?"

"Jeez-zuz, Flynn! Are we in the same world?"

"I'm not sure," he said. "Did your mother plan to meet me?"

"Don't you know?"

"No," he said. "I'm not sure. I don't know what I know."

"No wonder your life is full of piss," she said. "You have to believe in what you see, Flynn. Even I know that . . ."

They were getting nowhere, Flynn thought, going literally upstream and against the current.

Suddenly he had a mind to show her the skiff, maybe even take it out and let it catch the air, see if he could handle it. They needed to start over again.

"You want to see the boat your father fixed for me?"

She nearly leapt from the seat.

"Fan-fuckin-tastic!" she shrieked.

"Can you watch your mouth?" he said, and pulled the start rope, throttling up.

It was all a put-on, Molly knew, the scream and the potty mouth, all to get him to stop ozoning out on her. Sometimes you had to do something to shake things up, especially with Emma's men. It was just what she needed now, another boat, another one of Yves' creations. A boat made out of inlaid breadboards and full of vegetables. But it lit Flynn's eyes up and she knew enough to know he needed that.

How would it be, she thought, to just stop like that, to be always twelve years old, inside your head, a lady outside and a kid inside. There was a kid named Jason in their class, with big lips and the nicest eyes, and you could always see him thinking, and there was a big dumb smile he had when he got something right and Mrs. Mendel would hug him 'cause he liked that when he was right, just grab him around the head and pull him to her, reaching down around him from the aisle and hugging him in his seat, and some asshole would maybe make a dumb remark or a smooching noise, but nobody much would laugh 'cause you could see his eyes so happy looking out at everybody else from where Mendel hugged him, like there were sparklers in his eyes and he was so damn proud to be there, so proud it would almost make you cry.

But it wasn't like that for Flynn's sister, Molly knew, they didn't have mainstreaming then, although they had trained her some according to Emma. Probably, she wouldn't even be mainstreamed anyway, probably she was just too much a retard to do anything about, except dress her in those goofy, pretty cotton dresses and put ribbons in her hair and bring her oranges. She loved oranges, Molly knew, 'cause Emma brought her them before she was sick and couldn't take care of herself any more.

She studied Flynn, he was looking for something. Emma said he was gathering them all in like a lost family because he was looking for something.

The big ship with the Shell Oil shell was far to their right, to starboard in the deep channel, cutting the water with its deep grey bow, the butterfly-shaped radar thing spinning slowly round and round like the tin figures Emma had which ran around a candle in the wind. A couple of sailors looked down over the rail at the boats speeding up and back below.

Mainstreaming. Jason was the name of a real hero from the Greek stories and he sought a golden fleece. Aphrodite rose from the sea on a seashell like the Shell Oil thing. She rose in foam, born of the severed member of her titan father. All the assholes had really had a field day when Mendel told that story. A dick floating in the water, a jet-propelled cock. They made blubbing sounds with their lips like motorboats, but for once Mendel didn't yell at them. She just sat there and stared out half-smiling like some things were hard to understand. Jason had been grinning back at everyone and making the motorboat sounds.

The boat rocked on the slow wake from the Shell freighter, but Flynn kept them pointed upriver, holding fast and moving slowly through the wonderland surrounding Boldt Castle.

SEVENTEEN

My, he was a handsome one, tall and fine-boned, and he moved with a silent grace that reminded her of Red.

She had awakened out of sorts when the telephone rang, feeling slightly dyspeptic, her forehead sweaty, her hair out of place.

Despite the flush about her brow, the house had a chill in it, the uneasiness of shifting weather.

"Hello Bertie, are Jack and Molly there?"

Bertie poured a tumbler of water from the jug in the icebox, and lit herself a Virginia Slim, liking the contrast of the ice water and the dry smoke.

"I don't think so, darling. Would you like me to look? I've been napping."

He was in the doorway.

"Oh my!" she said, frighted.

"What is it Bertie?" Emma asked.

"I'm sorry to alarm you, Miss Alberta, my name is Romulus Hunt."

He bowed like a gentleman and extended his hand to grip hers. She felt herself redden, embarrassed that she had called out. She had pressed the phone against her shoulder while she took his hand, and she could hear Emma chattering in the receiver.

"I'm sorry, I . . ." She gestured to the phone.

Hunt made a sweeping gesture of acquiescence.

"Please . . . ," he said, then, pointing to the jug of water, "May I?"

"Jackie's not here?" she asked, and Hunt shook his head.

"Sorry, Emma, they're not here," she said into the receiver. "Is something wrong?"

"God, Bertie, is something wrong there?"

"It's only Willard," Bertie said, "scaring me half to death, creeping around."

Now why would she lie, she asked herself. Hunt did not seem to notice, or, if he did, he was too polite to show it.

"If he calls, tell him I'm heading back there," Emma said.

"Is something wrong, dear?"

Emma hesitated a moment. "No," she said, "no, it's only a mix-up about who should be where."

Isn't it all, Bertie thought, isn't it all a mix-up about who should be where?

Just then Willard swung around the doorway and posted himself between the black man and her, his long arms swimming before him exactly like the spider Molly claimed he was.

"This here's the fellow named Wolfman, Bert," Willard blurted, thumbing toward Mr. Hunt over his shoulder.

And who did he think she thought he was, she wondered. Just a passing troubadour? A tradesman come in for a drink? Yet she couldn't fault Willard his solicitousness. He was all a frazzle, the worst she had seen him since he arrived. The pollen mask was pushed up over his head and crushed, stray hairs fell frantic over his brow, his eyes were crusted with sleep, and his complexion flushed from the rush to protect her.

She and he both noticed simultaneously that his bedroom slipper was half off, and Willard commenced to speaking again while he hopped about on one foot, frantically trying to stuff the bony, pale-blue foot into the loose slipper. Mr. Hunt observed this circus with some curiosity but without laughter.

Whatever must he think of us, Bert thought.

"He's the one what clubbed Jack," Willard said, hopping still. "But it weren't exactly his fault entirely . . . That is, if you want to believe him . . ."

"Are you defending him or interrogating him, Mr. Walker?"

Willard still hopped, the ankle eluding his attempts to stuff the bony foot in.

"Dadgum booshwah, goddamn thumb!" he said.

It was a fine effort at sparing her sensibilities in the way she had insisted upon since his arrival, but you honestly could not help laughing. It was as if the foot itself went mad on him and would not settle, squirming out in front of him while he chased it down with the high-backed slipper.

But it was "thumb" that got her giggling, and, when she saw the slow, sweet smile unwinding on Mr. Hunt's face, and saw the merriment in his eyes, she began to laugh so hard she couldn't catch her breath. A neat little crease of pain in her diaphragm bent her over, and her eyes clouded, and she kept thinking thumb, thumb, each time the wave subsided, thumb. A blue foot all thumbs, by gum. Thum dum da dum, as the dam let loose, and all the foolish tension of the days and weeks past washed over her in a fit of laughing.

The great, strong arms gathered her up before she fell, his hand rubbing down along the backbone between her shoulder blades, smoothing out the crease of pain, putting the laughing fit to rest.

"There, mum," he said. "There, mum, it's okay. There, mum . . ."

"Dang dum loonybird!" Willard complained.

Thumb, mum, dum, she felt faint, the kitchen lights bright and the ceiling spinning. Mr. Hunt led her to her recliner, still holding her in his strong arms.

The room was dim in the gathering evening, only the flicker and flare of the color from the silent television washing over the walls. Richard Dawson was kissing the women of the Drum family on the Family Feud and Bertie felt a little bubble of laughter rise and break at the coincidental rhyme of the name. But everyone on the screen was laughing too, and so she felt it ease.

Mr. Hunt stood in the shadows of the screen, the flaring light playing against his dark green suit like the aurora borealis. Willard again stationed himself between them—whether linking himself to Hunt or holding him off, Bertie could not tell—the slipper in the hand at his side, the blue foot pale against the dark carpet, the mask now down over his ear.

"Well . . . ," she said and waited as another little bubble of laughter passed, "well . . . I must say I am sorry, Willard, and apologize also to you, Mr. Hunt."

"Don't trouble yourself, woman," Willard muttered. Mr. Hunt merely smiled.

"We have been under some tension here, haven't we, Willard?"

Willard agreed glumly, working his jaws.

The room smelled of tobacco and normally she would have said something, but she did not want to put Mr. Hunt in any further discomfort. The Drums won the game's first round and Richard Dawson hugged the young Drum woman as her brother or someone went off behind the curtain while she played the money round. Mr. Hunt wore a scent that mixed with the tobacco in a pleasant fashion, it reminded her of small white flowers she couldn't give a name.

"Well . . . ," she said again, "I should be thinking of feeding you gentlemen, and Emma's on her way . . ."

"Ah, LaChaise . . . ," Mr. Hunt said, pronouncing the syllables in a real French way.

Bertie felt a pang of jealous sadness for a lost past.

"LaChance," she said, meeting his white eyes in the dimness.

"Of course," he said. "It has been some time. I flew up here with Flynn then . . . for the boat he gave his father. I met her then with her husband. It was my last time here, except of course the ceremonies."

The ceremonies, Bertie thought with an awful sadness. It is why he is here now, why Jack has asked him. She remembered the scent of the flowers now, why she had thought it. Mr. Hunt all in white with a great white bouquet, he gave Joey that walking stick when Nell died.

"Wait," she said, and let the chair down and fled from the room. She found the stick in the umbrella stand in the front hall and brought it back, extending it to him with both hands, an offering.

"Well, hot damn," he said. He placed his two hands under hers on the stick and she let it roll to his palms.

"She don't like that talk none," Willard said quietly.

"Mr. Walker—" she said.

"No," Hunt protested, "I entirely agree. I'm your guest, Miss Alberta, and he is right to point it out." He winked at her then. "Especially after such a magnificent effort to avoid such talk on his part, don't you agree?"

Richard Dawson was holding the Drum girl with their backs to the camera as he pointed up to the tally board with the two sets of words. She had one hundred and sixty points on her responses alone, her brother only had to come up with forty and they would win.

"Yes," Bertie said, "yes."

"But I am afraid I cannot accept this," Hunt said, extending it to her again. "It was a gift to your brother, Miss Alberta, and it should as like remain with you. Consider it a gesture of support to your family in this difficult time . . ."

"Thank you," she whispered.

"Pshaw shit!" Willard muttered.

They neither looked at him, which was just as well, since his protest had only been half-hearted. Even Willard recognized a noble gesture.

"Ought to give him his dadgum bat if we're tradin' wampum," Willard grumbled, trying to work up a genuine complaint after failing to find real fault with Hunt's gesture. "Jack had it made up of ironwood, buck. But he never give it to you when you went and clubbed him."

"Willard!" she said sharply.

"We have an understanding, mum," Hunt said. "I know his kind."

"And I know your'n . . ."

Bertie chose to ignore this tussle and sat back down. The Drums were hanging on to each other and jumping up and down, turning round like a maypole or a carousel. They had won.

Willard sat himself down, Hunt stayed standing.

"There was more than one gift never given," Bertie said. Something in seeing the Drum family celebrate so made her sad, although she knew that it might only have been the lowering evening. It was a sad time for a woman alone, twilight.

"How's that?" Hunt asked.

"Hmmm?"

She was distracted by the beauty, by the scent of flowers, a cloud slipping in above the tobacco smell and the white-blossom cologne of Mr. Hunt, by the whole room blue-silver with the television light, and Willard stuffing his foot carefully into the old-fashioned slipper. Crickets rising, river in the air, Emma heading home without Jack and the child.

"You said something about a gift."

"The boat," she said, then, "Please make yourself comfortable, Mr. Hunt, please . . ."

He crouched way low on his haunches, steadying himself with a hand against the coffee table, and then slowly stretched out on the floor, first one long leg then the other, extending himself on the carpet and lying on his side. It was the most curious way to recline, as if he favored an injury, and yet he accomplished it with an unmistakable grace, stretching as comfortably as a great black cat, propping his head up with an elbow on the carpet, looking up at her from across the room.

She prayed it wasn't wrong to think of him as a cat, prayed it wasn't something he would mind her thinking.

"Jack never really had a chance to make the gift of the boat to my brother," she said. "Joey really wasn't the sort of man to go slowly into anything he'd begun, and when he faded it was swift. I don't know what the trouble was. Whether the carpenter wasn't ready yet, or Jackie didn't know quite what to do . . ."

"It was painful, was it, mum?"

She nodded in the silver light, watching Richard Dawson wave goodbye in silence.

Willard finally had the foot in and he stood to test it, scuffing about.

"Twisted the dadgum thing breaking up a double play a half century ago," he explained to no one in particular. "Acts up in the weather like the bursitey in my thumb. Can't pull the heel back proper . . ."

He scuffed again, a little two-step.

"Right as rain, boys, right as rain . . ."

She would sail off to sleep again if she didn't take care. She pulled the La-Z-Boy upright again, ejecting herself with a pop.

"Land's sakes," she said, "I ought to fix us supper."

I sound like the Waltons, she thought, talking like that. She twisted her hands together, feeling foolish.

Mr. Hunt started to rise again, unfolding the same way he had stretched down. Willard leaned back into the Morris chair with a satisfied huff.

He liked his supper, she thought with a quiet laugh, all my gentlemen callers like their supper. It was a good joke on herself, worthy of Richard Dawson.

Hunt was crouching again, watching her.

"Please . . . ," she said again, the same voice she had used with him before, "please . . ."

"But I insist," he said gently.

"Me too," Willard added. "Go on and fetch it if you're goin' ter . . ." and he made that cackling laugh.

"We could have roast," she said, "that is if you . . . Do you eat roast, Mr. Hunt?"

"She means do you fancy anything but poke chops," Willard explained.

"I don't at all," she said but she did she supposed.

Wolfman was back to his full height again.

"Don't stretch me, old man," he said quietly. "Get yo' bony butt off that chair, chump, we gonna get this lady some fancy steak!"

"No . . . ," she said, extending her hand.

"I insist," he said, and took her hand in his. "You do eat steak, don't you, Miss Alberta?"

"Why yes . . . ," she said before she saw the joke, and he broke into a broad laugh and squeezed her hand.

Willard scooted up and headed after them into the kitchen as fast as you can.

"Don't do to argue with no buck when he got his mind set, woman!"

"Don't do to stretch yo luck, chump," Hunt said. "You got yo' kite stretched high, old man, best be careful don't no one clip yo' line on you . . ."

And he smiled at her, so sweet, like Willard was some joke between them. Going to take you flying, mum, sometime when this be over. Take you high above them clouds to where the world stretch far and wide and birds slide beneath you. You ever looked out on the ocean an' seen the world tuck itself down on the edge uh the h'rizon? I take you so you see where the curve come down, where you see the actual shape uh the worl' . . .

"Now mind you go to the Grand Union," she said. "It's open all night and they've got those aisles of generic things. Black and yellow labels, as you first come in . . . Get some steak sauce!"

An' some Wheat Thins an cracklin's an Willard chaw an' hog maw.

Violet candies for my lady Emma.

Haagen Daaz for the girl, raspberry whirl.

Pickled clam fo' Flynn.

Jamaica pepper in a bottle.

Chinese hot oil.

Blue cheese an Pep'rich Farm cookies.

"An . . . mos' supr-i-i-i-i-i-sin' of all . . . yaas!"

Hunt paused, nearly whispering, he had them all laughing, even Willard, even Emma, making that raspy Muhammad Ali voice.

"Yasssuh!" he grunted. "Su-prize-in!"

He jumped up from the table and shadowboxed his way into the kitchen, dancing back out with the plate held high above him, a white towel over his arm.

"Shabazz sweet po-tay-toe pah! Righ'cheer in honkie heaven! Grand Union indeed! Can you believe, Mama, can you be-lieve!"

You see, it really had been quite a gay evening despite all. Emma had come along not long after the men left for the store, and though she was plainly distressed at whatever Jackie was up to, she had worked hard not to show it.

"They'll call," she said.

"Yes," Bertie said. "They'll call."

"It's an adventure," Emma said. "She probably put him up to it. Or maybe he was upset when I wasn't there when they got back . . ."

"Can't go wrong on dry land," Bertie said.

"If they're not here by midnight, Wolfman and I can drive along the highway."

"There you are," Bertie said, and hugged her. "There you are."

They both knew it was something to do with Esther, but they hadn't let themselves say it. An adventure was best, and meanwhile they had work to do, hauling the table out on the screen porch to get them out of the now muggy air, putting candles on, cutting roses in the night for the vase in the center.

The ceremonies, Bertie thought, we are making a funeral breakfast.

What Emma thought wasn't clear. She went into a fog for the most of the evening, smiling faintly whenever she caught Bertie studying her.

Though she had brightened when Hunt and Willard returned, after being gone the better part of two hours. The black man greeted her with a mighty whoop, setting the groceries down on the porch while he spun her round in his arms.

"Lookin' good, Frenchy Mama, look-in good . . . !"

"Been a long time, Wolfman," Emma said, her head down on his shoulder and a sad smile on her lips.

"You know each other then," Bertie said.

"Spent a whole life talking one night, didn't we, Mama?"

Wolfman set her down and touched her cheek, the dark finger lovely against the pale.

"Didn't we, Mama?" he said.

It was incredibly sad to Bertie, how he asked it. He knows, she thought. He knows why he is here. Jackie's gathered us all here, but the ceremonies belong to Mr. Hunt.

He looked into Emma's eyes a moment more, then jumped down from the porch as if he suddenly remembered something.

"Y'all wait right here," Wolfman said and trotted back to the car. It was the first Bertie had noticed that Willard hadn't appeared as yet.

He emerged from the car dressed as a spaceman, an astronaut, all in white from hood to booted feet, the paper jumpsuit scratching as he walked across the lawn, leaning on the arm of Mr. Hunt with white gloved fingers against the green arm. Only the dark canvas trunk of the gas mask broke the whiteness of the slowly moving apparition, and Hunt laughed with delight at the sight of their reaction to this walking cumulus. He freed his arm from Willard's grasp, and stood back to present him, his voice filling the night with gentle laughter, and yet somehow not just making fun.

"Here he be, ladies, the ultimate whitey! Free from stain and relieved of pain, unsullied as the lamb, the original white man, breathing sweet and ready to eat, gift wrapped and close yapped . . ."

Willard waddled on before him toward the porch, his eyes bright behind the transparent plastic visor, looking like nothing less than a blessed fool, a kid with candy.

"Oh Restless . . . ," Emma muttered like a prayer, and went down the stairs to help him. "Whatever has he done to you?"

Willard grunted an answer through the filtered snout, Wolfman interpreting for him.

"Done saved his life, Mama, what he said. Done saved his bony life . . ."

"Got ridda poison," Willard said, his voice sounding slightly amplified yet distant, like it was coming through a kazoo.

Emma had to laugh.

"You see," Hunt said and squeezed her arm, "man knows I saved him. Got to running his mouth at me all the way to the store, telling me how I poisoned him out on the porch, how he could feel himself failing."

"Wuz!" Willard grunted, breathy behind the mask.

"Had to buy him a half dozen plastic jugs uh spring water so's he could clear his system. Even then he still be complaining, pushin' that damn ol' cart on rattly wheels through the store and chugging on that water. So I remember me a army surplus store I seen on the way in from the airport up to Ogdensburg. We run down the highway but got there when they closed. Had to raise holy hell to rouse the man where he live upstairs, then tol' him how as Willard here be allergic to everything. I'll be damned if he don't scout up these here zootsuits, say they use 'em in aerospace and that be good enough for Willard, right, old man?"

Willard nodded. "Got me a pair," he rasped, as he moved into the house. "Never knew damn things existed. Coulda saved me long ago . . ."

It had been very gay, though Willard chewed tobacco behind his mask, though they each of them watched each hour pass as if noting how many hours it had been without Jackie calling, though Emma sank slowly into a worried and motionless fuss, her eyes staring out as if from underwater.

We are all waiting for Esther to die, Bertie thought, and it made her panic briefly, though she had to laugh when Mr. Hunt carried on, had to admit that the unaccustomed wine made her happier and less sleepy than her usual screwdriver nightcap.

And the candles burned down into slumping piles on the holders, and the June bugs vibrated against the screens of the porch, and the locusts began their long song, while Willard slept behind the mask, his paper suit rustling, and still Jack did not call, and Emma's eyes turned sadder each time Wolfman poured more of the champagne, until there were only her eyes and his in the dying light of the candles, Bertie watching them from far away and as if in a dream, her own eyes aching and occasionally dropping closed, dreaming of flying and of roses, not knowing what was said and what dreamed.

"Tell me, girl," he said to Emma, looking first at Bertie as if he did not see her.

It was as if hours had passed and morning was coming, Bertie thought, a gaining light in the east as the candles faded. She had eaten almonds and plums and thin, minted cookies from the sack of things he had brought along with the steaks from the store. She was slightly upset and very tired and unwilling to sleep, and yet unsure of things on account of the cold champagne. She could not be certain if what she heard at one moment followed upon what she thought she had heard at another.

It did not matter, they were all in a dream, waiting for a phone to ring. Red had gone out walking; she wondered if Mr. Hunt had brought any baseballs with him. She thought of their leather covers, smooth and tightly stitched in red, white as Willard's spacesuit.

"Bertie?" Emma whispered, but she wouldn't answer.

"I think he wants us to decide for him," Emma answered.

The black man started singing a hymn that began uh-hum.

They were sailing, leeward of the looming islands.

"That be about right for Bush . . ." Wolfman said. "That be about his style, Mama."

She knew he was talking about Jackie, and she thought it was a good name for him. There was something thin about him, something thorny. Bush seemed right and she tried to tell them, her tongue too thick to form the words. They looked toward her, looked away again toward the gaining light.

Why do you say that?

It happen with pitchers, Mama, it happen to them. They be different than other men, used to sitting three days with no worry on they mine, happy as ol' bony ass over here in he paper cocoon. Forf day they rule the worl', like some upside-down god, don't you know, work one day and three they rested. It go to you head, girl, it go to you head. Don't be used to knowin' what it is when you spen' the wrong side uh yo' life throwin' no ball, don't be used to knowin' . . .

What it is, Mama, what it is.

A chump's choice, you dig, ain't no choice at all.

Whether that sister be rigged to some machine, or whether she be free of it and hardly breathing, you dig? Ain't no percentage to that bet. You tell me how you gonna vote Mama do it come to that?

Tell me.

Bertie watched slow birds settle, coming across the sky in a slow glide, their feet reaching for water, skidding to a glide on folding wings afloat rippling water.

"Tell me."

"For life," she said.

"Ain' no life, bitch! Ain' no life . . . Not in the general sense, only the particulars we call existence, you dig? Up high rocking on the edge of the cloudbank, wings flashing, ain't no life! Only you, sweet Emma, you and the engine and the titanium skin, you dig? Rare metals and gases, oxygenlessness, blessed space, amazing grace . . ."

You think you vote on it up there? On top of the air?

Emma shook her head, again and again, her hair slashing like whips, stirring the candlelight.

No, she moaned, no, I don' know, and he moaned with her. The light swirled in the eddying air, shot off like silver moths.

I vote, Bertie thought, the words coming slow. I vote . . . to keep her, as Nell did, holding the moon in her arms. Let her sail on, like the Quinlan girl, watch eternity pass.

They watched her. They did not seem to hear. I am not the one who is dying, Bertie thought. The light was thin milk now, dazzling to one who has stayed up all night. Mr. Walker's suit was startling bright as the light gained, white as bone, and, as if it were a memory buried in light, she unaccountably recalled the bullhead fishing, the late March hunts from years past. The water would crawl with boats, flat punts, jonboats, smooth sailing things moving slow through the night. All the men with bamboo poles slung over their shoulders, arms wrapped round them like the crucified Christ, the air yellow with the lanterns' flare across the swamps and inlets, a low murmur on the water, the croak of awakening frogs, the rubber hips boots squeaking as they adjusted their weight, occasional drum beats as a punt pole struck a wooden hull.

The night smelled of life, of moss and worms and water and air, of cattail shoots, lily pads and the first exhalations of the fermenting muck of the shallows, a low mist rising from the swamp surface like the fog upon ice under the sour packing straw in the ice shed, and the fish down there somewhere dark and cold, iron-skinned and sweet-fleshed and Medusa-snouted.

Someone, for a lark, had thrown a phosphor flare out on the water where it hissed and sputtered and then sank slowly, sending the yellow light pooling from it, turning the water green, outlining the dark, slow shadows of the bullheads.

You could feel the fever rise in the men, even a little girl bundled in the center and looking out could feel it. They seemed to laugh all at once across the whole dark swamp. Bullheads there to harvest, a fry to come, the flare finally snuffing itself and the water dark again.

"Count 'em up, Emma, count 'em up. One vote already for the machine, and you know ol' Restless, he gonna vote for the paraphernalia.

"That leave me and you. Two and two, am I right?"

She nodded.

Two and two.

But you're forgetting Molly, she'll vote too, Emma thought. Though she fears so much, you could never be sure, never know what she was learning this long night on the water. No matter what Bertie thought, Emma knew they were on the water.

"They be some things in every life don't be no one can know, Mama. Everybody got at least one time in they life be unique, you dig, if it only be dyin' . . . Havin' babies, hit your first home run and see it rising, ride all night back an forf across a cold channel a million miles away from home, something be something . . .

"No telling for Flynn how he feel now, no telling for Bush. I remember exactly that last day myself, you dig. Once they pull me off and push me away and somebody got my arms pinned behind me, could feel that violence subsiding, you dig, like the taste of blood in your mouth when you bash you lip, flooding you like the taste of pennies all warm in you mouth and then fading away as she dries up. Violence be like that, rush at you head, press against you skull and forehead, makin' you eyes flare, then suddenly leavin' you weary. Jus' starin' out there at the circle, a whole pack of guys standing there over him, watchin' the blood flow down, watchin' the trainer press the towel against his head, watchin' you and the shadows fallin' . . . You mind?"

What.

You mind if I do some?

A gold lozenge in his pale palm, exactly like a compact, the lid flipped up, a mirror, a pale light flitting over his face as he emptied the snuff out on the tablecloth, twisted the bottom section, unscrewing it.

"No." She shook her head. "I mind nothing this morning."

"Finally," he said, "the saps let me go, you dig, give me a last push like they been waitin' to do that for a time. Push me off to where this constable waitin' to escort me into the clubhouse. Khaki shirt and blue pants with a stripe down the side, blue hat also with gold braid, patent leather Sam Brown belt. These Canadian boys they like to do it up, look more like a zoo guard, you dig, not no cop. Shy-town got cops, white shirts and blue lights makin' the street crazy . . ."

He sprinkled the powder carefully from the unfolded, waxy envelope, putting a little pile of white on the mirror lid. Took a steak knife from the table, wiped it with the napkin, then spread the powder carefully, marshalling it into a thin line with the tip of the blade. From his shirt pocket he took a small silver straw, covered a nostril, ran the straw along the thin line, snuffing it up, leaned back and sighed.

"Didn't do no nose until after then, if you believe me. Didn't need none of them, you dig . . ."

His voice was hollow now, the sinuses running, his eyes two silver disks in the gaining dawn.

"Life had its satisfaction, Mama, I'm tellin' you. You want to know the truth? Truth is I think I got to Flynn because I knew it was over, 'cause I knew he would let me go that way. I remember the constable's hand holding my arm, guiding me off, real careful and considerate like they do all up there in Can'da, but firm about it, you dig, no question we goin' . . ."

He made another little line and took it up the other side.

"But I make him stop, you dig. Not make him, but sort of indicate it's what I want to do, and he looks in my eye to let me know no more shit, then leaves the hand go. I look back at Flynn. He's up now, holding the towel over his head and eye like he just had a hangover. We meet just once then, you understand, our eyes just meeting for an instant. Twenty thousand people out there and no one seeing this instant.

"Asshole, I think. I love you, Bush. I owe you one.

"Then the constable's arm touches mine again and we start walking, Bush and me, walking in time with each other to different places. Skipper comes down the runway to the clubhouse. I can hear his cleats along the wood from far away, and I'm already showered, already packing my bag from the locker.

"You're gone, fuckhead, he says. You're gone from baseball, gone from earth. And he spits on the floor and walks back to the dugout before I can give him no static.

"I dress alone, answer the questions for the constable, promise I won't leave the Province of Ontario for the following twenty-four hours, tip the old fart clubhouse boy three twenties in Eskimo money to get rid of the stuff before I go off, then walk through the writers and the teevee people without sayin' nothin', drive out to the airport and get on my plane, fly away home.

"It was the end of the world for me, Emma, do you understand? Even under my circumstances, the end of the world. Had my leg shot up in '70 and played ball in six months, but when I had to quit playin', you understand, took me three full years to function again. You can't expect less of Bush, Mama, can't expect a whole lot less considering the troubles he's seen."

He had the gold lozenge together again, the sun in his hand, turning it to catch the light, holding it tightly in his palm when the phone rang.

EIGHTEEN

She had seen it before, both bigger and smaller, not propped like this on a rack of crossed timbers, but hanging in the air as if in a dream, the dark wood burnished and curving to a high narrow prow, the stem sheer as a knife, higher maybe than this was, although the boat wasn't much longer.

"My dad really made this?"

Her voice echoed in the tin building. Flynn was walking around her, around the boat, touching the seams and the places where the wood curved up from the bottom in a smooth slope that reminded you somehow of snakes.

"Make it?" he said. "No . . ." But then he changed his mind just as he ducked under the bottom of the boat near the far timbers, crawling under and coming back toward her, his voice softer.

"I suppose you could say he did," he said. "She wasn't much but a promise til he started at her. Didn't know a damn thing about them either, though lord knows he tried to act like it."

He turned to the old troll who had let them in the building. "Isn't that so, Jess?"

The old man grinned and spat. "Expect so, Jackie," he said, cackling just like Willard. "Frenchy feller talked himself into bein' a shipwright . . . though it took a heap a talk to convince himself he knew 'bout beveled lapstrake . . ."

It made her mad how he laughed, although she knew what they meant about Yves. You never could catch him pretending he didn't know anything, no matter what. It was just his way, though, and probably part of what made him and Emma split. Emma just didn't like lies.

Molly was starting to believe that every old croaker got to the point where he did nothing but chew and spit and cackle, moving around on spooky silent feet like spiders. This one and Willard both, you'd think they were born with sneakers instead of feet.

Leave it to Flynn, she had thought when they got to Fisher's Landing, leave it to Flynn to find the ugliest place on the river to keep his boat. From outside, the tin building was washed with rust in big splashes coming down from the roof, another set working up from the ground like brown teeth. Most of the windows were replaced with white sheets of metal with red flying horses and the ones that weren't were so grundged up with dirt and grease that it didn't matter. Even the old dock where they tied up was half-way falling into the water; an old-fashioned gas pump with no hose was rusting away next to the water and the deck boards were so rotten they chipped away and fell through some places where you walked.

"What happened to Floyd?" she asked the old man.

"How's that?" he said.

Flynn was crawling under the boat again, starting his second time around it.

"Floyd!" she said loud enough to blast his deaf, hairy ears.

If he cut out those little tufts of grey hair from his ears, maybe he would hear some shit now and again, she thought.

Just then he cackled again. They must think it's boss to cackle, Molly thought, real popular riff with the old codgers, cackling is.

"Nothing happened," the troll said. "He never was, so nothing could happen."

"Your name's Jess," she said. "The sign outside says Floyd's Marine."

"Yup," he said, like it explained everything.

Cackle again and you're dead, she thought. I'll drag you out there by your hairy ears and drive your head down through your crumbling, rotting dock.

For a minute she thought he was coming toward her, the way he looked at her and smiled.

Pat my head and you're really dead, you old fart!

Instead he crawled off after Flynn.

"She worthy?"

"What?" the troll yelled.

"She worthy?" Flynn repeated loudly.

Cackle. Choke. Spit. Then, "Thought you was asking 'sea worthy,'" he said. "Thought you had big plans, boy."

"Could," Flynn said. "Is she?"

"Prob'ly she is," Jesse said, "but she need a sweep for sure then,
and fair weather, and a helluva lotta luck with you at the helm . . ."

He just about cackled enough to die then, just creaming his
jeans about his lame joke. And there was Flynn laughing along with
him, laughing at himself really, you'd think big people had no sense
sometimes.

Still she had been surprised to see how neat the old man kept
the place inside, how—except for him spitting—the floor was clean
enough to eat off of, and how the whole place smelled like tar and
oil and something else like cotton, but real clean, clean as the ropes
coiled and hung on the pegs along the wall, clean as the beautiful,
smooth boat high on its padded timbers, the soon to be setting sun
flooding in upon it when the old man opened the big sliding door.

She had seen it before in the slides Mendel showed for mythol-
ogy. There was a boat in Oslo that they used to bury a king, only it
ended up on ice and so they saved it in this museum, hanging it in
the air. Mendel showed it to show what it was like when the mighty
Thor went fishing for the big serpent when he was a kid, and she
had another slide that showed a picture of him fishing, part of the
carving from an old stone cross somewhere in England. He held his
hammer in the air and in the other hand he held this giant line to
fish with. Under the boat big huge fish pushed against the bull's head
he used for bait.

It was real eerie. Both Thor and this other guy who was also a
giant, and whose bull it was before Thor twisted its head off, and
who later chickened out and cut the line and let the monster get
away, were bald, their heads exactly like eggs. Still, nobody much
laughed, probably because there was a superhero named Thor in the
comics and so he went over real well, not near as bad as that faggot
Apollo.

Mendel said the story about Thor fishing for the serpent showed
the wisdom of the Norse, it meant that even the gods weren't ready
to assume their powers when they were young.

"All young people wrestle against the elements," she had said,
"and eventually, like Thor, they do win their struggles. It is just that
you have to wait until the time is right."

Something about her saying that had seemed right at the time, though Molly got to wondering about whether Mendel wasn't being just a little bit of a bullshitter when she said they'd win for sure.

Besides showing that the carving on the stone cross was pretty realistic, Mendel said the real boat showed that the Norse weren't the dorks everybody thought they were, although she didn't put it quite like that. Then she asked if anybody saw some movie from a thousand years ago with Kirk Douglas or some other cretin getting burned up on a boat after he died.

He wouldn't, she thought, he wouldn't, would he?

Flynn and old Jesse Floyd were way in the back of the building up on a wooden balcony thing, above where the ropes hung on the wall. She shouted across at them.

"How long's this thing, Flynn?"

He was pulling something out of a big drawer built into the wall, and he paused and consulted with the troll before he answered.

"Twenty-three feet exactly," he shouted. "Why?"

"The king's boats were twenty to thirty!"

"That's nice," he yelled and went back to helping Jesse.

They were hauling out sails from the drawer, letting them drape down over the rail of the balcony like big banners. Big jerk probably thought she meant someone named King, or maybe didn't hear her at all. She walked down the floor toward the balcony end.

"You think I'm gonna go out in this with you, you're nuts, Flynn."

"Yes," he said.

"I mean it," she said. "I'll call my mother right now and have her come get me."

Flynn poked his head over the rail.

"What will you call," he asked, "Chippewa Bay dockside?"

He laughed then.

"Don't worry," he said. "The only sailing I'm gonna do now will be to see if I remember how to turn her. Then I thought we'd tow her back with us, that is, if you don't mind that . . ."

"You're not going to sail without me, are you?"

She heard the cackling come from behind the sailcloth, then saw the old man's head next to Flynn's.

"What are you staring at, Floyd-boy?"

For a minute she thought he was going to spit on her, the way he stared down at her.

"Looking at a natural woman, I expect," he said, his voice surprisingly nice. "Anybody who can jibe like that in short water, she got to be a woman . . . Wanted to check you out again, make sure my eyes ain't deceived me none about your age."

"What do you see?" she asked.

He ducked his head away and spit on the deck of the balcony.

"A woman fair enough . . . ," he said, "but a girl yet in the hull."

She floated on air.

Wouldn't you just know, she thought, it's what comes of hanging around Flynn and his band of merry maniacs. Got so used to Willard's crap, never noticed the old man was flirting all the while. He really was sweet, when she thought back, not quite like her Grandpère LaChaise, who she always remembered in his ridiculous swimming suit, his thing hanging down in a little nylon sack, spindly little legs and duck feet, a tight round belly and muscles in his arms, always smoothing back his black hair or fingering his pencil moustache. And not at all like Emma's father, changing from his black banker's vest to a green tartan vest on weekends, the shoes always polished so hard that the leather cracked, his sad blue eyes gleaming far away behind his face whenever, uneasily, he hugged her, the eyes watching her the same way they watched Emma.

But dead now, she thought, gone behind the grandmother she never met, but who seemed something like Bertie the way Emma talked about them.

And soon Esther will be dead too, Molly knew, and she'll know no more than I do now when she goes. Which isn't much, except probably there is a heaven, and it's something like a party where everybody's there but you can't go home. And there are friends in the air, if you believe Emma, and they shine on like the stars which aren't really there, only the light from them burning a million years ago.

Suddenly she felt real sad again and she wanted to go out. Flynn and Mr. Jesse were downstairs again, wheeling out a long wooden trailer thing and maneuvering it this way and that to steer it under the cross beams.

She slid the huge door open a crack and started to go.

"Take care on that dock, young woman," Mr. Jesse said, looking up at her. "'Tis fair to rotted away by now, I'm afraid."

She nodded and left. Flynn was still wheeling the trailer thing under the boat.

She went way down to the end of the dock and, when that wasn't far enough, she got into the rental boat and sat way at the back looking down through the kaleidoscope skim of oil that floated out from the motor, watching the sunfish or pumpkin eyes or whatever you wanted to call them nip at the pieces of stale corn chips she crumbled into the water.

They took what you gave them, she thought, and the little ones got more because they were faster, although now and then a big fat one would shoot out from the shadows under the dock and spear a fat crumb, chasing away the rest for a minute until they swirled back.

When you looked real close, you could see the tiniest little minnows swimming in and out of the sun eyes, so tiny and silver that you almost never noticed them, and yet all of them swimming in patterns, first one way then the other, flicking forward and back.

In this way she forgot.

Flynn brought the boat out with a big whoop that made her stand and clap her hands despite herself, as if this launching was a goddamn big deal she had been waiting all her life for. The boat rocked when she stood and she had to slip back down and grab the sides so she wouldn't fall out.

Out in the light the skiff was more beautiful than you could have imagined seeing it up on the timbers. There were two boss-looking caned seats facing each other at the rear, with spindles on the woven chair backs like old antiques and the top of the back and the arms all one piece of bentwood like Emma's rocking chair. Another woven seat bottom sat on the middle of the front bench near the pins for the oars.

All around the seating compartment there was a raised rail of inlaid wood in a pattern of pegs and diamonds. The whole cockpit seemed held together with pegs, even the curved wooden straps that held the benches for the seats to the ribs of the sides. There was a little deck in back and a bigger one in front, closed off around the cockpit kind of like a kayak, both decks inlaid with thin fanning wedges of honey wood in a sunburst pattern. The pins for the oars and the rings for the ropes at the front and the sides were polished brass, as was the handle at the top of the centerboard.

It was varnished inside and out, the dark wood gleaming. On the face of the rail at the front of the cockpit, dim little inlaid wooden letters said "A. Bain—Clayton, NY," and under that in smaller but brighter inlaid letters, "Restoration : Y. LaChaise—Gananoque," then "J. Flynn, Capt."

"My father," Flynn explained when she touched the letters.

"Mine too," she said and laughed.

It was just like her father to lie even when he signed a boat; he never lived in Gananoque but he always liked that name.

Jesse wheeled another trailer out, this one loaded with the sail and mast and oars. He had a coil of the new rope over his shoulder and he payed it out several times between his outstretched arms, measuring the painter. Tying the free end to the brass fitting at the bow, he cut to the measure with a huge folding knife from his pocket, then folded the blade back in and folded out a chromed spike which he used to splice off the loose strands of hemp at the cut end.

As he wove the rope back into itself, he talked softly to Flynn.

"When you want to bring her about, you rush forward smackdab to the mast cone, remember. That'll bury her bow for certain and rise her stern up and into the wind. Be damn certain when she sail shakes out in the wind you get your butt aft and raise her up. You follow?"

Words, Flynn thought, all words, however wonderful. Can't see anything to follow til you feel the wind in your hand.

"Mostly," he said.

"You mess up, you use your sweeps," Jesse said, his eyes following the spike in and out of the hemp. "Want me to handle the stepping up?"

"No," Flynn said, and he went to step the mast, careful to place the brass partners.

My father did this, Flynn thought, stepped and unstepped, spliced lines and wove his own nets, carved plugs, hammered spoons, tied leader, replaced eyelets and ferrules, broke down reels and motors and put them back together again. I have done little in my life aside from throwing baseballs, driving cars, riding airplanes. Now am I asked to decide on someone's life.

The girl's father knew more about how life actually works, tapping his little wedges into place to fit a board to a predestined curve, carving and fitting the walnut letters of his inlaid name.

Jesse kept after him.

"You using the running block, Flynn?"

"No."

Jesse nodded his head without looking up from the rope.

"Have to splice off another line for you then," he said, "so's you don't lose her coming about . . . Better that way, nonetheless, gauge the wind against your hand . . ."

"We don't have time to splice another," Flynn said. "Just wrap it for me and gunk it up with glue. You needn't worry that I'll drop her."

"Speaking of which, the young woman got a life vest?"

"Just cushions is all they give you, in the boat."

"Fix you both up then." Jesse looked up, tying it off. "Give the little lady a gift with my compliments. Vest and the whole doo, foul weather gear and sailing gloves and all. My pleasure," he said, cutting Flynn off. "When this one's gone, won't be no more Floyds . . ."

He smiled over at Molly when he said the name, it was a joke between them now.

"Flynn here's been my sole customer for years now, young lady. Made a mighty profit of him, didn't I, Flynn?"

No, Flynn thought, it was me who made the profit from this deal. You kept something alive for me, Jesse, and I owe you for that.

He had sailed her then, and not half bad in the smooth four-knot breeze, a little slow hitting the bow on a tack, a little clumsy getting the centerboard up and down, but satisfactory generally, making her turn on the breeze, keeping clear of the boom, sailing slack but with a fair plane, a decent wakeline. Feeling good enough about it that he could spare an arm to wave at the child and the old man arm in arm on the far dock.

Took in water only twice. Once when he couldn't get enough purchase for hiking out on a leeward tack and took some water, a second time capsizing her on purpose to slow her at the dock, feeling her sink to slow like a huge water-ski.

The capsize had them both laughing at him, but it served its purpose. Not going to sail her downriver, he thought, just tow her home.

"Hadn't meant it to be like this, you see," he told Emma on the phone. "Hadn't meant to sail her home."

He hadn't. It was maybe six o'clock by the time they left Jesse's with the skiff under tow, maybe twenty nautical miles down to

Chippewa with the throttle open as far as she'd go, the skiff riding well with an oar lashed for a rudder. They'd have made good time if the rental boat rode as well as the skiff. As it was they had the Evinrude rattling and smoking, pushing against their own wake, settling her down when there was too much traffic so as not to have the skiff take on water from the chop. It was probably an unnecessary caution since she rode in good trim, down slightly by the stern, the bow high and buoyant in the calm of their wake, the weight of the mast and gear enough to hold her trim.

Flynn's arm ached only mildly from handling the line in the test sail. All in all he felt extravagantly good, better than he ought to. It was kind of exciting. People waved from passing boats, saluting the skiff, and Molly was back to twenty questions again, sitting proudly, courtesy of Jesse, in her new ancient cork-filled life vest and her oilskin sou'wester, the slicker folded into a bundle on her lap.

What kind of things did he talk about with her father?

Did Yves tell fibs?

How long had he known Jesse?

Did he think there was a heaven?

Could fish smell things?

Had he ever tried to hurt someone throwing a baseball at their head?

Wasn't Boldt Castle really sappy?

Did stars ever die from the sky?

Why had he been so weird on the way upriver?

Could they sail it just once, if Emma said yes?

Then Emma wasn't there and he could see no reason not to, with the breeze picking up as night fell, and the sky still light, the water smooth lavender.

They stopped for a moment at the store where they had rented the boat, getting two Pepsis and two hot dogs for four dollars, Flynn buying a couple of battery-powered running lights, an aerosol horn, flares and an anchor on sort of a lark. A sad-eyed woman in a gardening apron waited on them, giving Molly a couple of chocolate bars and a single rose as gifts.

It was her day for gifts. Especially, Flynn thought, when the man she's with drops fifty bucks on impulse.

They didn't know then that Emma had been there and gone,

sent away by mistake because the woman's husband had pulled the wrong ticket on a previous rental return, and then put her note to them in his pocket without telling his wife.

Flynn hadn't meant to sail her. But the skiff hissed lightly as she caught the wind, Molly crooning to herself and leaning sideways to let him pass forward each time he had to bring her about; and Flynn began to catch himself in the rhythm of it, playing the sail out, hauling her tight, old lessons coming back to him, more recent lessons beginning to make sense.

Now and again he had to row her around when he missed a tack, but otherwise they ran easy, leaving a slight wake behind her as she ran on the fair southwestern breezes from the shore.

They had made Oak Point on the down leg when he knew he would have to bring her about for the way home, jibing across a stiff breeze to make the turn, running fore and aft for all the tacks to bring them back along the leeward side of Chippewa Point.

By then his arm and shoulder were aching like middle innings from the line and centerboard, and he was half afraid to jibe, and more afraid of the Chippewa lee. Anyway they were running well into the twilight, making maybe seven, eight knots, Flynn figured, and the girl was back in earnest to her twenty questions.

Seven knots would put them into Morristown by the time it was pitch dark, they could tie up there and call Emma, be back before midnight and greet Wolfman, wake early in the morning and attend to Esther.

It was a miscalculation, they were making only four knots at best in a fair breeze and a narrow river under a half moon, but they were running fair and he did not want to lose her now that he knew the feel of the wind in the sheet, the pause and dip as she slacked and lowered, the rush and tug as she climbed back on the wake. Flynn felt like they could sail forever, and he wasn't really sure if he could make her stop without swamping her again.

As night settled he set the forward running light, taking it forward in a slight hop on a mild tack, holding the sheet close as he bent to set it, dropping the centerboard again as he slid aft in the dark.

It made him grin to do this, by now it was all a dance in the dark, the thwarts and benches printed in his mind, Molly's form like some breathing dark. He set the aft light and sat, letting the sheet line extend his arm.

There were fishermen out tonight, you could see the lights up and down the line. With his free hand he fished through Jim's tackle box, setting the light on its cover like his father used to. He grabbed the girl's rod and chewed off the leader, attaching a ten-inch braided wire, tying the knot carefully with the free hand, holding it firm with the hand wrapped to the sheet. He hunted and found a number four gold spinner with what looked to be number two treble hooks trimmed in white bucktail, a good rig for muskie with an extra split-shot to make it run deep.

"Going after the white whale, Flynn?"

She had moved from the seat facing forward to the seat facing aft.

"Maybe," he said and laughed. "Maybe."

She told him the story of Thor and Midgard and what her teacher said. He let the line play out until the spinner ran deep and set the drag and reached the rod up to her.

"See if she's right, your teacher," he said.

"I thought you could tell me . . ."

They were running free, the wake splashing off the freeboards, the sheet taut and everything in good trim. It was a sledding silence.

"Why did you think my mother would trick you?"

Flynn watched the silvery water slide by, the half moon there in its hollows, the whole shore sighing as they slid by.

"It's all too neat, isn't it?" he asked her. "Emma just happens to be on that road, just happens to work at what she does. I just happen to be unable to function."

"You're functioning fine now," she said. "You are weird, Flynn, you know that?"

"I suppose," he said.

"You ever think that it might have been you who planned it?"

"What?" he said. The bow dipped and then rose again, the breeze hesitating. He felt the sheet go taut again.

"All of it," she said. "You knew Emma from way back, she even helped your father. You're on your way home to see about your sister, and you see Emma on the highway, her dippy car broke down. It gives you an excuse to lose it . . ."

It was all a story, like Thor and the boat.

"Which is it," he asked her, "Hardy Boys or young Sigmund Freud?"

"What?"

"Your questions. You sound like a bad detective."

He felt the skiff tip as she bent, then right as she scooped the water at his face, the silver flashing.

"You're so full of shit, Flynn!"

"Watch the potty-mouth, pre-pube," he said. They both laughed.

"She'll be pissed at you," Molly yawned. "We're not going back, are we, Flynn?"

He could tell from her voice she was getting tired, water did that, running in the damp air, the lulling sound of the hull racing on its plane.

Depends on what you mean as back, natural woman, depends on what you mean as back. There was truth in what she said, it was a plausible story. They were going downriver now on a long dark chute toward the ocean, now and then a long tack taking them over the line of the channel to Canada, another tack taking them back. Everything wound in and out. The stem cut the water under, the line ran on a deep angle to the spinner, the moon sailed eastward, already morning gained in the east over the ocean. Emma's fears wove with her daughter's, Flynn's with them both and with his sister. Bertie sat alone with Willard and Wolfman at her side, a sleepy nurse watched the green eye of the screen that was Esther's life. Flynn's child swam like a grotesque tadpole in whatever was heaven, pursued by the tears of his mother like the diamond splash of wake wash over the gunwale. A woman floated on a rubber raft somewhere in the water; Jim's lights illuminated the river, sunfish swimming in and out of the light, bullheads lurking in the muck at its edges.

"Gonna marry her, Flynn? Gonna marry Emma?"

She was yawning deeply now, slumped over in the woven seat, the slicker tucked under her head as a pillow.

I can't, he thought, I've struck her, no woman can trust her life to a man who's hit her.

"No," he said softly. "No, it isn't right."

"Why not!" she said sharply and raised her head. "Why can't life be right once? Why can't it end happy and pretty and right?"

"Because . . . ," he said, hearing the wind slap the sheet then let it go, the water splashing, the drag on the reel cranking slightly with the following swell. "Because there is more to it than love," he said, "more than a series of however many days. There's knowing things . . ." He was trying to find the words. "There's days and weeks of knowing things involved in it. You see how someone walks and combs her hair, see what makes her laugh, witness her crying . . . It's very complicated . . . .groceries and music and laundry and stopped sinks and oil changes . . . turning the channels, walking up stairs, making the bed again in the morning, shaking the sheets out . . . watching them billow and then settle, smoothing them across the mattress . . . I'm used to maids, you see, hang a little plastic sign on the doorknob, wait in the lobby while someone carries your bags . . . I don't know things . . ."

I am a foolish man, Flynn thought, to say this to a girl. He listened to the wind and prayed she slept.

"Crap," she whispered. "You know them if you can say them . . ."

She knew he knew it was right.

It was that with Jim, he thought, when he came back, what killed him. Things. He wasn't used to things, took it off the road near Sparrowhawk Point, the car flying, sunk in water.

"Tell me about your brother," she said.

It was not a dream, he asked her to repeat it. She was nearly sleeping. "Jim," she said, protesting. "Tell me about Jim."

"We are a great and beautiful family," Flynn said, "fortunate people, all in all. We have lived rich lives, even Esther, although we died young."

"You aren't dead, Flynn, you asshole. You didn't all die young."

And he knew then she was right. There was he thought she knew no doubt from the first, the road north and seeing her, the card about Esther in his hand. The child knew he knew.

She was right to say it. Jim had come home drunk, Mama was already dying though no one knew. She had a predisposition to it, you see, the vapors settling into her lungs bringing a mild case of pneumonia.

That wasn't right, it was a story, she died three years after Jim.

She was dying, each spring unable to get her breath, and Jim came back drunk, the war was over and he was always drunk. Their father met him at the door, it made Nell cry. She didn't like them at each other's throat. You know things, Joey, she would say, Jim doesn't know them yet, none of them do, not even Jackie, not certainly poor Esther. His mother was dying like the sliding, dimming moon, the water turning darker.

It wasn't true, only how we remember.

Flynn held her hand, it was long and cool, the nails colored silver like the moon. There was a scuffle in the hallway, shouts.

Go to them, Jackie. Your father is worried to death about him, it makes him crazy to see him like this. He wants so much for everything to be all right.

He was too late. Their father had decked him. He stood looking at his bloody hand. One punch and he took all Jim really had to fall back on.

I remember sailing in, Jack. They made us jump into a firefight so's we would get the idea we were there for real. After however many hours in the air from Okinawa, the compartment steamy on account of the lousy ventilation system, we were ready for some night air. I got them all out and then I jumped and the chute popped with a giant whacking noise. It was all silence then, floating down into the jungle night. Come all the way from San Francisco on a single flight with refueling stops, then floating down into the silent night.

I saw the tracers before I heard them screaming. My kiddies hanging below me while they shot them from the air. I pissed my pants, Jack, I'm not afraid to tell you I pissed my pants. Here I was the jumpmaster, head honcho, hot shit Ranger and they're shooting my babies below me, getting ready for me . . .

Next morning someone had some Asian sunshine, a little rush of grey powder, mix 'em up and smile . . . I started then, Jack, and ain't about to stop yet.

He heard the sheet pop, felt the silence take them downwind, sliding along the night, the dark chute to the sea.

Saw him lying there and Pop crying over his bloody hand.

You fucking asshole, you're killing her. You're killing them.

You're killing you, Flynn thought, and I'm sorry.

For we are a beautiful family, a trail of silvery foam follows us as we glide through the water.

They made it somewhere near St. Lawrence Park by early morning. Flynn's arm and eyes were worn and he couldn't go any longer, couldn't find the energy to anchor then wade in and call her. The girl . . . . the young woman slept, her legs curled over the bentwood arms, her arm over her face to ward off the insects.

She couldn't sleep. She thought of Eric the Red, he was here once, here in America, left little copper coins the shape of the sun up somewhere near Maine. It was a long way to sea, like Eric the Red, like Jason and the Golden Fleece. There were mosquitoes everywhere and she couldn't sleep. Heard Flynn crying, heard him gather in the sail and tie it back, drop the anchor with a plooking splash, heard him crank the line in.

"Whatta ya know, a big old bullhead!"

Midgard. The stars rocking high above her, the water still rocking in her stomach when you stopped.

She said she wished there was a radio.

So Flynn sang to her.

It's only a paper moon shining over a cardboard sky.

"We'll meet you at the hospital," he told Emma on the phone. "Get everyone dressed and meet us for a celebration."

"Meet us at the ballfields," he said. "That will be better. We're all all right, Emma, we really are."

NINETEEN

They met him at the ballpark. Bertie wore a great wide straw hat on account of the sun, Emma wore a long lavender dress and they sat in the bare bleacher stands, watching while Mr. Walker pitched to Wolfman from the peach basket full of balls they had taken from Bertie's closet.

They waited for Jack and Molly.

Mr. Walker wore the new white suit, the second one, the spare, and he kicked his leg up high as he pitched, the paper crinkling with his crazy corkscrew motion. Wolfman used the ironwood bat, the grey wood smooth as soap and probably all of forty ounces. It slowed him enough to keep him from getting an edge on the old bird dog. He too wore a white suit, it was like old-fashioned baseball seeing the two of them there, the ball cracking off the heavy bat and sailing far skyward, off high over the fence with its ragged edge of blue flax.

Some boys stopped to watch and laugh, but they cheered the high blasts. The ball rose from deep in the green meadow, the white leather cover spinning slowly in the high air, higher than the towers of the hospital, light and lofting above their gaze.

Willard threw one at the black man's head and he fell back, the red dust exploding in a puff, streaking the back and arm and legs of the suit, rising in a thin cloud as he laughed and slapped it off.

"Gonna put the next one in your teeth, old man!"

It was high and tight and Wolfman tomahawked it at him, hitting it with a dull clunk and setting it rocketing. Now Willard too bit the dust, setting a cloud rising and the boys laughing.

He pulled off the hood from his bony head, his hairs smeared madly with sweat, wound up and threw another which Wolfman set riding.

The boys began to shag them, running out deep in the field and climbing the chainlink fence, the fence making music as they climbed.

Willard stripped off the top of the paper suit and the shirt underneath. There was a great tattoo covering his chest and shoulder, a snake.

Wolfman swung with a grunt, unwinding like a great cat, the ball twanging against the chainlink behind him.

Willard cackled at the missed swing and stripped the rest of the suit off, down to his boxer shorts and the high-backed slippers. He was oiled with perspiration but moving slow and easy.

Jack and Molly arrived in a rusted red taxi. Emma came down from the seats to greet them. Wolfman set his bat down and walked toward her.

"No," Wolfman said to her. "He's mine first. We got a long thing to settle."

The sweat rolled from his dark brow, he smiled for her eyes. His eyes were bleary from the night, but with a little fire within them like the coke had made in the early hours of the morning, although she knew he hadn't taken any after that. He walked slowly toward Flynn as Emma signaled for Molly to come. Willard watched them from the mound, his skinny body gold with sweat, a new ball in his hand and ready to pitch.

"Yo Blood," Flynn called from a distance. He too was weary.

"Bush," Wolfman acknowledged, nodding slowly.

"I got to . . ." Flynn said.

"I know your story, Flynn," he said. He was huffing from the hitting, sweaty all over his body, the dust still staining the suit.

"What's it about, man?" Flynn said. "You tell me what it is . . ."

Wolfman spat into the dust.

"Ain't about nothing, Flynn. About you . . . About us . . ." He took them all in with a sweep of his arm, Flynn saw them watching him, the young boys gathered by the backstop far away.

"It about going on . . ." Wolfman said. "That's the point, my man. That is, as they say, the certainty of existence, do you understand?"

Flynn nodded. Bertie sat there in the stands, she looked worried and tired, as if she thought it would start between them again. He wanted to go tell Bertie about the motel where they had the skiff tied, wanted to tell her she could live there summers if she wished, that he had had Lenny buy it after all.

But they had work to do.

"Been a long time, Wolfman . . ."

"Ain't about nothin', Jack, ain't about nothing . . ."

"You go with me, Wolfman?"

"Why I'm here, jujuman, why I'm here."

So, in time, they went down to the water. The young doctor had waited for them in the staff room, faintly apprehensive when he heard them laughing as they came along the tile corridor. He was surprised to see the black man.

"Vitals are stable," he answered when the black man asked.

Flynn seemed relieved. It was impossible to tell what he had decided.

"Are you Mr. Flynn's attorney?" the doctor asked. He did not want to be double-crossed, it was not their agreement.

"Of a sort," Wolfman said. "Consider me a family advisor."

The doctor shook him off. "I'm sorry but I can't . . ."

The black man extended a hand, slowly, gently cutting him off.

"Not to worry, son," he said. "The family has agreed in conference to ask your opinion about the possibility of granting Miss Esther Flynn a day pass for an outing."

The young doctor searched the black man's eyes. It was clear that he meant what he meant. Still he had to have them say it.

"I'm sorry," he said, "but I need Mr. Flynn to tell me that he appreciates the risks of any action with this patient. I need him to state that he absolves this institution of any peril which might result coincidental with a day pass."

"I . . . ," Flynn said.

Wolfman cut him off.

"Doubtlessly, the good doctor has a release for such occasions."

The doctor nodded.

"I think what you are doing may be best, Mr. Flynn," he said. "There should be little suffering."

"Will she . . . ?" Flynn could not say.

"He can't say that, sap," the black man said. Then, more gently, "It isn't really some plug like in you toaster oven, Bush. Don't nobody just keel over and drop when you loose them from these things, ain't that right doc?"

"Generally . . . ," the doctor began, but Wolfman was orchestrating things his own way.

"It's just a little sugar water on one end, a drain on the other. A little oxygen to keep the respiration, a little electrolytes to keep the ticker pumping. It take some time to die, Flynn, maybe never . . ."

The doctor nodded grimly.

They went in to see her. "She's a beautiful girl, Flynn," the Wolfman said and hugged him. It was like standing over a coffin and Flynn didn't like it. She was alive.

"She's alive."

"That the point, chump! Didn' I say she's beautiful?"

Flynn nodded. He was still missing the point, even after what the girl showed him. He and Wolfman walked down together arm in arm and waited in the dayroom while the nurses prepared her, got her sitting in the wheelchair dressed in a blue cotton dress. Flynn cried all the while as Wolfman held him.

"Like old times, Bush," Wolfman murmured, "old times . . . I be laying awake at night in some chump-change hotel hearin' you cry over your hurting arm . . ."

Flynn didn't know. He hadn't thought the pain showed then. He had remembered it in mornings.

So they went down to the water, Flynn and Wolfman and Esther in the Maserati, the air conditioning seeming to ease her weary breath. Emma, Molly, and the other two followed behind them in Emma's rented car.

The motel was stucco over concrete block and green trimmed, fairly down on its luck but a bargain nonetheless. Sea Breeze Inn it was called and Flynn thought he would leave it at that.

They carried her down to the water in a fireman's carry, their linked arms under her for a seat. She was wide-eyed still and breathing fairly well, and not dead weight although unable to move to help herself. Bertie put the wide hat over Esther's head when they had her on the skiff in the forward-facing woven chair.

"I'll go with you," Wolfman said.

"No, someone has to row them," Flynn said. "The old two . . ."

Willard spat at the insult. He was dressed again in trousers and shirt, the white paper suit under his arm.

"Emma can sit in the other chair," Flynn said, and Emma nodded. Molly clung to her side, her eyes on Esther's eyes.

"And Molly will crew for me in the bow . . ."

She scampered on without him saying, and began to free the ties from the sail. Wolfman got Bertie and Willard into the rowboat from the motel.

"Just one time out and around," Flynn said and Wolfman nodded.

Bertie was crying as Molly rigged the sail.

"Wait!" Flynn said before they pushed off.

He pulled the heavy bullhead from the water on the stringer and tied it to the dock. "Supper," he said and then seated himself, poling carefully away from the dock. Wolfman rowed out beyond him and waited while Flynn adjusted the rig of the sprit, nodded to Molly, and climbed aft, letting the sheet out from the line in his hand. The breeze caught with a tug and they shot off. There was a big freighter out in the channel, heading downriver to the locks, the Selena Marie, heading home.

(Flynn is laughing with the memory, his eyes glazed.) We shot out from my landing, you see, the spray kicking high into thin rainbows drifting down in a mist, the skiff turning under our weight and facing full to the breeze, rocking hard on the chop from the freighter, the girl moving in time with me each time we tacked, sliding the centerboard up and down like she was born to it, and I'm leaning into the wind and letting the sheet out full, Emma talking all the while to Esther, encouraging her and telling her what they're seeing and holding the straw hat down on her head so it wouldn't fly off.

Wolfman rowed behind us, pulling the boat in long strokes, Willard whooping across the water, Bertie sitting primly, her eyes always on us.

"We're taking you sailing, Esther," I said. "In our father's boat, we're sailing."

She met the spray with blinking eyes, but did not acknowledge the words. Emma kept talking to her, but I hadn't the patience. I just wanted to say it before we were done, wanted Esther to hear. She sat stiffly in the cane seat, her eyes wide and her blue dress flapping; Emma whispered to her as we went. She was a sweet thing, my sister, and it was over, really, it was over but not quite anything.

The game taught me some things, you see, things which are useful, things which have their uses. I remembered feeling that way at least once before, one time coming to my mind. We were in Detroit my last season, a jewel of a ballpark, you know, with true infields and dark seats and a beautiful high sky and fair winds. It just smells like a ballpark there, between the lines, no chickens in Disney feathers, no gimmicks, only a happy black guy named Herbie Redmond dances when they dress the infields, pushing his broom and waving his cap and skip-dancing as they groom the base paths.

I was going good, better than good for that last year. Allowed only two hits into the eighth, one a four-seamer Parrish takes a mile. Still we're even coming into the home half of the eighth, one to one after we leave enough stranded Canadians on base to upset immigration. I get the first two on strikes and a long foul. I'm sailing and young again, but I let Whitaker get away from me. They bring in Wockenfuss and you can smell hit-run in the air. I take my time and watch the shadows settle halfway from the mound. I send Whitaker back once slow and then again fast to show him what I got. Each time he takes another walking lead, like he's hanging on me, you know, going to ride my shoulders. I shrug it off and line up Wockenfuss. Waste one way outside to see if he'll reach or Whitaker will go. Nothing doing. Take a guess he'll hit and run after one strike, so give him heat down the chute. The entire stadium groans with the strike call. It's tallying time and I give him a slider down damn near on his shoes. He turns that silly foot out and inside-outs it, golfs it with Whitaker running all the way. It hits the gap and skids but Bailor's over and cuts it off clean, except he never throws. Whitaker's motoring all the way and he's home clean.

Wockenfuss stands right on top of the bag, kicking dirt from his spikes. It's over, but it's not; it's over but it's not anything, you know. You just keep going on, get the next guy on a ground ball to short and run on in.

Knowing it's over. Three hits and a damn nice cut-off by Bailor and nothing to be done. Best damn hit-and-run man in the major leagues, Wockenfuss. Morris takes us one, two, three because no one cares, including him, now that it's over.

Won twenty games five times lifetime. It's over.

You learn that way, you know, how life is.

It was a fair day for sailing, a high sky, clouds careening, Esther dreaming.

You see. (He says this as if it is the whole statement, not a question, not a habit of speech. Even so he continues.)

You see, there are happy endings.

(There are tears in his eyes. We sit awhile in silence. I ask him if he has ever heard the quatrains which some claim to be the first mention of baseball in American writing. He shakes his head and I ask if he minds if I recite them. He looks toward me, as if encouraging me to go on, but I know he is watching elsewhere. I recite them nonetheless.)

The Ball once struck off,
Away flies the Boy,
To the next destin'd Post
And then Home with Joy.
Thus Seamen for Lucre
Fly over the Main,
But, with Pleasure transported,
Return back again.

(He sits as if struck, but then says yes.) "It's a good place, Sea Breeze," he says.

A beautiful morning he thought she said.

It's a beautiful morning, Esther, the men all in white and the waves dancing. They tip their caps like little Dutchmen then duck under one another, hurrying off like Willard in a rush. Aunt Bertie is here and my Molly too, and Bertie's cheek already has some color, no more than the blush on an ivory rose, and the sun is rising gradually now high in the sky, and Molly works the lines and dances with Flynn, turning the skiff about. Feel it drop beneath us, see her shake the wind off and sigh, she too now hurrying on, the spray glistening in the sun sheen, she would make your father proud.

Oh you would too, dear, don't be afraid. See the Selena Marie, she's outward bound, hurrying to Surinam, and she carves a single furrow of overturning silver. It echoes to either shore in a diminishing series like distant yawning. And Mr. Hunt is climbing now, working the oars as he works up the side of the swells, the dark wooden sweeps desperate and briefly empty at each peak, and then they slide down.

Now our skiff is rising, Esther, rising with them to meet the swells, each time easing into the breeze. We are aloft, my darling, gently rising, and you're not alone. None of us has slept this night, none of us sees.

It is a peaceful morning for sailing off, my friend, a soft and swollen feeling overtaking us all. Peace, my darling, the wave swirls are chrysanthemums, the shorebirds cry. We are beautiful and fortunate, hurrying off.

The End